Oceans
of Potential

By Saleah Micci

Conscious Dreams
PUBLISHING

First Printed in United Kingdom 2024

Published by Conscious Dreams Publishing
www.consciousdreamspublishing.com

Editor: Elise Abram

Typesetter: Oksana Kosovan

ISBN: 978-1-915522-79-5

Dedication

I thank God for the gift and courage to call myself
a writer. Out of the ashes of a most difficult time,
this story occupied my thoughts.

Acknowledgements

I could not have done this without the support of Andrea Best and Lilly Brown, who spurred me on every step of the way. They have my heartfelt gratitude. I also thank Conscious Dreams Publishing for their patience and for giving me time to calibrate. You know that you're a writer when, for years, you've always loved playing with words. Now, the words have come to life through this book.

Contents

1

Talent

IT'S FUNNY HOW friends can turn into lifelong soul mates. For Abi, Candice was the sister she never had but always wanted. The relationship cut both ways. She was the yin to her yang, sharing heartfelt conversations, a piece in the jigsaw puzzle of time slotting into place, plugging into snippets of each other's day . There were endless amounts of things to say, enough to pass the time of day or night.

The phone rang. 'Candice?' Abi said upon answering. 'I've got something important I want to talk to you about. I can't wait to see you.'

Hearing the effervescent tone in her voice, Candice asked, 'Can't you tell me now, on the phone?'

'No, we need to talk face-to-face. I need your help with something amazing.' It was a come-now-drop-everything kind of conversation as if she had won the lottery or something similar, and she had to show her the winning numbers on the ticket she was holding in her hand.

Abi had two girls, Ruby and Lacey, six and seven years old. It was often high drama with those two, arguing over toys and who was first. Whatever one had, the other wanted. It wasn't easy rounding them up and getting them into the car to go anywhere, much less to see her friend.

As for Candice, things were much simpler. Her two teenage boys—Reece and Jake—were happy enough with their Game Boys, which were all the rage in 1995. If she let them, they'd be occupied for hours, playing she didn't know what. All she knew was that the game was called 'Super Mario'. Mario was a pizza-chucking, Italian go-cart racer. 'If I were Italian, I'd be offended. Why not call it "Ferrari" or "Pasta"' was her go-to comment about the game.

The boys regularly corrected her on her lack of game savvy. Mario chucked bananas and turtle shells, which baffled her all the more. *God alone knows what on earth they have to do with anything*, she thought. It might all make sense when you consider that the advertising was not aimed at her age group. Of that, she was certain. Regardless, it had her kids hooked.

Candice was dying to know what the big reveal was, so she popped out of her house for a couple of hours to meet Abi, who was a ten-minute drive away.

Abi lived in a big house with a horseshoe drive in Bromley, South East London. In her divorce settlement, she got to stay in the house until the youngest had finished university. Then, the house would be sold and split fifty-fifty. Her ex-husband was a specialist consultant at a private practice in Harley Street. With the maintenance she received, she didn't need to work or worry about money. At least, not for the time being.

Abi and Candice met a year before through a mutual friend, and they'd hit it off from the start as they had many things in common. Both had divorced in 1993. Candice's marriage had been loveless; the spark went out a long time ago. Abi's marriage was riddled with abuse and drama which crushed her freedom and sense of wellbeing. Her liberation began the day she divorced him. Hidden behind her husband's profession as a specialist consultant—a caring occupation—he was, violent and abusive, which wasn't good for the kids. When he grew fearful he would not have a relationship with his daughters, he tried to take them away from her through the courts, accusing her of being an unfit mother. Abi loved those girls. She fought tooth and nail so it wouldn't happen.

Eventually, she broke free from the abusive marriage and now lived life in peace. As much as she hated her ex for what he put her through, she strongly believed that children needed to know their fathers, and she allowed him to have access to them every other weekend. While the kids got to stay with him, Abi carved out a new life for herself, doing everything she wasn't allowed to do before, like singing the songs she loved, partying, making new friends and seeing whomever she wanted without her ex's constant vetting.

Young children meeting new friends wouldn't ordinarily connect by discussing sad stories, but upon meeting a new friend, adults might open up to share their sad stories, discussing how to put the world to rights by talking about the unfairness of life.

While driving over to Abi's house, Candice remembered the first time they'd met. They got to talking, and Candice was just about to get into her story about her woes when Abi interrupted and said, 'Let's face it—when you walked down the aisle, you didn't really love him, did you?' They erupted into fits of laughter.

Candice was taken aback by her outburst! She hadn't known whether to be upset or offended that anyone would say anything like that to her, much less someone she'd just met. She thought about it. Yes, it was true: she'd married her husband for all the wrong reasons. She realized she hadn't loved him at all, and she joined in Abi's laughter.

Candice pulled up at Abi's house and rang the doorbell that chimed like Big Ben.

'Candice!' Abi said when she opened the door. 'Thanks for coming over so quickly. I'd come over to you, but I've got the kids.'

'What's going on? What's all this urgent, mysterious, face-to-face business?' Candice asked.

'You know how I'm interested in music, right? Well, someone gave me a ticket to an event where artists could promote themselves, and I met this guy called Sami. He's a songwriter and a music producer.'

'And?'

'We got on so well. He's tall, dark and handsome.'

'Yes, your type…so?'

'I told him I was a singer looking for a lucky break, and he said he would introduce me to some people. All I needed was to put together a demo, and he'd put my cassette in the hands of the right people.'

'Great. Do you believe this stranger?'

'He is kind-looking…yes, I believe him. Sometimes, you've got to take chances in life when opportunity knocks. Anyway, I've got nothing to lose.

'We got to talking about a project he was working on. He's looking to put together a boy band and get them signed to a record label. He's also a talent scout.'

'What's that?' Candice asked.

Abi responded in a condescending tone, as if it were obvious, 'A talent scout is someone on the lookout for talented singers and artists who matches them up with recording companies. He gets paid if they get signed, and if they use his songs, he gets royalties whenever the song is played or sold. As a scout, he sometimes goes to auditions and talent contests just to see if he can spot the next best thing.

'I'm really interested in helping young singers make it, too. I think that if I can show him how useful I am, perhaps I'll get a chance to make it big as a singer.'

'What are you thinking? If your connection with him is about gaining access to a recording company, don't you think it would be confusing getting involved with his boy band project, mixing the two things together?' Candice asked.

'No way! I scratch his back, and he scratches mine.'

'What a terrible thought.'

'What?'

'Back scratching, Abi.

'Do you fancy him?'

'Yes. We'd make a great team. A power couple. I can see it now: me singing like Oleta Adams and him producing my songs.' Abi stared into space as if dreaming about the potential of stardom her link with Sami could bring.

'But we're in the UK, not the USA. How many British soul-singing artists make it through to even the *Top of the Pops*? Not many. And if they do, they're only one-hit wonders, and you never see or hear of them again,' Candice said.

'Don't say that. Why couldn't I make it? My ex constantly put me down and tried to beat the shit out of me and my idea to become a famous singer for years. Don't come here and tell me I can't do this.' Abi said.

'Calm down. Sorry. I didn't mean it like that. You know the things you see and read these days — the statistics show the facts — but me? I'm your best friend. Team Abi all the way. Of course, I'll support you in whatever you want to do as long as it's legal and within reason, I might add. You're the wild and carefree one, while I'm reserved and very cautious,' Candice said, trying to calm the situation.

'Yes, extremely cautious,' Abi said, rolling her eyes.

'Yes, and don't we make a great team? I'm good at organising — what can I do to help?' Candice said.

'Let's meet Monday,' Abi suggested.

'I'm working,' Candice said.

'I mean evening. Monday evening. I want to discuss things in detail and put plans into action.'

'I've got to go now,' Candice said. 'It's school tomorrow for the boys, but I'll see you in the evening.'

Despite the minor hiccough about Candice's loyalty to the cause, Abi went to bed that night excited at the possibility of starting something new.

♫ ♫ ♫

Candice worked as an IT project manager for one of the top ten accountancy firms in the United Kingdom. For her, there was no such thing as an unsolvable problem. Her team had to find a solution for everything, and it had to be nothing less than excellent. Then, after reaching excellence, you couldn't just sit on your laurels. Being excellent meant always improving upon your last performance. These were the values drilled into every member of the staff at their induction to the firm. It was what the partners wanted. It was their way of working everyone extra hard and leaving the staff feeling unworthy of success at times. That meant the staff were in a constant state of trying to prove themselves to the management or were in competition with each other. On the other hand, they developed strong muscles when it came to faith and built their abilities and resilience in the face of negativity. Mostly, people feared losing their jobs.

In that work arena, so much like those in America, the pressure was on. One little mistake and chop—off with your head. If you slacked, even for a moment, you were gone.

Candice was always looking over her shoulder. Everything had to be tip-top. As a single parent, determined not to allow her circumstances to hold her back, she didn't want to lose her job. She had to manage the pressure skilfully, balancing her work and home lives.

Candice didn't know where she fit in on the creativity spectrum. She loved music and dancing—after a few drinks, she could dance for hours. She had fun singing with her workmates at the karaoke bar, though they were like meowing cats, nothing professional like Abi. Once, at a gig in a London nightclub, Candice came along with Abi to show her support. For some reason, one of Abi's backing singers dropped out at the last minute and Abi persuaded Candice to step in and pretend to sing. On that night, they looked like twin sisters in their slim-fitted, short, colourful dresses, killer heels, up-do and make up, and Candice could pass for being a singer. Abi assured her not to worry because the mic would be turned down. For Candice's performance, she only had to look the part and dance like the other backing singer. It was working up to a point until Candice's mic came alive in the chorus, and there was no mistaking her bum notes. The glare she got from the other singer, even with Abi staring back at her, made her realise that something was wrong and she was the cause of it, and she immediately stifled the sounds coming out of her mouth.

Workwise, things were different. Candice could organise anything, think through the layers that made up the whole, and break down the process to make the IT infrastructure work for the firm. At work, for one of her developmental goals, she'd stripped down a computer and built it back up again. Abi admired Candice because, personally, she knew zilch about IT. She thought everyone who worked in that field had to be brainy, but Candice had a great eye for detail that would serve Abi well. Abi was convinced that, with her involvement in the boy band project, it was bound to be a success, and it would be one step closer to her own dream of reaching stardom, no matter how convoluted.

♫ ♫ ♫

It was Monday evening when Abi and Candice set about making plans.

'Let's just brainstorm. We need a venue with PA facilities, some kind of waiting area, an advert in *The Voice* newspaper—'

'Why *The Voice* and not *The Underground*?'

'Everyone gets *The Voice*. There are loads of adverts about upcoming music events. *The Underground* is dry. I don't hear many people talking about it. It's good for bric-a-brac. A huge classified section, but nothing we'd be interested in.'

'Okay. *The Voice* it is. We'll need judges—who do you have in mind?'

'I'll be one. Then there's Sami, of course. I'll ask Mervyn, who's my vocal coach. I'll count him in. He won't say no. Shirlee and Robert… so that's five. Plenty,' Abi said.

'Sami, you've just met, so we know about him. Tell me about the others.'

'Mervyn used to be in a band called The Shakalakas. You must have heard of them. They were popular in the early eighties. I don't know the ins and outs, but many things changed for them.'

'What changed?' Candice asked.

'The lead singer died in a plane crash. It was tragic. They looked for another singer to replace him. Then a scandal broke out.

'And?' Candice was inquisitive to know.

'That finally removed them from the music landscape altogether—it was, 'inappropriate behaviour with a minor', which got him a prison sentence.' Abi continued. 'By the way, it wasn't Mervyn who couldn't resist the younger ladies. It was the replacement. Mervyn's happily married to a Brit he met in the States. They came over to the UK to live in Sydenham. They've got two kids. He works as a vocal coach for a living, and his wife is a schoolteacher at my girl's school.'

'Can't wait to meet him.'

'Mervyn is such a character. He's got these neat and tidy shoulder-length locks. He's tallish and rides a motorbike. When I see him pull up in his all-black leathers, he reminds me of the predator in that movie with Arnold Schwarzenegger. And when he removes his helmet, he shakes his locks to put them in place. Picture that in slow motion. He's a nice guy, though, and a good friend.'

'What do Shirlee and Robert do?'

'Shirlee is a Chaka Khan look alike. She's the spitting image of her, and she can sing. She almost had a hit in the eighties. Her song, 'Woman in Love', was in the top ten on the UK chart, but it didn't get any further. She went to the States to pursue her music career, but when she split from her manager, her then-husband, she decided to return to England. She met Robert, who plays the piano, and they got married. He's like a fish in water when he's on that piano. He could play morning, noon, and night. To him, time doesn't matter.

'They were both married before. Shirlee was like me. We both had violent-tempered husbands, envious of our beauty and talent, but a long while after the divorce, she met Robert. He was the session musician at an office gig, and she was the performing artist for the night, singing Chaka Khan songs. They've been married for ten years now. They're really great together.

'Oh, and Shirlee has a son called DeAngelo who's following in her footsteps. His voice has a sweet, melodic tone when he sings. When you hear him, you'll see what I mean. I'll invite him to the audition, but he's definitely in the group. I love his temperament, and he's friendly.'

'Abi, let's run through this. We've got the judging panel and the media. I'll put an ad out tomorrow in *The Voice* newspaper, but before that, we need a venue and a date. I know someone who runs a community centre in Lewisham. His name is Pete. They have a PA system, but there'll be hire charges and a deposit.' Candice was direct about the facts.

'Call him. Tell him what we're doing, and ask if we can use his facilities. Let's say in two Saturday's time, at the end of July. Kids are out of school for the summer, then. The ad can run for two weeks. Hopefully, we'll get a good selection of singers to choose from. Then, we'll be ready for the next stage.' Abi was in tune and on a roll.

'Should we put a contact number in the ad if anyone wants to know more?' Candice asked.

'No contact number. Let them all just show up.'

♫ ♫ ♫

The auditions came around fast, like a train travelling through a dark tunnel and bursting into the light, out in the open, clear as day, a change of scenery, a change of sound. There was a buzz about that day. Something great was about to happen. Abi and Candice sensed it. They would be written about in history books as the ones who'd set the trend in the UK, cultivating a boy group that had made it big using their formula for talent selection and turning two-penny talent into big-dollar talent.

The audition was set to start at 10 a.m. Candice was responsible for making sure everything was in place at the centre, while Abi took care of the sound and catered to the judges.

The centre was booked until 6 p.m. By then, it would all be over. Would they find the talent they were looking for, or would they have to do the auditions all over again, perhaps at another location? Abi pondered these questions, but her heart said, *Don't worry. They'll show up, and we'll select the best singers.*

Her thoughts turned to Sami. Would he be impressed by her resourcefulness? Would he honour his word and hook her up with the right people? Could this be the mega-breakthrough she was hoping for?

Candice went over the details again, muttering to herself.

'What we're looking for are young, talented singers with voices touched by angels,' Abi said. 'A blend of harmonies that will make the girls go wow! I can see it now.

'Why should all the singing fish be in the American ocean? Haven't we got fish, too?' Abi said. 'The USA is a long way away, and that marketplace rarely gives British artists a look, except for the Beatles, who got so big the US couldn't ignore them. Now, I'm not talking about pop—we want to start a new craze when it comes to homegrown boy talent.

'So, what're we doing? How're we doing it?' Candice needed to know if the plans had changed.

'There'll be a two-part selection process. We don't have years to do this, so we have to cut to the chase. We're only giving each singer ninety seconds to impress. If they pass that stage, we'll give them a second song choice, put them into groups, and ask them to organise the harmonies of the song.'

'How will the singers do that in such a short space of time?'

'It's not perfect, but we'll get to see who can adapt and who are willing to work together for a common goal. We'll end with our final selection. When the judges all agree, it'll be a wrap.'

♫ ♫ ♫

Abi and Candice arrived at the centre at 7.30 a.m., where they met Dave, the PA technician. Candice focused her energy on the layout and reception area for greeting and registration, while Abi went straight for the sound check, determined not to let a technical failure be her downfall that day. She'd seen it happen many times before, when people started faffing about two minutes before the performances started only to find there was no sound. It was so amateur.

'Dave, how many mics do you have?' Candice asked.

'How many do you want? We've got a cupboardful of them. We just got to check which ones work,' Dave said.

Deep in thought but speaking out loud, Abi calculated, 'Five judges — Sami, Shirlee, Mervyn, Robert, me — and four contestants. We need five to be on the safe side. There's no audience, so the judges won't need to project their voices, but the PA system — is it any good? No feedback nonsense?'

'Of course, the PA system works. I run a tight ship here,' Dave said.

Abi responded with, 'I hope so. Nothing less, right?' She gave him a sexy smile so he would see that she had a friendly side, linked arms with him, and asked to be taken to the cupboard where the kit was stored.

It was a good thing Abi arrived early. Ten mic checks later and they found a box of mics that actually worked.

'Testing…testing…one…two…three. Finally!

'Candice, what's the sound like back there?' Abi asked.

'Sounds good to me,' Candice said from the back of the room. 'Very clear.'

'Then, we're ready to go!'

It was now nine o'clock. They hadn't checked outside yet to see if anyone had queued up. Would anyone show up at all? Feeling anxious, Abi asked Candice to hold her hands and pray. Candice was not a believer, but she was happy to help.

Abi was a backslidden Christian. She'd fallen out of the Church through her divorce, but in her heart, she still held onto a thread of faith and wanted to say a prayer in case God was listening. 'Dear God, let today be successful. Bring boys who can sing from all over London to show up for the audition. Let the right voices be chosen, and the boys will be eternally blessed. Give us a breakthrough today, Lord. We pray for protection over the equipment—no gremlins and no hiccoughs. Bless our time together and make something special happen today. In Jesus' name. Amen.'

Candice managed to squeal out an amen. 'What about the judges?'

'Yes, Lord, let them arrive safely. Amen.

'I know it will work out. I'm expecting them to arrive by 11 a.m. Apart from Sami, I've already introduced Mervyn and Shirlee to each other. Sami is keen for this to work, so he has a vested interest. A success for him would be a win for me.'

'Do you hear that?' Candice asked.

'Hear what?' Abi answered.

'Shush!'

They stood frozen, like puppies with their ears pricked up. They heard Dave's voice, along with many others. Wondering what the fuss was about, they rushed to the main entrance and saw Dave trying to reassure everyone outside that they would be open at 9.30 a.m.

There was a window on the upper floor overlooking the front entrance. Abi and Candice looked at each other and went towards the stairs without saying a word, both of them thinking the same thing, and ran up the stairs to the window to see what was going on outside.

'My gosh, Abi. Look at that crowd. There must be at least a hundred boys with their supporters.' There were boys clowning around while trying to keep an orderly queue, wearing the jewels of youth fashion (Adidas, Nike, and Reebok), trying to look 'wicked' in their shell suits and tracksuits. The ad in *The Voice* newspaper had worked. The rest was up to the judges.

Nine-thirty struck like a starting pistol.

'How do you want to do this?' Dave asked, looking worried as he hadn't envisaged that many people showing up. 'Do we need security to keep order out there? I don't want any trouble. Some of them look a bit rough.'

'It'll be fine.' Abi said, hoping he'd find comfort in her words.

'I'll call Jaeger and ask him to come down.' Jaeger was extra security he called on when needed. 'He owes me a favour. Better to be on the safe side. He lives around the corner. He won't charge, so don't worry,' Dave said, anticipating their questions and answering them.

'I'll leave it to you. Whatever you think is best.' Abi's head seemed back in the game. 'Candice, let's start the registration process. We're only going to let a few in at a time.'

'I'll hand out the forms to get their information. They can complete it in the foyer, hand it back to me, and wait in the side hall. There should be enough space for them, but their entourages will have to wait outside.'

2

The Brief

PEOPLE CONTINUED TO arrive, but Abi made the decision to stop registering the boys once one hundred had been listed. There were more still waiting to register, but Candice put forward a convincing argument against that limit, saying, 'We don't know how far these boys have travelled, and there might just be one at the end of the line who could be it, and we'll have missed him. We need to find a quick way to sift through them, separating the sheep from the goats…or the horses from the donkeys. It's not obvious who can actually sing from their looks, so we've got to eliminate some of these guys quickly and brutally. Plus, I've only printed one hundred and fifty forms. We've used up one hundred so far, and many of them will be a waste of time.'

Abi went into the side hall, where the ones who had made it in were standing, and shouted, 'Guys—listen up! I know some of you have brought the backing tracks you've been rehearsing to. You can use those later when the judges arrive. Right now, I want you to come to the front and sing acapella, so prepare yourselves, limber up those voices, and show me what you've got.'

The boys had one minute to impress. They say you can sum up a person and whether you like them within the first sixty seconds of meeting them. Abi didn't just want cute looks but the voices to match. If they could whittle down the crowd to the boys who could sing, it would be better for the judges later on, and Abi didn't want to waste anyone's time, especially Sami's. He was the one person she wanted to impress the most.

Candice stopped handing out registration forms, resolving to take the boys' details if they made it through the first round with Abi. Age was an important criterion and another way to bring down the numbers. If they were under fifteen or over seventeen, they were thanked and asked to leave. The ad had specifically asked for fifteen to seventeen years old, but some must've come anyway, thinking they would take their chances.

Next was their height. Following the brief, the verbal mandate, agreed by Sami that initiated the project, Abi wanted them five-foot-eleven to six feet, which was another way to eliminate some of the boys. Dave, the community manager, was bang on six feet, so he was on hand to use as a measuring tool if needed. Again, the boys who were not the right height were thanked and asked to leave.

There was now a line of potentials waiting in the queue, ready for round one.

Candice took a chair, placed it in a prominent position, and stood on it to get everyone's attention. 'Let's have the first five!' she shouted. 'You can sing first. We can talk later!'

One of the good things about the community centre was that it had a number of smaller rooms used for afterschool lessons, clubs, Scouts, Beavers, Brownies, dance classes, and drama during the week, so there was a way to easily separate the groups of five.

Abi received word from Dave, who'd picked up a few messages on the office's answer service that the judges were on their way, and their ETA was between eleven and 11.30 a.m.

Mindful of the update, Abi smiled at the boys. With a commanding voice, she said, 'State your name and sing a song of your choice. I'll either tell you to stop or let you continue till you've finished.'

The first five were diabolical. They looked cool in their fashionable, on-trend garments, but they sang out of tune. Nerves, it seemed, had got the better of them, and their belief that they could sing outweighed the reality of the situation.

The next five were just like the first. History repeated itself over and over again, just like in the *Groundhog Day* movie.

Abi muttered under her breath, discreetly communicating with Candice. 'Someone should put them out of their misery.' She took a sharp intake of breath and exhaled with her shoulders lowered and with less enthusiasm, said, 'Next!'

'Abi, we're going to have to take a quick break to rethink our approach. This,' Candice gesticulated to the crowd, 'is not working. If we don't do something, we'll be here all night, registering every Tom, Dick, and Harry.' There was a tinge of panic in her voice.

'You need to go down the line and eliminate some of the boys,' was Abi's response. She was already feeling worn out from the mechanics, and the day was still young. She wished she could say, 'Would the best five singers meeting the brief reveal themselves by stepping forward,' but that was wishful thinking. What had to be done was very much a part of the process. She had to persevere and stick with it.

An idea jumped into her head. 'I'm not saying that every great singer can do any of this,' she said, 'but let's ask for all of the boys who either play an instrument, read music, write songs or poetry, or do backing vocals to come forward. That could be a way to bring the musically-minded boys to the front of the queue. I'm praying that we don't exclude the real singers that way, but we need to up the pace. Sometimes, it's not until you're right up against it that the answers come to you, just like that. Out of nowhere.'

'I get the instruments, reading music, and song-writing part, but poetry? They might be tone deaf,' Candice commented.

'Well, I feel that if you can write good poetry, you can transform it into the lyrics of a best-selling song. It all adds to the talent. At school, I was always good at poetry. That's how I'm able to write my own songs now.'

Following Abi's new approach to the selection criteria, Candice asked those boys to come to the front. The announcement couldn't have come at a better time. Abi was surprised to see how many boys had taken the initiative to bring their guitars, mouth organs, saxophones, flutes, and even a violin with them. It made her job much easier.

'Let's have the next five!' Abi yelled, with her fingers crossed, hoping not to get any more auditionees that couldn't sing.

This time, it was different. When each boy sang, Abi made some of the fastest decisions of the morning. From the first few notes, she knew there were actual singers standing in her presence.

'Yes, yes, yes, yes, and yes,' Abi said delightedly. 'We have lift-off.

'Send in the next five.'

There were looks of disappointment on the faces of the boys waiting in the queue when they saw the boys with their instruments go in first, and they sensed they either had to up their games or go home, their voices unheard. Adding to their anxiety were the boys who left early because they'd clearly been told, 'Thank you for your time, but this is the end of the process for you.' It was unnerving for those preparing for their shot at a place in the unknown boy band, but it also sent the message that the selection process would take no prisoners. Either you sang as if your life depended upon it or you didn't bother.

For Abi, there were a fair number of boys she could send through to the next round to sing in front of the judges. It would be better for them, as they could sing their own choice of song then.

The judges arrived on time and to schedule. First to arrive was Mervyn. He walked slowly past the line-up of boys, observing their presence and hoping there was a star in there somewhere,

Next was Shirlee, who'd also made it big in the US with her first husband, a genius producer, but who now lived in the UK, followed by her second husband, Robert, a brilliant keyboard player, and son, DeAngelo, from her first marriage. DeAngelo would also go through the motions of auditioning along with everyone else. Even if he was guaranteed to be picked, the healthy competition would be good for him. He could foul up, but the chance of that happening was slim. He qualified to come to the front in his own right, playing the piano and drums and reading music. To be fair, Abi agreed that if he got through, Shirlee would not be included in any voting concerning her son.

Finally, Sami arrived. Abi watched Sami's approach from a distance. Like a hound, Sami sized up the potential artists lined up in the queue. He smiled, said hello to the few bold enough to say something to him, and entered the reception area, where he was greeted by Candice, who was juggling everything but the kitchen sink. She ushered him into the main hall, where there was a long table and four chairs waiting for the panel of judges. There were bottles of Highland Spring Water, notepads, and pens neatly positioned for them to write their deliberations, which was Candice's touch to make the judges feel like VIPs. Whatever happened, Sami was the one with the final say. After all, it was his brief.

♫ ♫ ♫

Sami was Abi's knight in shining armour. She believed he'd be the one to launch her dream career of being a superstar. The steps she took now would be crucial for her trajectory. Her plan was to stay close to him. He knew how to get her up there by reaching the top people in the industry.

Sami — whose real name was Simon Achidi Achu, after a Cameroonian politician — was born in 1957, grew up in West Africa in a French-speaking colony in Cameroon, and was thirty-eight years old. He didn't like the name Simon, so he chose to call himself Sami. He studied French and English and came to the UK in the seventies, while still in his mid-teens, to live with his aunt. He was expected to better himself by becoming either a doctor or a lawyer, but he did neither. His passion was centred in the music world. He'd never played a musical instrument, but he had a good ear for music and was gifted with songwriting talent. After his college education — focusing on music studies and sound engineering — with no experience in the field, he applied for a job as an assistant junior sound technician at the London Coliseum and charmed his way in. He worked his way up to becoming a senior technician and received solid training in theatrical sound production.

Sami had an approachable demeanor, not overbearing but engaging, and he could hold conversations well. He came across as knowledgeable about anything involving music. He was soft-spoken but intentional with his words. On a deeper level, he was a man on a personal mission. His songwriting ability was enough to tap the strings of anyone's heart. He had the ambition to make it big by breaking into America with a stonking song. He charted a course and set a goal to be at the very top of his game by forty. All encounters with whoever he met were viewed as potential connections, points on a map to a destination.

Abi knew nothing of his life or inner desires. On the other hand, Abi saw their encounter as being about her connecting with influential people and being in the right places at the right times. Sami showed her a lot of attention by making time for her and taking her calls, and Abi was bewitched by his caring nature. She was convinced he'd been sent by God to wash away all of her past struggles while trying to get recognised as a professional singer.

It was Sami who got the official brief through various chains of connections, leading to the Faceless People who were a conglomerate of decision-makers, the real movers and shakers in the music world.

Vicky Valero was one of those stepping stones towards the decision-makers. Vicky was the singer and songwriter of 'Just Stop', a hit in the UK's Top Ten chart and massive in Europe. Sami met her at a gig a few years ago, and they'd remained friends ever since. It started as a brief fling, but it turned into a friendship. She always had her ear to the ground. If she heard of any requests from producers looking for talent, record labels looking to sign up new artists, or music event launches, she always kept him in the loop. They had regular chats, keeping up with their worlds, whatever they were doing, and projects in progress. They were allies who shared an affinity for their love of music, which was mutually valued as the industry was littered with fake friends.

Ten years back, in 1985, Sami had been badly let down after being contacted by a record label. Someone who was part of a network of contacts had liked his songs and promised to pitch one as a taster to producers at Zackeray Records. Gloria Estefan had been the target singer for the song.

For Sami, songwriting came easily. Writing while listening to classical music in the background was his favourite pastime. It helped him connect with the emotion behind the stories the songs would tell. After hearing opera at the Coliseum, he learned to interpret emotions from sound and words. The job at the Coliseum had been his lucky break, and from then on, he had a heavy involvement in music production, but he couldn't sing to save his life. From the moment he got the phone call from the producer at Zackeray, his hope was up. He invested in their promises, heart and soul, believing it was a done deal and that Gloria Estefan would love it.

He was naive and green. After two years of holding on, hoping and waiting for the call to come to America because his song was a hit, nothing came of it. His pride was hurt so badly that he vowed it would never happen again. Sami brushed off the failure and with a stiff upper lip, he sought out other lucky breaks.

By the time the brief had come his way, he had had some success with the songs in his repertoire that had been used on TV and radio, advertising jingles, singers looking for songs to audition with and pitch to get signed, and songs for films. The brief was the official request from Butterfly Records, endorsed by the Faceless People. Initially, they were once a small-time, independent label, but they had hit the big time on the world stage in the USA, Australia, and Europe, with UK bands and names signed to their catalogue. Heavy metal and rock were their things, but for years, American soul singers and emerging rap artists killed it on the UK charts traditionally dominated by Americans, and Butterfly Records UK wanted a piece of it. The American dominance needed to be broken by investing in some home-grown competition. For Sami, the boy group was a shot worth pursuing.

♫ ♫ ♫

Sami and the rest of the judges, who were now ready, stepped into their driving seats. Abi's selection had done a good job of weeding out the wannabes and teasing out the exceptionally hopeful. The judges were quite the team. Mervyn and Shirlee had never met Sami before, but they all seemed to feel at ease with each other, having come from the music world, albeit from different parts of it. They seemed to speak the same language and used similar words, like 'too pitchy', 'not enough rasp', and 'falsetto was on point', like lawyers, doctors, and IT geeks who knew their fields.

Abi and Candice did not stop once. They were on a roll, sifting and moving the boys from one room to another. What they had created in such a short space of time was commendable. 'Could you see yourself making a living setting up events for other organisations looking for artists?' Candice asked Abi.

'Are you mad? I'm a singer, not an organiser. If I get caught up doing this for the rest of my life, where would I find the time to be a professional singer? This has been great, but it's not my goal. I'm only doing this for Sami. I wanna get inside that door, and this is one way of doing it. By helping him with his project, I know I'll get a break,' Abi said with conviction, not wanting to be swayed from losing sight of her intended prize. She and Sami were both fully involved in the groundbreaking move to create something out of nothing, turning nobodies into somebodies who would be huge, phenomenal successes.

Narrowing down the selection to twenty contenders was not too difficult, as the ones who shone the most when it came to voice and stature tended to stand out. Plus, the selection process Abi and Candice had implemented saved a lot of time.

At last, the auditions came to an end. The last contestant sang. Everyone selected to sing and chosen to return after the judges' deliberation break was informed.

It was not, however, a high-five moment just yet.

Sami asked Abi to take Polaroids of the twenty boys, and Abi instructed Candice to do it as she was the one with the camera.

The judges glanced at each other and smiled, looking relieved once the discussions and debates began. They were interrupted when Candice poked her head through the door, and like the last gust of wind after a stormy day, she asked if there was time for just one more boy to sing.

Now Sami was a stickler for punctuality, and he expected the same level of respect from any of the artists he dealt with. When meeting an artist, he arrived at least fifteen minutes ahead of time, acclimatised himself to the setting, focused on what he wanted from the meeting, and waited. After ten minutes of waiting past the agreed-upon time, he'd been known to walk, even if the artist bumped into him as they hurried in. Sami's response would be, 'I'm busy. Don't waste my time. Call me.' This invariably led to the artist's desperate attempts to ring down his phone. Sami usually let them sweat for a bit until they got the message. If they were still keen and he was still interested, he would eventually take their call. This approach always seemed to work for him because the artist never made the mistake of arriving late again. It was his way of commanding respect.

'Really?' Sami asked. It went against his usual stance on punctuality, forcing him to pause for a few seconds. 'Okay, just one more. Let's see what he's got.'

The boy swaggered into the room, full of confidence. Any sign that he might have had any nerves had been thrown out the window. It was a good thing, too, for after their long day, the judges were totally devoid of patience for anyone with nerves.

The boy opened his mouth, and the tone of his voice was enough to make Sami regret thinking *Here's another one*, if he had at all. The boy sang, moving to the sway of non-existent music as if he was the only one who could hear it playing — there had been no time to load a tape for the audition.

Mervyn beamed from ear to ear as if wanting to proclaim, 'This boy can sing,' but he waited until the boy was done.

When he had finished the audition to the very last note, the judges, each of them wearing a poker face so as not to give anything away, gave him a nod.

There were now twenty-one hopefuls, including the last-minute singer, Eddie, who'd slipped in through the door as it was closing, while others were being turned away. He' managed to talk his way into the room where Abi was giving the boys one minute to impress before performing in front of the judges. Apart from him being the right height, fresh-faced, and clean-looking, he hadn't any of the special qualities on Abi's wish list, like playing an instrument, singing in a choir, backup singing, song-writing experience, or even writing poetry, but he was ballsy. Ballsy enough not to take no for an answer and push himself forward, even though the auditions had ended. He was well and truly late, arriving at 3 p.m. instead of 9.30 a.m. with the others. To be fair, it was by chance that he happened to see the advert in *The Voice* newspaper at 2 p.m., and it was like a calling. He'd had an instant compulsion to get up and go to the audition and the serendipitous anticipation that something good would come from it.

Although his audition was good, Sami had words with him before he'd even sung a note. 'Listen, I don't know you, but I'm a stickler for punctuality, and you are well and truly late. I personally don't give chances to latecomers who don't respect my time, but Abi has put you forward, and I'm allowing it, just this one time. So, show us what you've got.' The stern words indicated his card had been marked and by Sami. The pressure was on him to perform or cave in. Eddie didn't disappoint.

Sami spoke for the judges and said, 'We are about to break for two hours. See you back here at six o'clock.'

Abi left the room. She observed the boys and their entourages, either waiting in the reception area or outside the building by the glass doors. The remaining boys eyed each other up, not knowing if they would be friends or opponents. It was a competition, after all, and there would be winners and losers, but they all seemed to hold onto the hope they would be picked to join the group, and they kept their composure while hiding their anxieties.

The judges said they would finish their deliberation within two hours. So they hoped. The Polaroid pictures lay scattered on a Formica table in the hall. Like cards on a poker room table, each judge showed their hand of favourite singers. It could shape up to be a lengthy debate, as many of their choices seemed the polar opposites of others.

'How the heck are we going to form a group if we can't agree?' Speaking her thoughts out loud, Abi threw it out there as a rhetorical question.

3

The Group

'Last-minute Eddie is in, for sure,' Shirlee said, putting her vote out there to start things off. They walked around the table with the Polaroids on it as if carrying out some mystical ritual. There were no objections about Eddie. He was unanimously well-liked.

'Okay, let's make it easier — are we all in agreement about DeAngelo? Shirlee can't vote for her own son, that's for sure, but Sami, do you agree with that?' Abi smiled warmly at Sami, and he reciprocated with a resounding yes.

'That's two so far, and Candice's nephew, Karl, gets my vote,' Mervyn said. 'Is everyone cool with that?'

There were yeses all around.

That was three selected. Three pictures were pushed along one side of the table, like suspects on parade. They were still looking for two more boys to join the selection.

'I've got to say, these two here seem to have an edge over the others,' Shirlee said.

'That's just what I was thinking,' Mervyn said. 'Let's put them together.' They moved the Polaroids around again, like a deck of cards.

Sami said, 'Yes, those two were good, but I think the sound of this one would fit the brief and nail the line-up.'

'You really prefer Nathan's voice over Perry's?' Abi asked, not convinced it was a good blend.

'Yes, Nathan's voice will work well with the others,' Sami said.

'Well, if you're certain of that, then we have our five. Perhaps Perry could be a reserve?' Abi asked, giving him one more push as her mind was set on him.

'These five will work better for the production,' Sami said, resolute with his decision.

'Well, it's your gig and your party. You're going all out for these guys, so whatever you say, boss.' Mervyn gave a quick hand salute. 'Either way, they're all works in progress, right? By the time they've been polished up, we'll be amazed at what we've created. The "best boy group ever", hey?' Mervyn would be their vocal coach, and he had a reputation for making a gnat sing like a cricket.

'Give the bad news to the boys who didn't make it and the good news to the five who did,' Sami said, casting his final verdict.

Abi and Candice, the ones who would separate and address the boys, left the hall with their instructions.

Upon entering the hallway, the energy of emotions running high in the atmosphere was tangible. There were boys wearing looks of disappointment mingling with those who shouted for joy at the news of being selected. Abi gave a rousing speech to encourage the unsuccessful boys to continue with their singing, emphasising that it had been a tough decision as they were all good.

Time was moving fast. Besides the formal paperwork and Sami's insistence on the boys signing a non-disclosure agreement to remain quiet about the group, there were still some conversations to be had. There would be no public announcements about the forming of the group and no interviews with the newspaper. The project was to be kept under wraps for the time being.

After the boys had been chosen, Shirlee wondered about their families. 'Do we know anything about them? I believe the driving force behind the success of any group comes from the support of their families. Are they behind them or not? If they're against the idea, it might pose an obstacle.'

Sami piped up with, 'We don't need to worry about that at this stage.'

Shirlee fired back, 'But families are an important support. Let's ask the boys directly and hear what they have to say. Hopefully, we can read between the lines and judge the truth from their facial expressions.'

Sami stood to make a swift departure and said, 'I've got a meeting to get to with the record company. I'll leave this part to you guys. You don't need me.

'Abi? Call me later.'

'What time?' Abi shouted after him.

'Around 9 p.m.,' Sami answered as he disappeared through the doors.

The boys were in the hallway, laughing and joking, excited to be at their first meeting. As Sami passed, he smiled at them and said, 'You guys are going to be great. You've got good voices. Keep practising.' The pep talk was over in a flash, and Sami hurried out.

The five successful boys headed off into the room to see the judges while the unsuccessful boys slowly left the building. It had been a long day of milling about for everyone, getting their hopes up for something that could have been life-changing. They had come into the process as individuals competing against each other and were welcomed into the room where the judges had initially been seated as a group. The judges stood to give them a rousing applause, smiling to show their approval.

Outside of the judges' room, Perry, one of the auditionees, was with his family. There was Mum, Dad, and little brother, Stevie. They didn't take well to being told their son was not good enough, and the anguish of being rejected resulted in Perry's tears. He was quite a sensitive child, and that sensitivity had continued into his teens. He was now sixteen and getting better at controlling his emotions, but a hissy fit was not far off from an explosion of anger.

Dad reassured had Perry they would not leave without getting feedback.

Perry was the one Abi and the other judges had initially wanted to make up the five, but in the final deliberation session, Sami had switched Perry for Nathan as he felt he was a better fit.

While trying to leave in a hurry, Sami was met by Perry and his family.

'That's one of the judges. I think his name is Sami,' Perry said.

Dad took no chances in letting him slip away by blocking Sami's exit. 'Hey, are you Sami, one of the judges?' Dad asked.

'Yes, I am. I'm in a bit of a hurry, but what can I do for you?' Sami said. 'Our Perry is a great singer. He's young, talented, and plays many instruments. From what he described, he smashed it on all levels at the sessions. The comments from your people were all positive, and we thought he got through. It's really odd to be told he didn't make it.

'What's wrong with his voice? Is it his looks? He's a handsome young lad with a lot of potential — can't you keep him as a stand-by or on reserve in case one of the other boys doesn't work out?' Dad was doing his best to control his disappointment. It was obvious to see where Perry got his sensitivity from.

Sami was not someone to mince his words. 'I'm sorry you're disappointed, but he did make it to the final selection. It was very hard choosing between the boys, but I've made my decision. Perry didn't make it. It's just not his time right now. None of this is to say that he's not a brilliant singer, but for this project, he was not good enough. Someone else was better than him.' Sami realised the discussion could end up being a long one, and he was doing his best to get past the family and leave the building.

'Not good enough? What do you mean, not good enough?' Dad interrupted.

When Sami said, 'Brilliant singer', it was drowned out by Dad saying, 'Not good enough'.

'What's all this secrecy about, anyway? What kind of group are you forming? Perhaps your outfit is not good enough for our Perry,' Dad said mockingly. 'In fact, your outfit is pants!' Dad was getting worked up, and his irritation was evident. He'd been triggered after hearing the phrase 'not good enough'.

Sami intuited Dad's hate for those words, imagining it made him see red.

'We've been waiting all day from 9 a.m., only to be told by a trumped-up git like you that my son is not good enough? I ought to give you a slap right now!' Dad's accent had changed from a strong, East End cockney to raw Jamaican, and his voice was raised.

Mum, who was Irish, said, 'Charles, leave it. They're not going to change their minds, so let's leave it. It's been a day and a half. There'll be other auditions. This was just the tenth one of many more to come. We're not put off.

'Look, Perry is getting better every time we go to an audition.

'Sami, sorry about the outburst, but if you change your mind, you know how to reach us,' Mum said, using her calming influence and Irish charm to subvert any actions that might cause regret later. She didn't want word getting out that Perry's family was trouble.

Upon hearing the commotion, Abi came outside to see what was going on. She saw Sami, slightly dishevelled and surrounded by Perry's family, trying to edge his way towards the exit. 'What's going on here?' Abi asked.

'Oh, nothing. We just wanted some feedback about our Perry. We really thought he made it through to the group,' Mum explained.

Perry—who seemed to have forged a connection with Abi at the audition—broke through his shyness to ask her why he hadn't been chosen.

'Sami, I've got this. Remember that you've got that meeting. I'll speak to you later.'

Sami was relieved to have been rescued from the situation. He left the building, thinking that Shirlee had been right when she'd said they needed to know something about their families. He hoped the five selected boys did not have families even remotely similar to the flavour he'd tasted from Perry's people. He didn't want to be confronted like that again, but he was able to brush the incident off and get back into his stride. He was the one calling the shots, and if he had to tell himself that a thousand times, he was prepared to do so. This little infringement was only a part of it. Seeing how Abi had stepped in to tone things down and take control of what was an awkward situation only served to highlight her usefulness.

'Do you mind if I take Perry away, just for a brief chat?' Abi asked, addressing her question to Dad.

'Dad, let me go with her by myself,' Perry pleaded. Trying to assert himself with his parents was his way of taking a step towards becoming a grown-up, but Dad wasn't having any of it. He feared she would fill his head with lies if there was no one around to witness what they were saying.

'That's okay. Let's go into that room.' Abi led the way.

Mum and little brother Stevie sat down to wait in the foyer while Dad and Perry followed Abi. On their way, Abi poked her head into the main hall, where everyone was waiting to have their first meeting as a newly formed group. 'Give me five minutes, and I'll be back with you guys.'

In the side room, Abi positioned three chairs, two together for Perry and Dad and one facing them for herself. 'I just want to personally say thank you for coming to the audition. It's been quite a day, but don't look at this time as winning or losing or time wasted because it's not,' Abi said. She knew the feedback sessions could have the tendency to ramble on, but she didn't want that. Besides, she had to get to know the other guys. Still, she felt something of Perry's pain and wanted to help him in the process of what had gone down.

'Perry, you are an amazing singer, and you are so young, which means there are plenty more opportunities for you if you believe in yourself and don't give up. I can see that you have a mum and a dad who support you one hundred per cent—that's a real credit to you to have their backing.'

Abi looked at Dad and said, 'I have kids of my own. I'd give my right arm just to know they are happy and successful in whatever area they choose.' She hoped her comment would help soften his stance. 'But this is all about you now, Perry. You've got to want it, not for your mum and dad's sake, but for your own. Get grounded in yourself. Own your voice. Look after it. Practice those high notes we heard earlier today. Blend your sounds until it becomes second nature. I know you can do it. And keep going to auditions. Get a good vocal coach. Every good singer must learn how to protect their voice by using techniques. You don't want to ruin it by not understanding your vocals.

'We loved your voice, and you've got oceans of potential, but the brief for this group came from Sami, so, unfortunately, it wasn't up to me.

'The other thing to remember is this: when you're told something like "You're not good enough," say to yourself, "I can learn to be more than good enough," and that is the greatest revenge, showing others that don't believe in you or want you that you're successful or on your way to success. When your name, Perry Charles Baker, appears in lights, you'll know you've worked hard for it.

'That's all I've got to say.

'Now, do yourself proud. I wish you all the best. Just remember when you make it that we saw you here, and you walked out of the audition with your head held high.

'Okay? Are we good?'

Listening to Abi's encouraging words made Dad think about his mission to see his personal dream fulfilled through his son. Abi surmised that, yes, he'd wanted to taste the success from singing he'd been denied at a young age due to a lack of support and encouragement from his own parents, who never thought that singing could ever be a payable career for the likes of him, but Perry was the one who needed to do the hard work. Dad had to accept that it was no longer his idea that Perry could be a singer. He saw for himself that there was talent in him in his own right.

They walked away from the audition as a family, feeling much closer. It was a great moment for Perry, one he would never forget. After the other auditions, he'd walked away feeling deflated and rejected, but this time, the feelings were better than ever before. Perry's soul was alive with faith and an inner knowing that he would make it because he'd told himself that from his heart and vowed to do whatever it took. He was now well and truly lit, and nothing was going to put out that fire.

Abi went back into the hall, where everyone was waiting to have their very first briefing as a group.

'Are you okay? It sounded a bit heated out there,' Mervyn asked upon her return.

'Don't worry about it. It's all sorted now. We'll talk later,' Abi said, wanting to move on to the matter at hand. She knew how close Perry had been to getting into the group, and the commotion that had drawn Abi outside to investigate was, in fact, a divine moment, as she had the chance to say something to Perry that would not shatter his confidence but give him hope for his future.

Abi was good with people. Her friends often said this was one of her better qualities. She had come out of a mega Seventh Day Adventist Church with affiliations around London, Nottingham, Birmingham, and Wolverhampton. The church calendar was always filled with special events invariably involving music, singing, and production. If it wasn't the annual festivals like Christmas and Easter, it was the women's or men's conventions, visiting preachers, honorary elders, or funeral accolades in which choirs had to be mobilised and whipped into flawless perfection. There could be no bum notes there. It was typically the men's job to direct the choir and get that perfection out on stage unless it were children putting on a special performance for visiting guests or the nativity. Only then were women given permission to lead. Getting the right song choice required exceptional skills, and it was not without its drama when egos got in the way.

Once, Abi had an idea for the children to put on a biblical, musical production about Nicodemus, who had gone to visit Jesus after dark because he wanted to know what the phrase being 'born again' meant. The play was to be performed in song, with the scripture telling the story in rap. She wrote it and auditioned the parts with other members of the youth team, who loved the novel idea of the musical. This was the kind of creativity that Abi had in abundance, though it rarely came out.

Perry reminded her of the young boy who had played Jesus in her musical. He didn't believe in God, only coming to church because his parents had made him, but he was a natural at learning his lines and rapping. Everyone said they loved it, and the play went down in the archives, remembered as being a great performance, never to be forgotten.

This, however, was nothing like the church setting she was familiar with or had ever seen. This was secular, and on the real-world stage, but if anyone could make the group work and fit together like a perfect jigsaw puzzle, it would be Abi. The boys only needed to be honed into shape.

𝄞

4

———

The Family

Famous groups were often family-oriented. From these families, tribes emerged, incorporating their members. The Jacksons—as in Michael, Germain, Marlon, Randy, Tito and the rest of them—created a dynasty involving the whole family, like a family business that everyone profited from. The head of the family was Joe Jackson. It was no secret he was a tyrant of a father, but he whipped those boys into a shape he believed would make the brand—the tribe—successful. There was longevity in all of his motives. He might have called it tough love, but the ones upon whom it was afflicted called it abuse. Not that there was any comparison.

The Jacksons were all one family, which gave them a head start as they could practice together, morning, noon, and night until their performances were spotlessly orchestrated.

DeAngelo, Karl, Jay, Nathan, and Edward—whose name would be shortened to Eddie—were all perfect strangers. Only someone with a vision of the future in store for these boys would have the virtue to make something great out of them. How far would they go in the industry? How great would their popularity be? Would they be one-trick ponies? That all depended on the level of detail that would go into the crafting of the group and the belief and conviction they would serve up to the public as they converted them into fans.

Abi knew the brief Sami had shared with her. She was aware that there was much to work on. To some degree, the boys were all blank canvases with exceptional voices and fresh-faced looks. Each of them had their own swagger, a hallmark of the fashion and age, and they were all single entities. This family, as quirky as it seemed, had to start somewhere before they blended together.

Back in the room, Abi was left to lead, but Mervyn and Shirlee directed questions to the boys while Candice observed and took notes. Always quick to get to the point, Abi began with, 'Hi. You've made it, guys. Well done. Woo hoo! Thanks for being here.

'We've put together a timetable so you can be at the right places and at the right times. This area will be our central location. As most of you live in the south, it will be easier for you to get to. We want to know some things about you, mainly your family background. Not that we want to be nosey or anything, but families are important. There are no right or wrong answers here, so relax. We just want to get to know you better.

'Let's start with Karl.'

Although Karl was related to Candice through her brother — it didn't omit him from auditioning just like everyone else. At the time, only Abi knew he was related, but he wasn't chosen because Candice was Abi's best friend — he was a hands-down favourite of Sami and Mervyn, and as Mervyn was the vocal coach, he made sure Karl got everyone's attention. His voice was like that of a natural-born singer who could sing 'La Traviata', if you asked.

Karl had never had singing lessons. The group would be the first time he'd ever be anything close to a professional lead.

'Tell us about your family.'

'As you know, I'm fifteen, one of five children. I'm the third oldest, with two brothers and two younger sisters. My mum and dad are together. Lots of my friends don't have that.

'Our house is noisy, with everyone playing their own music. I get on with everyone in my family, but I'm closest to my second-oldest brother. We are like twins because we're ten months apart.

'Our family is big on both sides, so we have lots of aunts and uncles, and our cousins live locally, so I get to see them coming in and out of our houses regular. My best friend is my cousin, Jake, Aunty Candy's son.'

Candice interjected with, 'For the record, there is no nepotism here. Everyone who made this group did so on their own merit, and there were no favours from anyone,' hoping to head off any accusations that Karl was only there because of his aunty.

Mervyn asked, 'How would you describe your childhood from zero to seven years old?'

Karl didn't want to alarm anyone by talking about his health issues. It wasn't that they stopped him from doing everything a child of his age might want to do, but from zero to seven years, he was in and out of the hospital because of his congenital heart condition. It wasn't quite a hole in his heart, but he had a slightly collapsed artery that had to be addressed with multiple heart operations. They called Karl a little fighter because he withstood two operations. Each year, he attended the Great Ormond Street Hospital for an annual review with his consultant, Dr Martin, who was always amazed that his heart was strong, functioning, and as sound as a bell.

'My family is solid. Everyone knows us in the area, so I don't get bullied at school or anything.' That was correct—no one would dare to mess with his family, as they were well known for being outspoken in the community.

Abi smiled. 'Thanks for that, Karl. Let's have DeAngelo.'

'Yo. Well…um…I'm DeAngelo. I'm fifteen years old. My mum and dad split when I was five, but my mum got married again when I was ten.

'I've got a little sister, Shanice. She's five. I love her, man.

'So, I've got two dads. Robert, my stepdad, has been the father I never could have wished for. He came into my life, and we were instantly friends. He's great. So, I'm blessed both ways. I'm not dissing my real dad, but I know I can talk to Robert about anything. He's on the piano, I swear, like twenty-four-seven, trying to figure out a new rift or something. I love to sing, so I practice my vocals while he plays.

'My mum's happy, so I'm happy.

'I've been around music all my life. Both my mum and birth-dad were in the music business. We travelled on tours a lot in the States. By the way, my mum is Shirlee.'

Shirlee also voiced a disclaimer: 'When it came to making the decision on DeAngelo, in no way did I try to influence any of the other judges.'

Mervyn and Sami had been none the wiser when the choices were being discussed.

Shirlee continued, 'I asked Abi if I could put forward DeAngelo, and she agreed. She made it clear that if he didn't measure up, he would not get a place in the group, and I accepted that.' Shirlee was as kind-hearted and fair-minded as you could get, which was why her first husband, Lewis, always seemed to get the better of her. He could talk her around even if he was in the wrong, and he often was, cheating on her with any backing singer he fancied.

Although DeAngelo was born in England, the family had moved to the US when he was three because Shirlee's singing career had taken off with a big hit single. His father, Lewis, was both her manager and producer. Lewis was a respected producer when it came to contemporary soul record labels. He managed Shirlee, gaining her recognition with the likes of Teddy Pendergrass and Luther Vandross. Shirlee once sang a duet at a concert with Isaac Hayes — it was a sell-out! To this day, whenever Isaac Hayes's concert is mentioned, Shirlee is in the clip.

Lewis's over-possessiveness and his infidelity eventually drove them apart. They officially separated when DeAngelo was five and divorced when he was seven. She left the US and returned to London, living off her royalties and the agreed-upon alimony from Lewis. It was not a bad split, as they agreed that DeAngelo should always be in contact with his father plus visit at least once a year. Though he was a long-distance father, he did it well.

Lewis was still riding high off of his successes, and he had no intention of returning to England unless it was on business. Whenever he did have business, he made it seem as if he was coming over to see his son.

By the time DeAngelo was nine, Shirlee had met Robert at a music festival. He was the polar opposite of Lewis. They married and had one child, Shanice. Whenever Robert had the opportunity to introduce his family to anyone, he always said, 'I have two children,' and he loved them both dearly.

Shirlee sometimes felt guilty about the upheaval they experienced after going to the US, and she wondered what the effect might be on DeAngelo — would it cause him to be wayward? — but Robert put her fears to rest whenever she saw their bond, and there was no denying they were father and son. DeAngelo was fifteen, but he still enjoyed hanging out with his family.

Mervyn was an American with an accent to match. 'Aah. I see now why your accent has a slight American twang. You've lived in the States. Some of your words are pronounced like an American would.'

'I thought I'd lost my accent,' DeAngelo answered jokingly with a pronounced American accent and a smile.

'I like the phrasing of the lyrics in your tone. Don't lose it. It's going to serve you well,' Abi said.

DeAngelo smiled.

'Next up, let's have Nathan.' Abi turned her head to look directly at him.

'Well, I'm sixteen, from the Brockwell Park area. I live in foster care with two other teenagers around my age, one a girl and one a boy. My carers are John and Molly. They're good people.' Nathan stopped. All eyes were on him, expecting more information. Nathan smiled but at the same time, he shifted in his seat, trying hard not to look uncomfortable.

Mervyn came swiftly in with, 'Thanks for sharing that with us. You've got a great voice—a tad pitchy, but with my training, you'll have excellent vocals. Just wondering: where did you get that singing voice from?'

Nathan shrugged his shoulders and said, 'I don't know. I just love to sing.'

'Well, you must be singing and listening to a lot of music to have harmonies on point like that. Congratulations. I can see you'll bring a lot of balance to the group.'

Nathan was the quietest of the boys, and Mervyn's praise was like water for thirsty ground, and his eyes lit up as praise was something he didn't often get. This was his first venture at stepping out on his own, fulfilling his dreams and proving to everyone and anyone that he could sing and be rich and famous. Underneath the dream was a hunger for his birth father to, just for once, acknowledge the son he had missed out on and be a part of his success. He imagined TV shows, constant appearances in the news, reports of what Nathan had for breakfast and paps taking pictures of his every waking move at nightclubs, restaurants and award ceremonies. At the famous acceptance speeches stars gave at award ceremonies in which they always give thanks to their mums and dads, Nathan would say, 'I want to give thanks to… myself for doing a good job of raising myself. Without my efforts, resilience, and perseverance, I would not have made it. I thank myself for believing in me.'

Nathan wrote that speech one day while his foster carers, John and Molly, had stood at the bottom of the stairs, shouting, 'Stop that racket. You can't sing to save your life.' It made Nathan even more determined to practice, practice, practice.

Sarah, one of the other teenagers living in the house, had heard the comments. She knocked gently on his door, as she often did, and said, 'Don't listen to them. They wouldn't know a star if it were shining right in their faces. You've got a wicked voice, and I love it. Don't give up because of them. They don't care about us, anyway. They're only doing this fostering thing for the money.'

Sarah was sixteen. She'd moved in only a year before because the relationship between her and her mum was fractious. The problem between Sarah and her mother was that it was hard to set boundaries when they both acted like children. Her mother had been fifteen when she'd had Sarah, so they were sometimes great friends but often sworn enemies. That was when social services stepped in.

Nathan had gone into the care system when he was three years old. His mother, Chantel, had given birth to him when she was sixteen. She had been thrown out by her mum for getting pregnant and ended up in a mother and baby's home, where Nathan was born. Later, she was given a flat to start out with her own independence. She tried to care for Nathan, but she was always out partying, wanting to enjoy her youth.

One night, while she was out, a meddlesome neighbour reported that a young child had been left at home alone. The police and social services came, and they took Nathan away.

Chantel had continued her relationship with him through supervised visits, always promising that when things got better, she would come back to take him away. In her time away, substance and alcohol abuse slowly ravaged her life. There had been times when Chantel turned up, but she was not fully coherent and was not allowed to see Nathan. Although she was often in that state, she somehow never missed a visit.

Then, thirteen years later, after repeating that she was getting herself cleaned up, she said, 'I've met a nice guy who said he loves me. I told him about you, and he's going to buy a nice house where we can all live together.' Her new beaus were regular topics of conversation, but this time, she genuinely seemed to believe her new lover's intentions.

At first, Nathan was fully invested in the stories, but over time, his expectancy and hope dwindled as he could see it was not going to happen.

In those early years, until he was taken into foster care, Nathan remembered his mother playing music all day long, singing and dancing to it. He loved to see her happy. She would sing to him, cuddle with him and dance to her favourite song, 'My baby just cares for me,' by Nina Simone. It was when he felt the most secure. For him, singing was a connection back to that happy time and place.

'Jay, you're next.' Abi seemed to have startled him with her voice. 'Tell us about your family.'

'Jay is in the house.' He often talked about himself in the third person. It was one of Jay's habits.

For Abi, it was a bit jarring. 'Jay, stop doing that. Just speak normally. We are all here.'

'I've just turned seventeen. I don't have any brothers or sisters, just my mum and dad and lots of aunties and uncles and cousins. I play the piano, guitar and drums. My family loves music. Yeah, they encouraged me to follow my passion, so I connected with some local guys, and we started a group, but they weren't going anywhere, so I saw this audition and went for it.'

'What area did you grow up in? You don't have a London accent,' Shirlee asked.

'I was born in Birmingham. I didn't think anyone would notice. I've lived in London for five years now.' Jay nodded his head. 'I like Birmingham. It will always be my hometown, but London's great.'

'You guys are so vague about your families,' Shirlee smiled sweetly and said what was on her mind. 'There are no prizes for the best family. This is not a grilling. Come on — relax.'

'That's what guys do,' Mervyn retorted. 'It's a man thing, ain't it, guys?' Collectively, the boys laughed.

Presenting one thing while masking the reality of his family came naturally to Jay. Jason was his real name, but he preferred to be called Jay. He came from a middle-class, family of Black lawyers. Even his two aunts on his mother's side in Canada were lawyers. That was the family's legacy. His grandparents in Barbados (on his father's side) had studied law to help struggling people with their rights. His mum and dad were both born in the UK to Bajan migrants who came to England, 'the Mother Country', back in the late fifties. They met at college and went on to study law at Birmingham University. Their whole lives revolved around civil rights law. They had both become barristers, then solicitors, treading in familiar territory. However, they never planned to have children. Then, unexpectedly, in their late thirties, Jay came along.

Whenever his grandparents came to visit from Barbados, they'd say, 'Jason, come here, boy. I'm gonna spoil you rotten.' The word 'no' was not in their vocabulary, to the very slight annoyance of his mother, but she understood.

Jason was their first and only grandchild from their one and only child: Jason's dad. They thought he'd never produce an heir, but they felt truly blessed to have one, even if it had been an accident. When asked about children, his mum and dad had told their parents many times, 'Sorry, we don't want any,' but his grandparents wouldn't accept that. They told Jason they sincerely prayed they would have a grandchild, and God heard their prayers. They'd say, 'You were handpicked for us.' Jay was seventeen, but they still hugged him as if he were a little child, even if he towered over them and little Jason had become big Jay.

Jay loved his parents. What he admired most were their strength and cohesiveness. At home, there were many heated debates that always ended in hilarious laughter. His dad was the one to usually bring in the humour. It worked every time and cut through any tension. Jay saw that they had each other's backs, and they were solid.

After hearing everyone's stories about their families, Eddie racked his brain to concoct a story that might match any of the others.

When it was his turn, Abi gestured with her hands towards him like a conductor and said, 'Eddie, tell us about your family.'

'I live in Lewisham with my mum and my twin sisters, Bianca and Jessica. They're six. I'm the oldest. Mum and Dad were like soul mates. They married young and had me. My dad was a fireman, but there was a massive fire at some sixteenth birthday party. Something went wrong, and he died trying to rescue some of the kids.'

'Oh, I'm sorry to hear that.' There was a sharp intake of breath from everyone in the room, and just like Abi, everyone's faces quickly switched to show empathy for Eddie's loss. 'Sorry to bring up painful memories. How old were you when it happened?'

'The fire happened on a Saturday, and my second birthday was on the Sunday.'

Being inquisitive, Abi asked, 'What year was that?'

Eddie did a quick calculation and said, 'Nineteen-eighty-one.'

'Oh, my God—was it the Deptford fire? I think eight teenagers died.' Abi turned to look at everyone and continued, 'It was all over the newspapers and on TV. That would be around thirteen years ago. I didn't know that a fireman also lost his life. I'm so sorry to hear that.'

Eddie neither confirmed nor denied Abi's assumption of his story.

'And your sisters—did your mother remarry?'

'Yes, but it didn't work out. My stepdad left the house when my sisters were two.'

'It must have been so distressing for your mother,' said Shirlee, who was now teary-eyed.

'My mum's been a single parent ever since, raising all of us, so I wanna be successful in the music business, make my family proud of me and buy our own house.'

'And we want you to be successful, too.' Mervyn said this with a serious face. 'Let's make this happen, guys.'

There was the truth, and then there was the real truth. Eddie *did* have twin sisters who were six years old, and his mother *was* a single parent. Two truths out of ten lies. His mother never married Eddie's father. They were casual acquaintances who had got together one drunken night out at a nightclub. Two months later, she realised she was pregnant. For the sake of the baby, they tried to forge a relationship together, but they had irreconcilable differences. He was a musician, footloose and fancy-free. Starting a family was not on his agenda, at least not any time soon.

His mother's relationships were always complicated because she craved the love she never had from her father. She grew up seeing the faults in her parents' relationship, which was rocky at best, caused by infidelity, and at worst, violent behind closed doors, yet her parents stayed together. This left her longing to be in the ideal picture of a happy family, and as far as she was concerned, every new relationship was going to be 'the one'.

Eddie loved his mother, but he also hated her poor choices in men. He often thought it would have been better if he hadn't been born. Every attempt his mother had made to create an ideal family picture led Eddie towards a fortified city of dissatisfaction. Whoever the man was, she would include him in their lives, going to the cinema, on holidays and short breaks, or to parks to appear like a unit, but there was nothing she could do to make things right in Eddie's eyes. Then, when she'd met the twins' father, Eddie caused so much unease through rebellion just for the sake of it that it drove a wedge between them. Eddie had made it clear: 'Ain't no way this man's gonna be my dad.'

His own father had never really been in his life, and he had no idea where he was.

On the other hand, Eddie resented the fact that the twins' father never missed a weekend to see his girls despite the break-up with his mother. Eddie observed the love their father gave his children, and it made him burn with anger whenever he saw it. It only served to remind him of his lack of paternal love.

'Thanks, everyone. You all have something in common.'

Eddie asked Abi, 'What's that?'

'Great families,' answered Abi.

For a moment, Eddie thought she was a mind reader and knew the reality of his world, but he smiled and realised that she couldn't possibly know anything about his family life.

Being the mother hen she was, Shirlee said, 'We've all have to get to know each other, so we need to get you guys bonding. We need to create a family unit. When I was touring in the States, it was the relationships I formed with my band and entourage that kept me going. Although I live in the UK now, they are family, and we'll always be friends for life.'

Mervyn added, 'Have you guys got each other's numbers yet?' Some had, but not all. 'I want you to stay in contact. Talk every day about anything—the weather, what you are doing…get to know each other. Become friends. Find things in common. Do you guys like soccer?'

Eddie ignored Mervyn's reference to soccer and subtly corrected him by saying, 'I like football. I support Arsenal.'

Having lived in the States, DeAngelo said, 'We call it football in the US, and it's huge. Like, the NFL is a religion. American football is a bit like English rugby. Anyway, to answer your question, I'm more into basketball. I play it and watch it.'

'I'm a basketball player, too, so I'm with you on that,' said Jay.

'I like basketball and football,' Nathan said. 'I can play both. I support Man U.'

'How can you do that, man? You're in London.'

Eddie shook his head as if to say, 'Shame on you.'

Karl didn't want to feel left out. 'I support Arsenal, but I'm useless at playing football.' Although his heart was stronger after all the operations he'd had as a child, he was never encouraged to join a football team like some of the other boys. His mother was always anxious that he might get hurt if he got into a hard tackle, but that never stopped him from having a kickabout with his friends. His thing was gaming. He was the first at his school to have a Gameboy device and a Sega home console. It went without saying that he was popular with the boys in the neighbourhood, who'd pay a fortune in the arcade playing *Street Fighter*. Karl could play at home whenever he wanted, and it didn't cost him a penny.

'That's great. We're getting somewhere,' added Abi. 'You've all got fabulous families, and you're all sporty. Perhaps you can hang out together one Sunday and play a game of whatever, but for now, let's do something less competitive but fun — any suggestions?'

5

Watch Over Me

THE BOYS DID not lack a sense of adventure, given the myriad suggestions presented. Everyone talked at once, suggesting everything from skydiving to go-kart racing, dry snowboarding, drag bike riding and speed skating. The options came in thick and fast.

'Guys, guys, those are all too dangerous. I'm not doing any of that,' Candice interrupted. 'Don't get me wrong — they're great ideas — but you can do those things together in your own time outside of this room. We need something simple and safe.'

Abi jumped in with, 'What about theme parks?'

The animated chatter that followed made it evident they were all kids at heart — they reacted as if they'd been promised a dream trip to Disneyland. Apart from Jay and DeAngelo, whose parents could easily afford it, none of the others had ever ventured out to a theme park, let alone tried any of the other suggestions they made. Local parks or the occasional trip to the seaside were about it.

Candice was well aware that it was not the trip that was important but the bonding. The boys had all been strangers and now they were looking to have a future together in the music business.

There was a general consensus for the theme park idea, and Disneyland, Paris, seemed to be at the top of the boys' bucket lists, along with Chessington World of Adventure, Thorpe Park, Alton Towers and Blackpool thrown in for good measure. They each seemed to have their own bucket list of theme parks.

'Disneyland Paris is out of the question. Alton Towers and Blackpool are too far, so hands up for Thorpe Park,' Abi said.

Eddie's hand went up.

'Hands up for Chessington World of Adventure.'

All hands went up.

Eddie did not mind either way. For him, it was about the adventure.

'Chessington, it is,' Abi said.

The date for the theme park was set for the following Saturday at 10 a.m. It would be their first trip out as a group. They were to meet at Waterloo Station at 8.30 a.m.

'Do we have to pay for this?' Eddie asked. He struggled with money like a bucket with a hole in it leaking water.

'Good question, Eddie. Thanks for raising it. We do have a budget that Sami asked me to manage.' Abi was responsible for arranging the bonding interactions for the group. For this trip, Sami had given her six hundred to cover the rides, food, transportation and anything miscellaneous. 'Is everyone okay with getting to Chessington?' Abi asked.

Everyone except for Eddie said they were okay to get there but would need reimbursement after the fact. Eddie spoke up. 'Sorry, but I don't have the money for travel.'

'No problem. Travel shouldn't be more than twenty pounds.' Abi reached into her bag, searched for her purse, pulled out two ten-pound notes, and handed them to Eddie.

'Thanks. That's great. My mum struggles with money, so she doesn't have much spare cash. I'm looking for a part-time job to get my own money. It's hard to find one at fifteen, but I'll be sixteen soon.'

♫ ♫ ♫

Eddie and Jay had established that they didn't live far from each other. At seventeen, Jay had a car, and he offered to give Eddie a lift home.

'That's so cool, man. How come you drive?' Eddie said in his excitement at his first time being alone in a car with a peer.

'There was this young guy who got murdered in Eltham, so my mother said it would be better to have me driving to keep me off the streets. It's just an old banger, but I've got to put my own petrol in it. I work a few hours a week in Safeway's Supermarket to get some money.'

Eddie thought about the kind of parents Jay must have had to even think about him taking on such responsibility. 'If I had wheels,

I'd be set, man. I'd drive everywhere—up north to Birmingham, even Manchester. Go to Brighton Beach.' Lost in the moment, Eddie smiled as he talked out loud. 'Today's my lucky day.'

'What?' Jay was puzzled by Eddie's random comment. 'Where do you want me to drop you off?'

'Over there, on the left.'

Jay pulled over, and Eddie got out of the car. He didn't want Jay to know where he actually lived, and he had no plans to invite him around anytime soon.

'Next week, man,' Eddie shouted. 'Laters!'

Jay sped off.

Eddie strode towards the newsagent, walking with a swagger. His head was filled with thoughts of being in a boy band and having a manager, vocal coach, and music producer. The past couple of hours had felt surreal, as if being in the slipstream of a dream that was programmed to get him to his destiny, which was to be a member of a popular group and signed to a successful record label. Like a warm breeze, he felt the vibes of good fortune all around him. 'This is my lucky day.'

He went into the newsagents', handed over one of the ten-pound notes, and bought ten pounds' worth of scratch cards.

Walking home was like a cool dance. The song playing in his head was 'Here Comes the Hotstepper' by Ini Kamoze. Humming and singing the words to the song uplifted his state of mind.

He put the key in the door and walked into the kitchen. Dinner was being served. Usually, the family gathering would have infuriated Eddie, but on that day, he was not bothered.

Eddie said, 'Hi, everyone. I'm home.' It was more than he would normally say when seeing his sisters, their father, and his mother all together, playing happy family and eating dinner at the table.

When he entered, there was a deathly silence as everyone waited for him to start banging the kitchen cupboards in disapproval or annoyance as he foraged for something to eat or found something to kick off about — like 'Who moved my cup?' — anything to put the blame on someone else for his bad mood. But this time, there was something remarkably different about him.

Theresa, his mother, saw the smile on his face, and she took advantage of it to invite him to sit with them. 'Would you like me to get you a plate?' she asked him. There was a pot of chicken stew in the centre of the table with other dishes.

Eddie thought about it for a few seconds, then said, 'Yes.' He was onto a winner today. Sitting down with them did not mean that he was joining them — he was joining another family with the band members, after all. This cosy family dinner he felt as if he had gate-crashed was unimportant.

Bianca, one of the twins, spoke up: 'Hi, Eddie. I won a prize at school for reading.'

'That's good. And what about you, Jessica?'

'I won a prize for drawing.'

'Look at that—my two bright sisters. I wonder where they get their talent from?' Eddie looked at them sweetly. The comment was said sarcastically and meant to niggle at George and his mum. With that being said, he did love his sisters, and he always made time for them.

'You know what? I shall take this lovely food upstairs and leave you lovely people to carry on.' Eddie picked up his plate and left the room.

For a brief moment, no one said anything. George shook his head in a kind of disbelief. 'What's going on with him? He's blowing hot and cold. Theresa, that boy needs help. He could be on drugs, for all I know.'

'Come on, don't be silly. Of course, he's not. He's just a bit troubled sometimes.'

'But I've always shown him kindness and respect—what more can I do? That's why I can't—'

Theresa interjected with, 'That's why you should take the time to think about what you say in front of the girls, right?'

George realised it was not the time or place to air his grievances against Eddie's hostility, and he stopped talking.

After five years of trying to be friends with Eddie, George had left the house. The day he moved out—twelve months ago to the day—he was sad that he would not wake up beside Theresa and in the same home as his daughters, but he was happy to be out of the inferno he had endured from Eddie's wroth. George almost felt comfortable having what seemed like a perfectly normal dinner with his family until Eddie arrived, displaying what he could only describe as strange behaviour, but his rose-coloured glasses soon fell off, and he deduced that nothing had changed, and things were not quite as they might appear.

'What? Oh, My God!' came a loud shout from Eddie's bedroom, along with banging and crashing noises.

Theresa went into the hallway to shout upstairs in the direction of his room. 'Eddie, are you okay?'

Eddie shouted back, 'What do you want? Mind your own business.'

Theresa went back to the dining room.

With a saddened tone in his voice, George said, 'I rest my case.' He took in a long breath, and equally as slow, breathed out a sigh.

♫ ♫ ♫

Eddie sat on his bed, staring at the discarded scratch card duds. There was not a penny in sight. He truly believed he'd win something this time, but he'd lost ten quid instead. Ten quid that was not his to lose in the first place and that he needed for his train ticket to the theme park the following Saturday. He thought it through, shook off the disappointment, and as usual, resolved to cross that bridge when he came to it.

Eddie's week was taken up with his final school assignments and coursework that needed to be handed in. The one thing he did well was to keep up with his studies. His thoughts were that if the singing didn't pan out, he would become a successful businessman and a millionaire. One way or another, his personal pursuit of something great was going to happen; he felt certain of that.

For now, he had the problem of finding the money to get to the theme park. Borrowing from his friends was complicated because he had run out of people to ask. He sometimes gave back what he owed, but his promise to return it within twenty-four hours had lost its power and trust.

He packed his lunch and walked to school instead of catching the bus more days than not, as he tended to spend money as soon as it arrived, only this time, he had to find the money. Eddie wondered how it might look if he did not turn up at the theme park.

He rationalised his next move by telling himself that if he didn't get any money, he'd say he was too sick to travel due to food poisoning. That was it. He was slightly uncomfortable about not showing up for the first bonding event, so he tentatively explored what other options he had.

'Mum?' Eddie had not exchanged many words with her since the previous Saturday, and it was now Friday, the day before the trip.

Theresa was surprised to hear him involuntarily initiate a conversation. She had resolved to give him a lot of space to work through his teenage angst. 'You haven't spoken to me all week—what's up?'

'I need ten pounds to buy some paints for my final assignment deadline that I've got to hand in on Monday. I didn't want to ask, but there's no one else. Mum, can you help me? Please?' Eddie smiled and tilted his head like a puppy waiting to be given a treat.

'Eddie, do you think I am stupid or something? Why are you spending all of your money on scratch cards?' Theresa asked.

Trying to switch the subject to the invasion of his privacy, his sacred space, Eddie said, 'Have you been snooping around in my room again?'

'No, Eddie. You're not clever enough to hide it for me to need to snoop. I went to the outside bin and saw a load of scratch cards in it.'

'That was not me. It could have been anyone passing by who happened to put them in our bin. Why does it have to be me? That's what I mean—you never trust me.' Eddie walked away as if he were the offended party.

'Are you going to give me an explanation for this or not?' Theresa waited for a response but got nothing. Eddie was already at the front door, getting ready to leave. He opened the door and slammed it shut behind him.

The weight of his situation played on his mind, but he thought that a long walk might clear his head and help him find a solution. 'What have I got to lose? I might as well spend the other ten pounds on scratch cards. And if I win nothing, I'm going to be sick with food poisoning anyway,' Eddie said, talking himself into finding another newsagent to buy another set of scratch cards.

He heard a car's horn blow and looked up to see that it was Jay.

Jay pulled over. 'Hey, man, what you doing around here?'

'I don't live far from here, and I was just going somewhere.' Eddie was pleased to see him, but he was still preoccupied with his dilemma.

'Let's meet tomorrow at 7 a.m. We can catch the bus to London Bridge and then go to Waterloo,' Jay said.

'Yeah, man…I'm not feeling too good right now with my stomach. I ate some dodgy wings or something. If I can make it, I'll be there at seven.' Eddie tried to look sick by touching his tummy as if in pain.

'You'll be fine. You've gotta be there tomorrow, man. You can't miss this. Be positive. Don't think about it.

'My mum gives me peppermint tea when I have a bad stomach. It seems to work and calm things down a bit.

'See you tomorrow. Seven o'clock, sharp! Don't be late.' It seemed as if Jay would not take 'No, I'm not coming' for an answer.

Eddie continued walking. It didn't worry him that he was only fifteen years old. He could pass as seventeen or even eighteen at the newsagent's because he had the height and the build of a handsome young man.

When George had first moved into the house with Theresa after the twins were born, Eddie was short in stature, but six years later, he almost towered over George at five-foot-ten inches and as a result, wherever he went, he was never challenged about his age.

Eddie purchased the cards without investing much thought or emotion into buying them. It wasn't like before, when he'd pumped himself up, trying to lure Lady Luck his way with positive energy. This time, he was plain neutral. He walked away, stuffing the cards into his pocket, unlike the last time, when he'd felt as if he were carrying tickets of gold, and he would not go home to check their status. He saw that, across the road, there was a green space and a bench, not fully in plain sight but slightly hidden. He looked to see if anyone was watching, but there was no one passing by or heading his way.

He went over to sit on the bench and looked up at the sky, perhaps for divine inspiration, but said nothing, not even a prayer. One by one, he checked the cards. This was a matter of course. It had to be done: win something or play sick.

Nothing.

Not one line of jacks among the cards he had bought.

'Blow it, man!' Eddie said to himself.

He was down to his last card. Why bother to expect anything?

Eddie was so engrossed in what he was doing that he didn't notice the police officer coming his way. 'Hello, young man — are you okay?' he said, jolting Eddie from his concentration.

'Yes, I'm fine.'

'You look a bit lost — do you live around here?'

'Yes, not too far. I've just fallen out with my mother, so I thought I would go for a walk to clear my head,' Eddie said.

'You know, mums are kinda special, so don't be too hard on her. She's only showing you that she cares. My mother died a few years ago, and I miss her nagging. I'd give anything to hear her nag me again.

'Son, go home. It's gonna be all right, you'll see.'

Eddie got up from his seat and headed for home. It had been a strange encounter with the police officer, especially when he'd called him 'son'. Eddie didn't know why other than that he thought it weird.

Just as he was about to pass by the newsagent's a second time, he took out the remaining scratch card and checked.

Bingo!

He got a line of jacks.

'OMG! I won! I actually won something.' He went into the shop and handed over the scratch card.

The shopkeeper checked, and yes, it was true: he had won fifty pounds. The shopkeeper asked, 'How old are you?'

Eddie swiftly replied, 'Eighteen.'

The shopkeeper accepted him at his word. Besides, it was late, and he didn't want to argue his gut feeling about Eddie's age.

He counted out the money into five ten-pound notes and handed it to Eddie, who left the shop, thinking, Chessington, here I come.

A song by Dennis Emmanuel Brown popped into his head, making him smile. It was called 'Love and Hate'. Eddie sang the words, marvelling at the fact that his voice was truly so versatile that he could also sing reggae music.

6

The Sidekick

IT WAS A STRANGE morning, and therefore, it was hard to judge how the day would pan out. A thick early morning fog hovered in the air. If it were winter, one could almost certainly write the day off, but it was the start of June, and the weather forecast said it was going to be a scorcher, with temperatures expected to reach record levels.

In Eddie's household, Theresa was awoken by the swift sound of someone moving back and forth in the bathroom. Then, there was a loud sound as the front door was slammed shut. Eddie had left the house. Theresa checked her bedroom clock, and it was only 6.45 a.m., too early to get up on a Saturday and still time for a lie-in.

'Mum, can we have breakfast?' Like a dawn chorus it was Bianca and Jessica, awakened by the bang from the front door.

'Go back to bed, honey. It's too early.'

♫ ♫ ♫

Jay was at the bus stop, waiting for the bus to arrive to take him to London Bridge. As the bus arrived, he saw Eddie running in the distance, and he asked the driver to wait for his friend.

Eddie made it. Breathless, he paid for his ticket.

'You made it, man, by the skin of your teeth.' They both laughed.

The connections to Waterloo ran like clockwork. Eddie and Jay were the first to arrive. There had been no time for breakfast at home as it had taken every ounce of discipline for them to leave their houses on time. The real reward would be a pancake breakfast at McD's.

It seemed as if the others had the same idea. DeAngelo, Karl and Nathan came in one by one, like stars aligning. They hailed each other with hi-fives, yesses, and yos. Like synchronicity, they had all worn black, baggy jeans, hoodies, and Nike trainers. People around them seemed to do a double-take as they couldn't quite make out who they were, but they could see there was an aura of something special about them.

'I'm so glad to see you guys again. This is it, man; we're stars,' DeAngelo said.

The crescendo rose to another level, with everyone talking all at once to the point where the manager came over to ask them to keep the noise down. 'Where you all going so early this morning?' the manager asked.

DeAngelo spoke up: 'We're on a special covert mission to Chessington.'

They all laughed. Her chat with them only seemed to increase the noise level, but she was not about to spoil their jovial mood. 'Tone it down a bit.

'What time is your train?'

Karl said, 'Eight twenty-seven.' He looked at his watch, which said eight twenty-four. They had three minutes to get out of McD's, run down the concourse to their platform, and catch the train.

So as not to get pushed out of the way, the manager stepped quickly aside. She had never seen anyone move so fast. As they were leaving, she shouted, 'Have a nice day, now.'

With one second to spare, they got onto the train and through the doors before it swooped shut. Out of breath from running, they staggered towards some seats. The carriage was completely empty, so they had it all to themselves.

Who would have thought they hadn't known each other before the auditions; not even in passing on the street or at an event. Little did they know their bonding expedition would forge relationships for life.

'Next week, we start singing with the vocal coach. I can't believe it—we've got our own coach,' DeAngelo said. 'And a manager.'

Nathan expressed his uncertainty about the whole experience: 'I'm here for the ride. If we make it, we make it. If we don't, we don't.'

'Of course, we're going to make it. That's what all this is about, right?' Jay was the eternal optimist. 'Not making it isn't on my mind. We've got this one chance in a million—let's take it.' Jay put his hand on the centre of the carriage table and said, 'Are you with me?'

Eddie put his hand on top of Jay's, followed by Karl and then DeAngelo.

'Nathan, are you with us?' Jay asked.

'I'm with us, man.' Nathan's hand was the last on the pile. Like swearing allegiance to the flag, each one had made their own declaration of commitment.

'I've got a good feeling about this.' Karl said.

DeAngelo confirmed Karl's sentiment with, 'I hear you, man.' It was easy for Karl and DeAngelo to say this because they had access to the inside track from Candice and Shirlee.

Jay was all in for his own reasons. He started to sing the song, 'This is How We Do It' by Montell Jordon.

Eddie jumped up out of his seat to repeat the words in time to an imaginary beat, which was infectious because they all knew the song, and they all joined in.

Karl rapped, showing a quick wit by twisting the lyrics of the song to reflect his own version of the south and southeast sides of London, much to everyone's amusement.

'Tickets, please!' The ticket collector seemed to rock into their carriage to the beat of the song, which they found hilarious.

♫ ♫ ♫

It was an all-round smooth journey to Chessington. Candice picked up Abi from her home and planned to drive on the M25. Abi didn't like motorways and was happy she wasn't the one driving. By contrast,

Candice loved the picture that driving painted in her mind. It gave her the sense of getting away from it all, throwing stuff into the back of the car and the freedom to 'just drive' wherever and whenever she wanted. It was the thrill of being in the driving seat, not having to wait for someone to take her to the places she wanted to go. The adventures she had would be her own choices.

'So, when we get there, what's the plan?' Candice asked.

'I don't know. This is not a babysitting expedition. They just need to get used to each other so they'll have a better chance of coming across as authentic when they sing together.'

'Yes, look at that Boyz 2 Men group—they're not the best-looking guys (not my type), but do they look as if they've been singing together from birth in the same household.'

'Yeah, you're too right,' Abi said. 'Our boys are handsome. They've got the vocals, too. We've just got to put the package together.'

'How many weeks do we have to get them ready?'

Abi had the schedule mapped out in her head. 'We've got June, July, and August, about twelve weeks. Vocal practice every day—that's a must. They can also do that at home. They've got to learn how to warm up. Mervyn will teach them that.

'Then, they need to sing together every week. I've got a friend who runs a choir at a church. Although I'm not in the church anymore, I still have contacts, and I've arranged for them to turn up for choir practice twice a month. My friend, Trevor, is up for it.'

'Not that I've ever been to church, but I've seen the programme that comes on every Sunday called *Songs of Praise*. Those singers can belt out those notes. They're so talented at controlling their voices like that. I can sing in tune, but there's no guarantee I won't throw out a bum note—how embarrassing is that?' Candice sniggered at her thoughts.

'One day, I'll go back to church. I just miss opening my mouth and allowing my breath to carry the song out into the atmosphere. We call it worship when the sound comes from a place deep in your soul, and you pour it out to God. Singers like Aretha Franklin, Ann Nesby, Dionne Warwick, Roberta Flack—they sing from that place. That's why they're called soul singers. What a gift to have, to be able to connect people to their emotions.'

'It's incredible to me,' Candice said, not fully understanding what the concept of worship was.

'It's a gift from God.' Abi started to feel emotional. She allowed the tears to flow freely down her cheeks.

'What's up? Are you okay?' Candice asked.

'Yes, I'm fine, but I get teary-eyed when I think of how good God has been to me, even when I don't feel as if I deserve it. But hey, what we're doing will work out for the better; I know it.' Abi wiped her face and did her best to push back the tears with tiny snuffles. This wasn't the place to be overwhelmed by melancholy about her divorce, leaving the church or how they tried to silence her voice. 'When I stepped away from the church, they almost convinced me I was leaving God. It still pains me when I think about it.' Abi had also left because she wanted to find out if God existed outside of the box of their managed building that was the church.

Abi changed the subject. 'Sami's amazing. We talk almost twice a day and meet up once a week. He said the boys will be ready to go into the studio to lay down the vocals by the end of July or early August.' All Abi had to do was to get them ready for the big day. She, of all people, knew that studio time meant money, the kind of which she didn't have. Her ex-husband had been the one to hold the purse strings in the relationship, and he would have none of his money spent on recording. He didn't mind her singing in the church choir, but becoming a star was out of the question. That simply was not the life he wanted for his family. He often raged at her whenever she tried to do something on her own, and his 'controlling demons', as she described them, would not allow her to venture beyond the confines of singing practice. But she was no longer under his control, and Sami had all expenses covered, including the studio. Abi was willing to wait for her time to shine, allowing the boys to go first. She trusted that Sami would be her ticket to greatness, hope, and freedom.

Abi continued talking: 'And he promised he'd get me in the studio to record one of his songs. He said he loved my voice. Hearing it from someone like him means something to me.' In her eyes, Sami was a well-connected producer in the music industry, the inside man she needed.

Candice felt happy for her friend. She could see that Abi was infatuated with Sami—or was it the power she believed he had? It had not even been a year since they'd met, but Abi had placed her trust wholly in him.

'You look like you're in love,' Candice said with a smirk on her pursed lips.

'What are you talking about?' Abi turned her head towards her and smiled as if being caught out about something. Her cheeks seemed to radiate the sun, and it was not from the tears of emotions she'd cried earlier.

'We're just good friends. We're having fun.'

Candice was not from the music world. She had no idea of the wiles of cutthroat characters willing to do anything for fame and fortune. Whether contemporary, pop, or Christian gospel, there was always a clique and ruling hierarchy of power and control, and as Abi had found out, the Christian scene was no different. She'd been promised so much from her church and got so little back. Her ex-husband was influential through his generous donations, which, bizarrely, did not earn Abi the exposure one might expect at big Christian gospel singing events. Those rejections were what had pushed her out of the church doors and into the secular world. Abi was convinced she'd find her fame and fortune there, where her voice would finally be free for everyone to hear.

♬ ♬ ♬

It was not long before they arrived at Thorpe Park to meet the boys. Candice looked straight ahead, her mind flashing back to the first time she'd heard Abi sing publicly.

It was at a big shopping mall that had recently opened. Candice and Abi had always promised that one day, they'd visit to browse around. Unbeknownst to them, they happened to pick a day when the mall management had planned a publicity event to create excitement. It was a live talent promotion, a crowd-puller. The audience were invited to step up to the microphone to sing in public. This would be a daunting experience for any singer, as it could go either way, good or bad, but the organisers felt it would be hilarious, harmless entertainment. There was a pianist on hand on the small platform, ready to play anything on demand.

Abi saw the sign: 'Step up. If you can sing, come over here.'

'I'm going up.' She bounced ahead.

'Really?' Candice would never be brave enough to do anything like that, but for Abi, it was liberating.

'I'd like to put my name down to sing Oleta Adams' "Get Here".'

The organiser looked over at the pianist and asked, 'Can you play "Get Here" by Oleta Adams?'

The pianist looked back and said confidently, 'Yes, I can.'

Abi was called forward and went straight into a discussion with the pianist about which key to play in. There was no 'one-two, one-two' mic check, but they both seemed on the same page about the key. Then, he played a soft, casual melody that floated in like a beautiful butterfly. As the shoppers moved back and forth about their business, Abi opened her mouth and sang with power and conviction. Her voice and words sounded incredibly believable as she sang about a love that had no distance, time or boundaries. The busy crowd had stopped, having been wooed by her story. Time seemed to have been suspended, yet those three minutes passed in the blink of an eye.

When she reached the end of the song, the pianist tinkled the keys, continuing to play until the final note.

The crowd burst into spontaneous applause, a melange of clapping and loud cheers.

The pianist stood up, faced Abi, and joined in with the applause as if to say, 'This is all for you.' It was the first time Candice had heard her sing a complete song, and to a public audience, no less.

Abi was professional, graciously receiving the applause. She thanked the pianist and applauded him in return.

'Abi, you're amazing. Truly amazing. You should be someone famous like Whitney Houston. Sooner or later, someone's bound to snap you up,' Candice said.

'Hi, I'm Justin,' the pianist said once the applause had died down and the crowd dispersed, 'how or where did you get that voice?

'Look at you—so unassuming. You're gorgeous.

'Do you have an agent?'

'No, I don't. At least, not yet. It's just me for now, but I'm looking to start a singing career.' Abi was of the mind that you never knew who you might meet, so after the divorce she paid to have professional demo cassettes and a profile made, and she carried them wherever she went, just in case she met someone. She handed three demo tapes to Justin.

'I know the best place for you to meet people. I'll introduce you, and the rest will be up to you.' He gave Abi a VIP invitation to a prestigious event at the Empire's Equinox Nightclub, an annual event attended by influential people from the music industry.

It was a wonderful moment for Abi to be recognised for her singing outside of the Christian circle in which she'd spent all of her singing life closeted away from the secular music world.

She held the VIP invitation in her hand, like a golden ticket, but she wanted Candice to be with her at the event too. 'I can't go on my own — can I bring my friend?'

'She looks stunning, too — can she sing?' Justin asked, looking Candice up and down with approval.

'Not as a lead. She's my sidekick and a backing singer, aren't you, Candice?' Abi looked at Candice with widened eyes, trying to communicate an unspoken, 'Back me up here.'

That was it. Abi's leap to fame rested on whether Candice would accompany her to the music event of the year.

'Well, when you put it that way, here's another invitation.' Justin moved closer to the two of them and whispered, 'No one is going to ask you to sing at the event, so don't worry about it. Take this opportunity with my compliments. Go, girl.'

At the party, Justin would vouch for Abi's singing ability as she had just smashed it out of the shopping mall in front of the general public. His intuition told him that Candice only looked as if she could sing without the voice to match. His eye was on Abi as she was the real deal.

As they walked away, Candice said, 'Thanks a lot. I can't sing to save my life.'

'Don't worry. He said no one would ask you to sing. We'll look the part. We'll be dressed to kill.' Indeed, they would catch the attention of many. Some months after the Empire event, Abi met Sami.

♫ ♫ ♫

Candice followed the signs to the parking area. They had arrived in Chessington without any traffic hitches.

'I want to find a good spot to park. Once, I forgot where I parked my car, and it took me ages to find it,' It had been one of Candice's worst nightmares. 'I'm going to park over there, just under that sign. It'll help me remember the space.'

'Sure! Write it down so we won't forget. Let's get this day started, shall we?'

Abi's comment didn't warrant an answer, but Candice responded, 'I'm not joking about these big car parks. When everyone's had their fun, it's easy to forget something as simple as this.'

'Come on. It's not that deep. I promise we'll find the car at the end of the day, and we'll get back home safely.

'See? I said it, and it's going to happen. The boys are waiting for us somewhere. Let's go find them.' Abi shook off Candice's concerns and walked in the direction of the big Chessington World of Adventure sign at the entrance.

'Are you coming, or are you just going to stay there, worrying?'

'I'm trusting you with this,' Candice answered.

♫ ♫ ♫

It was a reassuring sight for the boys when they saw Abi and Candice walking towards them. They had been waiting for around ten minutes by then.

'Hi, you guys. So great you all made it. How was the train?' Abi asked.

They all gave their version of the journey.

'I admire your perseverance. You've all worked together to get here—well done. First task accomplished.' Abi bought the tickets for the park and reimbursed everyone for their travel money, all except Eddie, who had already been given twenty pounds.

'Who's wearing a watch?' Abi asked.

'I've got one.' DeAngelo had a Swatch, which was fashionable in the US but had not yet caught on in the UK.

'You're the timekeeper for today. Let's meet again at 12.30 p.m. for lunch. I'm not going on any of the rides with you guys, so knock yourselves out.'

'Not even one ride with us? Come on, Aunty Candy,' Karl pleaded.

'Look, we want you guys to have fun and make some good memories. It's good for the group and good for business.'

Karl loved his aunt, but he knew how unadventurous she could be, not to mention that she was fearful of excitement. Still, he wanted her to at least try something new.

'Okay, then. If you can find the tamest ride in the park, then perhaps—and only maybe—we'll go on it, right, Candice?' Abi said.

'But for now, let's take a picture.' Candice pulled out her camera and called to a passer-by to take the shot. As soon as the boys heard the word 'camera', they assumed a pose, including Abi.

'One…two…three…everyone, say cheese,' said the passer-by.

This was followed by a chorus of 'CHEESE' from the boys.

'Now, go wild and have some fun.' Abi's words rang out like a starter pistol at the races.

7

Driven

WHILE THE BOYS were having their fun without a care in the world, Sami was charting the map, calculating their every move. To get the best out of anyone, he felt he must first make them believers. Without belief, things would be wooden and inauthentic. He wanted to serve them their dreams on a platter. Like the best steak, he wanted to let them see it, smell it and taste it. Sami saw that he could get exactly what he desired from the group, and he was the one driving the vehicle. He was willing to do anything to keep Abi sweet, as he had no time to micromanage the group. The boys were firmly seated on the train, and he was ultimately at the controls.

Rameses' Revenge was in Chessington World's Forbidden Kingdom section. It was the park's biggest thrill ride and the most popular. The boys agreed they would head there. According to the map, it was located on the far side of the park. Ignoring the other rides, they wove their way through the growing crowds to reach their first ride of the day.

Rameses' Revenge was at the top of their list. Undeterred by the thought of queuing for hours, they continued on their quest.

'Did you know that Rameses' reign as a pharaoh was the shortest? He ruled for five months before he died. In fact, he was murdered. His throat was cut with a knife. Many conspirators wanted to rule,' Jay said.

Nathan seemed to take offence to Jay's 'know it all' air. 'How do you know so much about Rameses?'

'I went to Egypt to see the pyramids with my mum and dad. Wherever we go on holiday, they always seem to do some kind of research to find interesting places to see that I might enjoy,' Jay replied.

Nathan found it hard to hide his envy of Jay's having two loving parents who went out of their way to give their son experiences that Nathan could never have. From then on, Nathan took a dislike to him, making snide remarks to put him down whenever possible.

'Well, look at you, Mr Encyclopaedia. If I want to know anything, I can come to you, right?' Nathan said.

Jay chose to take his comment as a compliment and not an irritation. He nodded and laughed it off along with the other boys.

'I'm interested in things like that. Egyptians were so intelligent,' Karl said, showing his love of history. 'It took so many years to build those pyramids — that's cool, man.'

'Yeah, it was on the backs of slaves, but where are the ancient Egyptians now? If they were so intelligent, they'd have something else to offer instead of just pyramids and old stones.' Nathan was growing more agitated by the second.

'Come on, guys. It's only a ride. Forget the history, man,' said Eddie, dismissing the discussion. He was there to have fun, and no petty argument was about to ruin his day.

They finally reached the front of the queue, and it was their turn to get into the seats. Jay sat with Eddie and DeAngelo, and Nathan sat with Karl, but on the opposite side, away from Jay. Not that any of the group noticed, but their body language indicated that alliances were already forming.

Once firmly secured in a gondola, the ride set off, making its slow assent towards the point where it would loop in a three-hundred-and-sixty-degree motion, with multiple spins.

'Oh, my God...I don't like this,' Nathan shouted. He had a real fear of heights but didn't want to appear like a wimp in front of the others, so he kept the secret to himself. He tried hard to hold in his scream until he couldn't hold it any longer. 'Stop the ride!' he shouted at the top of his lungs. 'I want to get off.' A part of his earlier agitation with Jay was his ability to mask his feelings about the ride, but now, he was well and truly scared.

Karl showed some concern. He swallowed the laugh building in his throat and said, 'Relax. It's not like we're going to die. It's just a ride. It's gonna stop soon.' He drowned out Nathan's screams by hollering, 'Yes, man—this is what I'm talking about.' Given Karl's heart condition, he might be expected to be extra careful, but the thought never once entered his mind. He had gone through many operations for any one person to have in a lifetime, and he had survived them all. His family often told him to be careful, but he always ignored them. His philosophy was that if he were going to die, he wanted to die happy, doing something he enjoyed. No challenge was too hard or difficult once he put his mind to it. Now that his heart had been stable for a number of years, he took more risks outside of the cotton wool bubble that had been his world for so long. He was no longer the tiny, vulnerable baby with a heart condition. He was now a young adult, a teenager.

No one had expected him to survive. For his family, each birthday was a big celebration in case it was his last. In a couple of months' time, he would turn sixteen, and it would, undoubtedly, be another reason for the family to celebrate yet another milestone.

Karl's life was filled with special memories that his family never took for granted. As a big plus, Karl's temperament was grounded and non-egotistical, and he was good fun to be around. He was surrounded by people who loved him immensely, people who never treated him like someone to be pitied or tiptoed around. His dad had given him the nickname of Braveheart. He wasn't quite William Wallis leading the revolt against the English, but he was strong, had a strong sense of justice, and stood up for others Wherever he went, he was well-liked and popular. These traits came out whenever he saw someone being bullied at school. He'd never side with a crowd that was afraid of and enabled the bully, but he was skilful enough not to get into fights. Everyone at school knew about his condition, and they didn't want to be the ones to cause his heart to fail and have his death on their hands, so they often backed off in arguments, which were mainly trivial.

The ride began its descent downward at a slow, gentle pace as if nothing had ever happened. Why it was called Rameses' Revenge was way beyond Nathan's capacity to think straight, and he struggled to get out of his seat once the ride came to a halt.

Exhilarated by the experience, DeAngelo said, 'That was some ride. I swear it would be enough to wake the dead. It was mad! Did you feel that three-hundred-and-sixty-degree twist? My head and stomach went into overdrive.'

'I thought I was going to fall out,' Jay said, equally as exhilarated and buzzing with excitement.

Nathan was sheepishly quiet, which was unusual for him. In fact, Karl noticed that he looked rather pale and less vibrant. It was the first ride of the day, and Nathan was already mashed. 'My head is spinning,' Nathan said, and before he could get the words, 'I feel sick' fully out, he ran over to the nearest corner and vomited. It was real gut-wrenching stuff as if he had been food poisoned.

'That's the Rameses' Revenge effect,' Jay said.

Karl joined in with the laughter, but when he saw that his friend was in some real distress, he said, 'Come on, guys, he's mashed up.' He walked over to him. 'It's better out than in, so it won't mess up your day. Let's find some sort of sick bay where you can sleep it off. After an hour, you'll be good to go again.'

Nathan gave him a look that said he was in no mood to joke.

'Look, you guys carry on. I'll take Nathan to wherever, and we'll meet up with you again for lunch. There's so much to do around here—we can join you later and do something else.

'Oh, if you bump into Abi and Candice, tell them where we are. If they turn up at the sick bay, I'll get them to stay with Nathan, and I'll try to find you, but I'm okay about it otherwise. We've got the whole day ahead of us. See you laters!'

'Look at that—the first ride, and he's already KO'd. How does everyone else feel?' DeAngelo asked.

In unison, they said, 'We're good.'

'I'm ready to go again—who's up for it?' Jay asked.

'You know what? I'm here for the long haul, so let's pace ourselves. We can't go on one mad ride after another or we'll end up joining Nathan in the sick bay.' DeAngelo was talking sense.

'Okay, let's go on some less intense rides. Check out the area.' As Eddie was talking, two girls sauntered by and gave him a cheeky smile. 'And I've spied some nice-looking girls in the house, too.'

Jay, who had the map, said, 'Let's just walk for now,'

They all agreed that they liked penguins, so they found the Sea Life section on the map and headed there.

DeAngelo had lived in the US for a few years of his young life. He'd been to Disneyland, Florida, twice, gone to SeaWorld and seen the dolphin shows, seals, and whales. It was every child's dream to visit such magnificent places, but he could not hide his disappointment when he saw Sea Life. It was nothing like he'd imagined it to be or anything like the publicity picture. The setup and shows seemed even worse than a low-budget movie, but that was England for you, always trying to make a carbon copy of the original and resulting only in the whisper of something.

DeAngelo couldn't help telling them about SeaWorld, but he didn't want to totally diss the place, so he tried to embrace the experience and not spoil it for the others. However, he couldn't help saying, 'I swear when we have money rolling in, we'll go to Disneyland, Florida, so you can see how it's done for real. I don't care—I'll pay. Hey, we'll be able to afford it anyway.'

Jay agreed as he had been to Disneyland, Florida, once before. Eddie thought the Sea Life exhibit was cool. He had never been to an aquarium and was fascinated by sea life. He was grateful for even being there, but he played it cool as if it was no big deal.

♫ ♫ ♫

Meanwhile, Abi and Candice created their own version of the day, walking, talking and planning.

'I'm not interested in any of those crazy rides,' Abi said. 'It's a nice day—let's go to the picnic area and sit out in the sun.' When they saw the hive of activity, Abi and Candice couldn't help but feel uplifted by everyone's energy. It was a great day out, and they expected many more like it.

Sami had given Abi free reign over whatever she felt was the best way to create unity amongst the boys. She had even more ideas that she wanted to run by Candice. 'The boys are bonding. I can't see them not having fun here. They're like little kids at heart.'

They sat down, Candice took out her camera, and they flicked through the picture storage, laughing and commenting on how they all looked. She had taken shots of the boys before the audition, but as much as they tried to appear confident, you could still see tinges of stress. On the other hand, today was perfect. Away from that pressurized environment, the boys looked great together.

'You've done a good job,' Candice said.

'With what?'

'This whole thing. You're the manager of a boy band. They're hidden stars in the making, and boy, can they can sing. You're going to go far, and you'll be rewarded,' Candice said, giving her take on the experience thus far.

'Thanks, Candice. I know I can always count on you. You're in this, as well.' Abi wanted her to feel as if it was not all one-sided and that if it were the other way round, where Candice needed that level of support, she would be there for her.

Abi was willing to push hard and try every avenue to get into the music industry. Helping the boys was an avenue that just seemed to open up for her, and she didn't mind waiting. She had been singing ever since she was a toddler and had dreamed of being a singer for almost as long, but she was now twenty-eight years old and still trying to find an open door into the arena. Life had taken her on some funny detours, which was partly due to her rebelliousness. Always thinking she knew best and no one could stop her if she wanted to do something, her plan in life had been to get married young, have two girls by the time she was twenty, and be a singer.

Although the plan was back on track, she'd married her pig of a husband at nineteen, though she hadn't seen the pig in him until she was already in the relationship way too deep. Her mother tried to tell her the man was not right for her, but being strong-willed, she refused to listen. Her mother had seen the red flags through her discerning, spiritual eyes. It was the same internal instinct that told her the man was not in the least bit kind.

Abi's own ambition of becoming a singer was never in the picture and out of the question. She hadn't seen it until after they'd married and moved to Jenson's church, where he was well established. Also, Abi had no academic qualifications, so she was relegated to play the role of being a pretty, dutiful trophy housewife, projecting the public façade of a loving couple.

These thoughts were far from Abi's mind at the time, and her head was up in Fantasy Land's clouds. She had wanted a kind, loving man who would do anything for her, which was not outside the realm of possibility, but her picker had been off, making her totally blind when it came to what others had seen so clearly.

It didn't take long for their relationship to fall apart. It had been a living hell for nine years of their marriage. Outside of that relationship, she hadn't had any further intimate encounters…until Sami. Killing two birds with one stone was what she felt she was doing with him. He was the kind man she'd been looking for, and he would do anything for her. At least, that was what she believed to be true of his character, but Abi was quite naive. Not everything that everyone said should be taken at face value, but she was never really able to exercise discernment.

Wanting to get close to her, only one day after they'd met, Sami told her about having to find a project that industry moguls would be interested in financing. Sami had found her sweet and attractive, and he'd listened to her talk about her dreams of being a top singer. From that moment on, they had a connection. It wasn't long afterwards that he showed his affection towards her, and she reciprocated. Sleeping with him went against her Christian values and upbringing, but she felt that the act of intimacy would show how much trust she had in him.

Being completely worldly, Sami didn't see their encounter the same way. They were coming at their relationship from two very different perspectives, Abi, as a truthful, backslidden Christian, and Sami, as a man of the world where money talked, and sex didn't equal power unless you understood the game, which Abi didn't. As far as Sami was concerned, kindness was considered a weakness. Abi would have her uses as he was hell-bent on using any man, woman or child as he climbed his way to the top.

They had been close ever since their first meeting at the music event. When the idea of forming a group actually came together, Abi got even closer.

Abi and Candice did not know about the Nathan incident on the Rameses ride, so they never made it to the sick bay to relieve Karl.

It was now lunchtime, and everyone headed for the restaurant area as planned. Abi and Candice were the first to arrive, followed by DeAngelo, Jay and Eddie.

The boys filled in Abi and Candice about the effect Rameses' Revenge had on Nathan. They were still laughing when he and Karl showed up.

'You made it—sorry to hear about the ride,' Abi said.

'Look, it was nothing. I'm feeling much better now. I'm just hungry—what can I eat?'

'Having some food is better than having an empty stomach, but I think it needs to be something light—do you like bananas?' Candice asked.

'Yes, but that's not going to be enough.'

'Ginger ale or something gingery will help. I'll see if I can get some toast at the restaurant. Then, by 3 p.m., you'll be completely fine and perhaps have a burger or whatever you fancy.' Candice had sold him on eating light for the time being and warned him to stay away from the big rides for the rest of the day.

Nathan knew there was no chance of his ever getting back on another coaster. He also felt slightly embarrassed, but everyone had welcomed him back into the group. Nothing had been wasted besides, as he'd spent the time in sick bay getting to know more about Karl and sharing their hopes and dreams. Being a part of the group was a huge morale booster for Nathan. He was starting to feel a part of something bigger than himself, and he had friends who wanted the same things.

'I've got some good news for you,' Abi said. 'Sami has booked the studio for the first of July, so we've got six weeks of practice, practice, practice before that date.'

The boys were delighted, each of them stating their take on 'I can't wait!'

'But don't get carried away. I don't want anyone who can't pull their weight during practice,' Abi warned them. 'Enjoy your weekend, because on Monday, the practice begins.

'I've arranged for you to meet with Mervyn. He'll get you started and give you the programme he's prepared. You'll get on fine with him. He's hard but fair, so I want you to get along with him famously. I've not detected any issues with ego from any of you, so don't let me down now, okay?

'Candice and I are going to head off around 3 p.m., so you guys can stay as long as you want.'

'I'm not leaving for now,' Eddie said. 'And Nathan, you've got to come on the log ride, even if it's the last ride of the day. This one is all about the water and trying not to get wet. I hear it's less of an impact when you sit at the front. If you sit at the back, it might be a bit too jerky.' Eddie wasn't telling the truth. Sitting in the middle section had the least impact, but Eddie wanted to get one last prank in before they left the park.

The last ride was the most enjoyable for the boys. Eddie sat at the back and was somehow showered with the most water. The laugh was now on him. Everyone commented on how wet he looked. In the spirit of it all, Eddie found it hilarious that he'd been caught out. 'Karma is a…umm,' Jay said. In some way, they were all wet to varying degrees as they made their way to the drying-off point.

By the end of the day, the boys knew so much more about each other. Eddie's eyes were for the ladies. Karl was caring, having looked after Nathan when he was sick. DeAngelo might have bragged about having gone to Disneyland a few times, but he had a generous heart and swore to pay for them to go there one day when he had the money. Jay was the knowledgeable one who knew all about the pyramids in Egypt and held seemingly insignificant facts in his head about everything. Nathan had a fear of heights and roller coasters, and he appreciated Karl's selflessness, not leaving him to die in the sick bay on his own.

The joking didn't stop when they left the park, carrying on all the way back to London, where they branched off to their different locations. It was fair to say that a good time was had by all, and friendships that would last a lifetime were forged.

Abi left the park with a feeling of accomplishment. Round one was coming together. That the five boys who had been strangers were now bonding and finding levels of commonality was a big tick.

8

The Practice

Shirlee, DeAngelo's mother and a friend of Abi, met Mervyn when she'd lived in the States, and her singing career had skyrocketed. Requests were coming in left, right and centre to perform at various events. From the East Coast all the way to the West Coast, she was becoming a renowned, sought-after singer on the R&B circuit. Her then-manager and ex-husband held the reins and was in charge of everything, from handling all the contracts to scheduling her appearances. One such request came from The Shakalakas, who were looking for something special to be the supporting warm-up act for their performance at the Apollo in New York City. This would be no ordinary show, as not only would they be singing to a live audience, but the big revenue would come from televising the live performance on two major TV network stations. The viewing rights alone were phenomenal and worth a fortune, as lucrative a deal as selling millions of records. Besides, this was sure to lead to other new, profitable contracts. It really was a big deal, and it had to be handled correctly. They were looking for someone who had talent, was up-and-coming, and to whom the crowd would warm. Shirlee fit that bill.

They had heard about the singer from the UK who had settled in the States. Not only was she pretty and petite with a cheeky personality, but her voice matched their expectations, and they loved her. Her English accent would get her far in America, but to have a voice that would match the likes of Chaka Khan was quite unique.

Originally from Jefferson City in Missouri, Mervyn was The Shakalakas' tenor. He had a singing range that could stretch from falsetto to low base in a moment, hitting rifts like the tones of a song thrush. As a vocal quartet, The Shakalakas were not considered ordinary. They worked their craft and were skilled in charming their audience with their silky smooth, romantic ballads, four-part harmonies, and layered productions of groovy, synchronised dance movements. Needless to say, the brightly coloured, outfits made them look like proud peacocks, strutting their stuff. The tight-fitted outfits showing off their physiques, adding to the ensemble of stage performance. It was the craze back in the seventies, along with grown-out and immaculately honed afros. The ladies loved it, and it drove them wild. Seeing them on stage was a sight to behold. At one concert, someone threw her knickers on stage with her telephone number written on them. It must have been pre-planned and not a spur-of-the-moment thing. Red roses were also regularly thrown on the stage.

That was the charm they had on the ladies, and they knew how to work a crowd. To this day, they still had a loyal following of fans and kept their fan club, managed by a publicity organisation, going for years. When the time was right, they'd launch a comeback reunion and possibly re-release some of their older, popular ballads, followed by a new song. There were plans for life after death for The Shakalakas.

Many groups from the sixties and seventies were increasing in popularity on the R&B soul scene. Motown was strongly holding their own and building momentum against the likes of pop, country and Western, and contemporary music, but The Shakalakas maintained their position with many top ten singles like 'You're, My Lady' and 'Searching for My Love'. They were three-time winners of the Best Album of the Year awards. As an outsider coming in, if you could break into the American music market, it meant you'd made it big.

Mervyn was now in his late forties. He'd left the group after Tommy Parkerson, the lead singer and songwriter, died in a plane crash in the late eighties. They tried to re-group, soliciting other singers to join them, but when the infamous child molesting scandal broke out—which led to a prison sentence for their new lead—they lost their mojo. (He was caught with a girl who looked older but was underage.) It damaged their credibility for a while, but they managed to distance themselves from the singer, regroup and find another lead. They also gave public interviews to reassure the fans that the scandal was not what they were about. Adding to the loss of Tommy Parkerson, the tide was changing in the music scene, moving far away from the peacock outfits and synchronised moves. Hip-hop was now up and rising and the demand for their type of songs was little more than back samples, which they found most distasteful. One of the old group members had tried his hand at starting his own record label, but it was too cash-intensive, which made Mervyn all the more resolute when it came to holding onto his money and living off of his royalties. With that in mind, he vowed that if ever things got really tough, he would sell one or two of his rights, but for now, he was happy with his lot, and that 'ride' he was fortunate enough to have been on was indelibly printed on his heart.

Mervyn had been married once before, but he divorced in the heyday of the group's rolling success. As a matter of fact, most of the group's marriages ended in break-ups, excluding Tommy Parkerson, who'd stayed married to his childhood sweetheart until that fatal day. Long hours and tours away from home multiplied the stress toll and the sworn commitment to stay at the top of the industry, whatever the cost. Their families were never allowed to travel with them as business always came first, and the families were expected to be given the short shrift, in last place. If they couldn't get with the programme, they would be left behind. Either you had a supportive, understanding, forgiving wife, or she left, but the second time around was the charm for Mervyn. He was older and wiser, and he'd married an English rose who loved him exactly how he needed to be loved. Then, he stepped out of the crazy limelight and into the sunset, across the pond to the fair isles of England.

Mervyn lived in Sydenham, South London. It was a good location for all of the boys to get to, as most of them (excluding Karl) lived in the South, but Candice said he could stay with her a couple of nights a week for practice sessions. She was also in the South and could drop him off and pick him up without a problem.

Jay and Eddie were the first to arrive for the practice session. They'd made arrangements to drive from Jay's house to the practice, and Eddie was well-chuffed to have a friend with wheels. This was often the attraction Jay had with some of his friends, but he made it clear that he wasn't their chauffeur. He would make the odd one or two trips, but as he regularly told them, 'Cars don't run on water.' This led to offers of money for petrol, but he was okay with that and astute to know who were genuine friends or just interested in having access to a car.

They pulled up at the house, which was slightly off the main road and down a short, tree-lined lane with very few houses. This was suburbia but not too far away from the urban life they were used to. There was a horseshoe drive up to a quaint, detached house that looked deceivingly small from the front yet backed onto a large garden overlooking a field. There were no neighbours peering in from any windows as nothing overlooked their house. It was pretty impressive by anyone's standards. Eddie had never known anyone with a house like that. Jay's parents had many wealthy friends who did, but it was still stunning for him, nevertheless.

With his mouth wide open, Eddie stepped out of the car onto the gravelled drive. In complete awe of the exterior, he looked up at the house and said, 'One day, I'm going to live in a house just like this.' It was a bold statement, but words often had power when said with conviction, and Eddie meant every word of it.

Jay was about to ring the bell when Mervyn, having heard the car pulling up, came out to greet them. 'Welcome to my home.' Mervyn beckoned them in.

They entered into a hallway set up like a picture gallery of family, friends, and successes. There were two platinum discs in a picture frame, signifying how many records had been sold in a particular year. The boys didn't know much about The Shakalakas, but at the end of the hallway was a large framed picture of the group in their all-in-one, tight-fitted jumpsuits with bell-bottomed flares in canary yellow. To complete the look, they had huge afros. The pose had been captured when they appeared on a music show called *Soul Train*, which was not dissimilar to the *UK Top of the Pops*. The only difference was that *Soul Train* had mainly Black artists performing from the soul and R&B scene, although Elton John had once sung on the show. As the story went, he asked the organisers of *Soul Train* if he could appear, and they'd agreed. *Top of the Pops* was the British equivalent for pop artists who were predominately white, but they occasionally had soul groups like the Jackson 5, The Temptations, Marvin Gaye, and sometimes other reggae and R&B artists performing.

The Shakalakas reached number twenty-two in the UK charts in 1974, with 'Ella, Cinderella'. They never appeared on the show live, but the song was played, and the dance group Pan's People did a staged choreography to it.

♫ ♫ ♫

Not too long after, DeAngelo and Nathan arrived. They were followed by Karl, who was dropped off by Candice. She did not stop in because she had a midday meeting to get to, but she sent her regards to everyone.

Abi was aware of this, and she didn't expect Candice to be at any of the practice sessions. She was in the lounge, waiting for the boys to arrive. Abi intended only to run through the programme, which had already been discussed and agreed upon with Mervyn. Then, it would be up to the boys to arrive on time and attend every practice session without exception.

'Morning, guys. It's great that you're here. I want to let you know the plan for the next six weeks. We are entering exciting times, and this is where the hard work begins. When you all came in, did you see those awards and accolades in the hallway?'

They each responded with either a 'Yes' or a nod of the head. Showing just how naïve he was and his young age, Nathan asked, 'Who's the group?' The others didn't know either, but they kept quiet.

'Didn't you recognise one of the members?' Abi asked.

They all shook their heads as if to say no and wore blank faces.

'It's The Shakalakas. Mervyn was one of the singers in the quartet.' All eyes turned to Mervyn, whose appearance was now neatly kept, with shoulder-length dreadlocks and a Mexican-style moustache he frequently fiddled with.

'Woo,' Eddie exclaimed. 'Which one were you?'

Mervyn walked out into the hallway to the big *Soul Train* picture and pointed to himself. 'This was me back in the day. They were wild times!' He said this with a wide smile as he reminisced.

'Come back in. Come, come,' Abi said. 'I won't be staying for any of the practice sessions, but I know you're in capable hands. He's my vocal coach, too, so I know you're getting the best. It's your time to learn from a great. He's done it, got the scars, made the money, and has the royalties to prove it.

'Mervyn is such a humble and genuine man. We are honoured to have him on this project, guys. Please remember that his time is precious, and Sami's the one paying for it, so don't mess up. Make a commitment to come to every practice session starting today. This should come first. It's a good time, too, because we're in the summer holiday period. Does anyone have anything or any holidays booked for the next eight weeks?'

Everyone except for Jay said no. 'I usually go away with my parents, but they're expecting me to go to Birmingham University if I get the right grades. Plus, I already have a conditional offer. The A-level results are announced in August.' Jay was the oldest of the boys, though he was always the youngest in his class as he had a late birthday on 31 August, which was the last date for the year's school intake.

'What will you be studying at uni?' Abi asked.

'Law. It's my family's dream that I follow in their footsteps, but that isn't what I want. I want to be a successful artist in my own right. I'm committed to this, and I'll give it my all,' Jay answered, reassuring everyone of his commitment to the group. He had already thought about taking time out from his studies should the project really take off. 'When—and not if—we get signed to a record label, I can always take a gap year or defer my place to start later.'

'You've told your parents about this opportunity, right?' Abi asked.

'Yes, but they think it's just a hobby. I'll prove them wrong.

'I promise, I'm gonna work so hard. You'll see,'

'Well, I'm glad to hear it. Thanks for sharing. At least we have a lawyer in the group. You can make sure we don't get ripped off with any of the contracts you'll be expected to sign.

'Well, guys, I've got to go. Have a good session. Mervyn, over to you. Update me later.' Abi left the room to head back to her life at home.

The coaching began now that the pep talk was over. 'Up until now, you've been singing for fun, but now your careers will depend on your voices, so you have to protect them. Your vocal cords are delicate. Are any of you smokers?' Mervyn asked.

Nathan was sixteen, and when he was around Sarah, the other teenager at his foster home, they often shared a cheeky cigarette over at the rec. 'Yes, sometimes.'

'My advice to you is to quit now while you're still young enough to. You'll thank me for it later. Anyone else?'

The others shook their heads to say no.

'Coffee or alcohol?'

'No.'

'Good. Coffee and alcohol are diuretics that help you lose water, and what do you need?'

'Water for hydration?' Eddie said.

'You're the clever one. So, coffee is out, alcohol is out, smoking is out, and taking drugs? Out. Stay clean, you know what I'm saying?' Mervyn really knew what he was talking about. In the past, not only did he have to deal with his own drinking demons, but he also had to help some of the other band members sober up or come down from being high just before a performance. But these were fresh-faced, young kids, and he could train them up so they would know which way they should go. If they ever strayed, he hoped they could, one day, get back on the right path.

Getting five strangers to sing together wasn't going to be a walk in the park, let alone getting them to act as if they'd been best friends since nursery school, but if anyone could do it, there was no doubt it would be Mervyn. He had a job on his hands, but he was excited to rise to the challenge of creating and blending the vocal abilities of these five young Black boys into UK pop stars. Though Mervyn knew it would be difficult, he believed all things were possible.

The boys had to learn a routine to protect their vocal cords, warm up before singing and learn the importance of hydration and the morning ritual of lemon, honey, ginger, and hot water. Then there were breathing techniques, mirror work for posture, singing from the diaphragm and not the chest or throat, meditation, clearing mucus from their throats, and throat massage. All of that prep work before even singing a note.

This would be followed by voice clarity. Mervyn hated it when he couldn't hear the words the others were singing because they had no voice control and couldn't pronounce the words properly in a song. Worst of all was when they sang from their noses. If he heard it from any of the boys, he would pull them up on it immediately because if it went unchecked, it would easily become a habit.

Next was voice balancing, running through the scales, and controlling the notes to produce the right tone and pitch, plus the G-sound exercise to help the boys close and open their cords. He knew it would enrich their singing so their voices would be stronger and have more power. There would also be lip trills, similar to what babies naturally do when they start forming words and hearing their own sounds, not realising it's practice for speaking. They'd love these exercises with a passion, he joked to himself.

'I'm not going to lie—you'll look and feel silly, but it'll be worth it.'

There was no end to the repertoire of practice exercises Mervyn had lined up, and he planned to have fun with it.

Mervyn broke down the routine and put it on typed-up sheets so the boys would know what to do first thing in the morning and when to do the exercises, and for the first time, he gave them a cassette tape with the songs they would be recording in the studio. 'Don't give the cassette to anyone, you hear me? There's a copyright attached to it. For now, it's absolutely confidential.'

Everything had to be kept under wraps. These were Sami's strict instructions.

For the boys, the secrecy added more credence to the adventure and excited them.

'This is a top-secret mission, like on *Mission Impossible*,' Eddie said, immaturely referencing a favourite film.

'I want you to spend at least three hours a day doing these exercises, and I mean six days a week. God rested on the seventh day, so I'll give you one day off.

'I hope you all have headphones. I want you to listen to the songs, love the songs, and hear yourself singing them. I want you to see yourself sing the words in your sleep. They should come as if second nature.'

'I really hope I like these songs,' Nathan remarked.

'I don't care whether you like the songs or not. I want you to love them. The crowd will believe you if you believe what you're singing when you sing it—does that make sense?' Mervyn said. 'If you yourself aren't convinced by the words you're singing, why should anyone buy your records? Whatever you have to sing, do it with passion. In your mind, find someone you love or loved and sing it to them. Connect with every ounce of nerves you might have and transfer that into passion.'

They listened tentatively.

'Don't look at me with blank faces—do you get what I'm saying?'

They all said yes.

'This is huge,' Karl said.

He was about to say that he was not sure if he could achieve the level of perfection Mervyn demanded, but Mervyn quickly interjected with, 'I know, I know, but the journey of a thousand steps begins with one step at a time. I can assure you that within one week of doing these exercises, you'll hear a difference in your voice. Your range will have clarity, and singing will be much easier than before and less of a struggle. Trust me.'

They were once more stunned into silence, but they had to trust what the expert was telling them.

'I'm going to run through some of the exercises so you'll know what to do when you leave here.

'I want you guys to start singing from your diaphragm. Now, it's going to throw you back a bit, and you'll feel like rubbish singers, but we've got to get you singing from the right place. This is the foundation we're going to build on.

'Get on the floor.' Mervyn had already cleared a space for them to lie down on the ground.

They all started to laugh.

'I told you you're going to feel and look silly, but if that's what you gotta do, then that's what you gotta do.'

The boys started having conversations about how silly they felt on the floor.

'Listen — listen up, guys.' Mervyn got their attention back. 'Place your hands on your stomachs, not on your chests. Now, breathe in through your noses. Feel how naturally your stomachs rise as they expand with air? Hold it for five seconds, then push the air out through your mouths and notice how your stomachs contract when they're emptying. Let's do this again.

'Now, this time, when you breathe in, I want you to do it slowly to the count of five. Feel your stomachs expanding as you do it, then hold for five, and finally breathe out to the count of five.

'Ready? Let's go. Breathe in: one…two…three…four…five; hold it: one…two…three…four…five. Now, relax. And again: one…two…three…'

The drilling had begun. Some of the breathing exercises made them feel light-headed.

'This is a natural reaction to your brain finally getting some air to circulate through your whole body.

'Some people haven't taken a deep breath since the day they were born when they were slapped on their backsides as babies. They walk around in life, shallow-breathing everything from the neck upwards. Did you know that your lungs, if expanded, are as big as tennis courts?' He used his hands to demonstrate.

'It's your rib cage that restricts them. The aim of the breathing exercises is to get your lungs filled with air, like a balloon that expands; then, you let the air out slowly—not all at once, but a bit at a time, in small amounts, larger amounts, and so on. Balloons go flat when they're emptied of air, but as singers, you have to know when to go for that quick intake of a breath so you can still hit the notes with power and be in control.

'Don't worry now. I've got you. Get up on your feet—we're going to do these exercises again standing up. Let's go!'

9

———

Studio

THE BOYS' COMMITMENT to stay on track with their practice was phenomenal! True to Mervyn's words, their voices became richer. Even after the first few days of exercises, they felt the benefit in their posture and voice control, and their confidence skyrocketed. Each time they met Mervyn, he drilled them hard, not allowing anyone to miss a beat, and he could see it was paying off. He always showed a poker face in front of the boys, but deep down, he was smiling. They were fast becoming his prodigies, and he was proud of them. It was like seeing eagles learn to fly.

At first, Nathan struggled to understand the breathing techniques, not knowing how to really connect with the air from his stomach and not from his chest. It was like learning to speak again, using different vocal cords, and it initially seemed alien. On one occasion, he panicked as he thought it was proving too difficult, and he started to doubt whether he would measure up in time. Abi made her routine check-ins with the boys, but Nathan didn't want her to know the turmoil he was going through.

He spoke with Sarah about how he felt. It wasn't that she was a singer or could advise on the subject, but there were elements of wisdom in her suggestions. She encouraged him to link up with the others, so he took her advice and reached out to DeAngelo between practice sessions. DeAngelo was more than happy to pair up, and he was glad for the company.

DeAngelo welcomed Nathan around to his house, and together, they worked through his mental barriers of self-doubt. Robert, DeAngelo's stepdad, was on hand playing the piano, keeping them both in key. Then, soon after, Nathan finally cracked it. 'I feel like I've reached the top of Mount Everest. I'm ready,' he said.

They say that opera singers practice daily how to sing from their diaphragms, and if they switched to singing pop music, they could ruin their voices, but Mervyn was skilful, and he had the moves and the techniques. He worked hard to impart his wisdom to the boys to make them sound naturally brilliant with ease by flexing with the air in their lungs.

Nathan was now turning up for practice sessions able to hit the notes, and he experimented with riffs in the harmonies. Nathan didn't have to say anything, as his newly found singing ability said it all to the point where Mervyn had to ask him whether someone had banged him on his head when he woke up that morning.

'What do you mean—is that good or bad?' Nathan asked.

'Yeah, it's good. Whatever you're doing, keep on doing it. I like it a lot.' Mervyn had a funny way of paying compliments, but after weeks of practice, they managed to get a handle on his humour.

Not everything went smoothly and without a hitch. Halfway through the practice weeks, Karl caught a cold. He tried to push through, but it only made him feel worse. Mervyn advised him to take the week off to rest his voice. There would be no singing for a week, but he had to keep listening to the songs and memorising the lead vocal parts and the four-part harmonies. The cold was put down to overdoing it at practice and the to-ing and fro-ing between his house and Candice's, mingled with his final school assignments and the pressure of the deadlines.

The week off did him a world of good, which meant he could clear the assignments. It seemed to release spurts of energy in him, and he recovered his health. With the assignments completely out of the way, he could put his full attention back into singing again.

♫ ♫ ♫

'Mervyn? Hi. It's Sami. How's it going?'

'It's going just great.' Mervyn reported.

Sami was fully interested in his investment and had weekly chats with him over the phone.

Abi had been faithful in giving him updates, but he wanted to hear it from the horse's mouth. Mervyn went to the trouble of sending weekly recordings of the boys singing on labelled cassette tapes and posting them to Sami. This kept him involved as much as possible, albeit remotely, so he could keep tabs on everything.

Each week, as the tapes arrived, Sami heard the progress Mervyn was making with the boys. Both DeAngelo's and Karl's voices stood out the most, which posed a dilemma for Sami, making it hard to choose which one to use for lead vocals. They were both very good, but the time was approaching when he would have to decide which one to go with. This was a special project, one he had never attempted before, and he was not about to fail at it.

The harmonies came second after the lead vocals. From what Sami had in mind, Mervyn made his work so much easier than he could imagine. Harmonies were Mervyn's thing, having come from a group that had sold millions of records built on harmonies and ballads. Like a touch of salt after a meal was prepared, it was the final ingredient after the lead.

'I'm whipping those boys into shape, Sami,' Mervyn said. 'Have you decided who's going to be the lead? I've got the harmonies locked down. Did you notice those trailing trills and inflexions?'

Sami trusted no one, but Mervyn gave him the weekly assurances he desired, and if he said it was great, then you'd better believe it. In Mervyn's professional opinion, the pitch had to be at the right level to tap into the listeners' feelings and emotions.

'That's good. Thanks for that.' Sami wanted to downplay the conversation. He didn't want to give him too much props, although inside, he felt as if he had struck gold to get even this far with five boys who'd been picked off the streets of London. It was all working well, but he needed to keep a lid on it.

'What do you mean it's good? It's magnificent, dude. Their voices are gonna go far. All around the world. You'll see,' Mervyn declared.

♫ ♫ ♫

They were only one week away from the next phase, which was in the studio. Then, Mervyn's job would finally be over. From then on, it would be over to Sami to pull it together. Once the boys were in the studio, everything would become clear, and every wrinkle or kink would be ironed out. For the studio work, Sami was allocated a 'wicked' studio producer and engineer whom he had heard of many times in the past but never met up close and in person. He was a rock star in his field, the best man for the job, and the record label used him for different genres of music for his magical versatility. If there was anyone who could make R&B pop, it was him.

He was known throughout the industry as 'Dizziboy', a short guy who walked as if he were six feet tall. What he didn't know about mixing down tracks wasn't worth knowing or writing home about. That is, everything that was significant and trending. He was wired for sound. Born with an ear for music, he had the Midas touch. He was rumoured to have been born with a tuning fork in his mouth.

Dizziboy would have his time to shine. He was a blue-eyed boy up there with the Faceless People who controlled and influenced the sway of music that entered the slipstream of the world's music entertainment portals. The faceless people were the dictators of what would be sold to the general public at large, nationwide and worldwide, this year or the next.

The studio was based at 44 Cressington Gardens, W8, the home of Butterfly Records. It was a building so unassuming you would never know that big stars like Cher, Elton John, Prince, and other world-renowned mega-stars had once recorded some of their greatest hits there. The studio facilities — state of the art — were also hired out for other special projects financed by the faceless people. These special projects were always kept under wraps until fully verified, proof of concept achieved, checks and balances tested, and schedules made to enter the music queue, waiting for the release date. Then (and only then), boom! The button was pressed! Another bullseye hit.

For the past six weeks, the excitement emanating from the boys was electric. They began by not believing they'd been selected at a singing audition out of many potentials, to having survived the gruelling practice sessions with Mervyn, who was like a drill sergeant, but it was worth it. They were booked to record in a real studio, and the next step was signing with a record label. They didn't know which one yet, but they focused on being able to deliver on Sami's investment. For a group of inexperienced young boys, it was impressive by any standard.

Keeping the whole thing confidential from their close friends, had been a struggle, but the boys had agreed, and they didn't want to break that trust. They were in this together, and they guarded their activities like a hidden entrance to a world they thought was all bright and beautiful.

♫ ♫ ♫

Sami booked the studio for one week with an option for a second. The hours spent in the studio would be long and hard, but it would be the making of his biggest success yet.

Day one was about to begin.

'I've never been so excited in all my life. Not like this. I couldn't sleep, but I listened to some of that meditation stuff Mervyn gave us to calm myself down. I even drank chamomile tea, and I don't drink tea at all,' Eddie said.

'We've made it to Butterfly Record Studios.' Jay had travelled with Eddie from the South to West of London, but this time, they'd taken public transportation. Jay didn't drive as traffic and parking would have been a nightmare at that time of the morning, plus they didn't know how long they'd be spending each day in the studio. The road was a few minutes' walk from the 295 bus stop.

'This is happening,' Jay said.

The smiles on their faces said it all: the experience was priceless.

As they waited outside the unassuming building observing their surroundings, there was a moment of realisation that this was where stars of greatness had been born. The day was one of those warm days in July, one of the few that wasn't dull and overcast. It was nothing special to speak of, but it was, nonetheless, significant.

Walking towards them were Karl, DeAngelo and Nathan. It was a gruelling six-week sprint to make it to that day, so for them, it would never be just ordinary. Rather, it would be extraordinary.

'Hey, we've made it,' Jay said. There were high-fives and man-hugs all around.

'We're all on time. Let's go in. We're not gonna be late.'

'Do you think I'd be late for this? You must be joking, man. Never in a million years,' Eddie said with seriousness, and there was another round of high-fives.

They walked into the thoughtfully constructed foyer, and like tourists, gawked at the sight. Plush leather sofas were scattered about in small clusters for people to sit in huddles and talk. Huge posters of rock stars, some of which they recognised, like Jimi Hendrix and Bob Dylan, and others they didn't know at all, decorated the room. There were also country and Western singers with cowboy hats on their heads. Music came from concealed speakers, the latest releases by their signed artists. There was also a lot of light streaming in from the windows, bouncing off a psychedelic strip, and a number of Picasso paintings on the wall, along with other abstract art.

'Can I help you, gentlemen?' a security guard asked as he approached the boys.

'Yes. We're here to see Sami Achu. We have an appointment for ten o'clock,' Jay—who was not in the least bit intimidated by the security guard's question—answered.

'Follow me. I'll take you to the reception where there'll locate him for you.'

They followed him to the desk where a pretty woman — fully made up, with auburn-coloured spikey hair, who looked like a rock chick groupie — faced them. 'Hi, Trevor. Who do we have here, then?' The receptionist smiled flirtatiously at him, and Trevor's face lit up with a beaming smile whenever she spoke.

'These young gentlemen have an appointment with Sami. I'll leave them in your capable hands.' Trevor turned and went back to his post. In the past, fans had once stormed the studio just to get autographs and pictures of their idols. Since then, the studio had a duty of care to protect its artists and had a regular security presence. Whenever big names came to town, they were known to enlist extra security.

'Hi. I'm Amie. Nice to meet you. Please write your names down here, and I'll prepare your security tags for the day. Is it your first time here?'

'Yes,' DeAngelo answered as the others were too star-struck, but he didn't elaborate as he remembered that everything was supposed to be confidential.

'I'll let Sami know you're here.' Amie handed out their passes, calling out their names one by one.

Like a sacrament, each boy said thank you as they received their tags. Then, they moved over to where a cluster of leather sofas was positioned and sat down.

'This sofa is nice, man,' Nathan said.

Karl gave his approval. 'I could sit here for hours. It's so damn comfortable.'

They didn't have too much time to revel in the moment of the experience before Sami appeared. 'Hi, guys. How was your journey getting here?' Sami hadn't seen them since the audition over two months before.

There was a chorus of 'It was easy' and 'No problem.' Sami sat in one of the armchairs to talk about the programme. The boys felt a little anxious as they didn't know what to expect. They leaned forward to hear what Sami had to say, but the sofa seemed to swallow them up.

'Have any of you been in a studio before?' Sami asked, checking out what, if anything, they knew.

'I've been with my mother, but not for anything I've ever done.' DeAngelo's mother, Shirlee, had taken him with her many times, so he was familiar with the environment.

'No problem. That's okay.' Sami took out a sheet of paper that contained the plan for the day's schedule and gave them a brief overview, assuring them he had it all mapped out.

'Who's who? DeAngelo?' Sami looked to see who had responded.

DeAngelo answered, 'here!'

'Karl?'

'That's me!'

'Nathan?'

Nathan said, 'Yes,' and he put his hand up slightly as if answering to his name on a school register.

'Eddie?'

'Here.'

'And you must be Jay.'

'Yes.' Jay wasn't at all fazed by being called last.

'It's going to be a busy few weeks. If we get everything done in time, that'll be fine, but we have the option of using more weeks if we need them — is everyone okay with that?'

Everyone said yes and nodded.

'So, come to the studio every day at 10 a.m. It's going to be a long day, and we'll finish late, but I've arranged for you to be taken home by transport.' For certain projects, it was Butterfly Records' policy to allow the artists to be taken to their place of stay by a driver and even to collect them, if necessary. They had a charging account with Addison Luxury Transport, who could pick up and drop off on-demand.

'Food will be provided. We'll take breaks at the point when we need them. Drink plenty of liquids.

'I'll direct you through the tracks. Much of it will be repetitive stuff, but I want you to relax and have fun with it. We are not pulling teeth here; we're making music, right?' It sounded like a political party campaign speech.

Sami's chat didn't register and went over their heads because, they were too excited, but they'd been prepped by Mervyn, so they were ready.

'Oh, and some of the breaks might be long, so there's a gym and a swimming pool in the basement. I've arranged clearance so you'll have access to them. They don't get used much, but the company felt it would be good to have something recreational in case anyone wanted to use it. Also, there's a cinema room with some game consoles, so there are plenty of alternatives. And there's a garden area if you need to get out to stretch your legs. Does anyone have any questions?' Sami asked.

The boys liked the sound of that.

Eddie wondered if this was how all artists spent their time in the studio. 'I'm cool with that,' he said

'I'm sure I'll have questions later, but nothing from me for now,' Jay said confidently.

'Let's go.' Sami stood up, and one by one, the boys followed him.

♬ ♬ ♬

The studios were located at the back of the building. The front of the building was deceiving as it obscured the small courtyard out back that looked quite like an atrium, full of greenery, shrubs and flowers. There were benches where people could sit, reflect or meditate. There was even a hammock if anyone dared try to sit in it. There was concrete paving and a small water fountain in the middle, trickling water at a slow, calming pace. On the ground, set into some of the stones, were handprints and the names of artists. This was a spin-off of how artists cast their feet and handprints in cement in Hollywood and throughout the world.

At the far back were two arches with two solid oak doors. Sami walked towards the one on the left and opened it, taking them into a semi-wide hallway with doors on both sides. Each door was numbered.

They walked to the end of the hallway to a door with the number eight on it for studio room eight.

'This is going to be our home for this week, but when we're ready, we'll move to room number one.'

10

───────

Conflict

THE WEEK BEFORE the boys were scheduled to go into the studio, Sami had already selected the musicians to play the instruments on all of the songs he would use for the *My Bella Angelica* album and project. They were seasoned musicians that he used regularly, and they were called in for different sessions to record their parts. The music was built up layer-by-layer, ready for Dizziboy, the great god, to remix into masterpieces. Up until then, the boys would rehearse with a single piano accompaniment to the songs rather than hear the full ensemble arrangement, so they would be familiar with the tunes. Although the rhythms would be recognisable, they would now have to get used to hearing the songs with the other instruments in them. Sami and Jimmy, the sound technician on the project, went meticulously over the melodies, capturing samples of each instrument to build the layers for the tracks.

Sami had never played an instrument before, nor had he ever read music. He didn't have the time or patience to put in the hours of practice necessary to be the professional he would have wanted to be. Nonetheless, he had an instinctive ear for what would work best, but he relied on proper musicians to play and improvise their interpretations of the songs and said either yay or nay to whatever they'd produced. This was the adrenaline rush he lived for. It gave him goosebumps but in a good way. When he was in that zone, nothing else mattered. He aimed for the top, like those big hit songs that reverberated around the world, played over and over again, bringing in the royalties forever. Then, every so many years—or every so many decades—it would be re-released for another spin to generate more royalties. That's what Sami wanted. It was one of his life-long ambitions. He was the *My Bella Angelica* songwriter. There were two other collaborators on a few of the tracks, but it was mostly him.

'This is sounding really good, but the piano part needs to be refreshed, don't you think?' Jimmy asked Sami as he adjusted the levels of the instruments fading in and out.

'Yes, you're right. Beth played the piano on the songs for all the tracks to help me get the project started. She did a great job, but I agree we need a better cut of it in the studio. Give me a minute. I'll give her a call and get her in.' Sami got up, left the studio, and went next door, where there was a phone.

'Hey, babe, it's me. Listen: we've got to redo the piano parts in the songs. I've been so busy focusing on getting the other musicians ready that it totally slipped my mind. When can you come to the studio?' Sami asked Beth.

'I can come in tomorrow. We can travel in together. As soon as my bit is done, I can make my way back home. I'm getting really tired these days. By late afternoon, I could do with a nap. I think our baby's a morning bird. By six o'clock, I'm so wide awake.'

'Okay. Let's talk later when I get home. Bye.' Sami ended the conversation.

Beth was Sami's wife, whom he'd lived with for five years. She wasn't a part of the music industry. Nonetheless, Sami had a great admiration for her, as she worked as a music teacher at a secondary school in South London. She was a talented, classically-trained pianist with a private school education who had gone on to study music at Cambridge University. Beth had no intentions of being a great pianist, but she did have a keen interest in teaching children.

She had been born and raised in Lancaster and moved to London ten years before. After years of living with various flatmates, she'd met Sami at a mutual friend's house party. They'd hit it off and got on so well they decided to rent a flat together. Both agreed it would be an economical move and a good way to really get to know each other. At least, that was the line she'd sold to her parents.

Five years later, Beth found out she was pregnant, and Sami seized the moment to propose to her. He'd never been married before and didn't have any children, although a long time ago, when the subject had come up in their conversations about marriage, Beth made it absolutely clear she didn't want to raise children out of wedlock. It just wasn't acceptable, not only for her but it would be absolutely frowned upon by her middle-class parents and upbringing, and Beth didn't want to raise children on her own. She wanted the assurance of marriage to set a good foundation for a family.

They were married—nothing fancy—just a small affair attended by her parents and a few close friends. Sami's parents were not at all happy about the wedding arrangements. They suspected Beth must be pregnant for them to get married so quickly. In his African culture, it was not uncommon to have hundreds of people attend a wedding. Two hundred was classified as a small wedding, but forty people was classified as eloping and having a wedding in secret. Though his parents were accepting of her being white British and not African, they couldn't help comment on how pale and anaemic she looked, as well as that she had no meat on her bones. It was not the African way for a bride to be.

The next day, Beth didn't feel well when she woke up. 'Sami,' she said, 'I feel awful this morning. I'm sorry, but I can't come with you to the studio today.' She was seven months pregnant. In the early trimesters, she had had a hard time keeping food down, but this feeling was different.

'It's early—should I call an ambulance?' Sami asked.

'No, I don't want to cause a fuss. I just want to take it easy. Let's see my doctor. The surgery opens at 8 a.m.'

Beth had the energy to walk the distance round the corner to the surgery, but she couldn't see herself travelling so early on public transport from South to West London to go into the studio.

It was a first come, first served, no appointment surgery. There were a few people in the queue, waiting outside for the doors to open, which wasn't too long a wait. They walked in, and Beth sat down while Sami waited his turn to see the receptionist, but when it was his turn, while he was giving the details, Beth fainted and slid slowly off of her seat.

Sami looked over his shoulder to see what the commotion was. To his surprise, he saw Beth passed out on the floor. 'Beth! Beth!' Sami shouted in a panic. He ran towards her and collapsed on the floor beside her. 'Beth, oh, my God.'

The receptionist called for the nurse who was in the back room and the closest to the scene. She hadn't yet started seeing her patients, and the doctors were still upstairs in their rooms.

The nurse took charge of the situation and went into action. 'What's her name?'

'Beth. She's seven months pregnant. She woke up feeling unwell with tight pains in her stomach,' Sami said.

'Thank you, and you are?'

'Her husband, Sami.'

'Well, you sit right here.' The nurse asked the receptionist to make him a cup of tea while she attended to Beth.

'Beth? Beth, can you hear me?' the nurse asked.

Beth moved her head slowly and said, 'Yes.'

'You fainted, my love. I'm going to help you get up very slowly. Are you in pain?'

Beth shook her head to say no, but she was a little phased out and not quite with it.

The nurse helped her sit up, got Beth onto a chair and walked her into her consulting room. Sami followed behind them, carrying her handbag.

'I'm just going to do a few checks. You're seven months pregnant—when did you last feel the baby moving?'

'This morning, but my stomach started to get tight, then it contracted,' Beth explained.

'Have you eaten anything this morning?' the nurse asked.

'Not yet. I didn't feel much like eating,' Beth said.

'Beth, it's very important that you eat, especially after a long night's sleep.' The nurse took out her stethoscope and placed it on Beth's stomach.

She finished her observation checks and saw nothing apparently wrong with the baby's position or development. 'The baby is fine, and the heart is beating beautifully. Do you know what Braxton Hicks is?'

'What's that?' Beth asked.

'Well, Braxton Hicks are like a dummy run of the contractions you'll get when the baby is due, but on a milder scale. Don't be alarmed. They'll pass, and they won't last long. You're in good shape, but you might need to eat something, even before you get out of bed.

'Sami, I trust that you can serve Beth breakfast in bed, right?'

She looked at Beth, gave her a wink, and told Sami that it was okay to spoil her. 'You're both going to need your strength when the baby is here. Come and see me again next week. I'll bring forward your monthly checks to weekly ones, but if anything happens in between, please call the surgery or 999 out of hours if it's an emergency.

'You're good for now. Take it easy today.'

Beth was fully alert when they left the surgery.

It was unfortunate that Beth's trip to the studio to record her piano part had to be cancelled. 'I'm staying here with you today in case you need something or anything happens.' Sami felt powerless, and he didn't know what else to do.

'Sami, go to the studio. You've got so much to do. Look at me—I'm back to my normal self. I'm fine. Please go." Beth tried her hardest to reassure Sami that she was, in fact, okay. "I'll potter around here like a mother hen, and I'll come to the studio next week on Tuesday, but I'll come in around midday instead of travelling early morning with you. The rush hour would have been madness. I probably wouldn't have got a seat anyway.'

♫ ♫ ♫

Monday, the first day at the studio with the boys, started well. In turn, the boys warmed up their voices, aligning them to the right pitch for the songs they knew like the backs of their hands. The techniques and need for hydration Mervyn had drilled into them had a positive effect. The sound checks were admirable. Progress was being made.

Tuesday, the following day, Sami clean forgot he'd told Abi she could come to the studio to see how things were shaping up. That morning, when Beth had said, 'I'll see you later,' he thought she meant when he got back home after the studio. Even if he had remembered, it was far too late now to reorganise the day. Abi was already there, and Beth was coming at midday to finish her part on the tracks. To his detriment, Sami miscalculated putting two and two together.

'Hi Sami, how's it going?' Abi greeted him with a kiss on the cheek.

'It's going really well. Come in. Take a seat. Mervyn has done a heck of a job with the boys.'

Abi smiled, feeling proud of what they had achieved. 'They were fast learners, and they're young—this is a dream come true for them.'

'You're welcome to stay as long as you want. I'll get cracking,' Sami said.

'DeAngelo? Let's start with you in the sound booth, then Karl, Nathan, Jay and Eddie.'

DeAngelo left the room and went next door to the sound booth. It was a medium-sized space where the walls were greyish and foam-padded. There was also a solid, soundproof glass partition. He could see everyone on the other side, but directly above the partition was a darkened glass area through which he couldn't see that seemed to overlook the sound booth.

Sami signalled with his hands over his ears for DeAngelo to put on the headphones hanging on the mic stand. While in the booth, this was the only way to communicate with the sound team.

'Hey, let's start with the song "My Bella Angelica". Can you see that red light in our room, the one that says "On Air"? I'll turn it on now, so you can see where it is,' Sami said.

'Yes, I see it.' DeAngelo waved at the others to say he was ready.

'I'm going to count you in, then the red light will come on. Listen to the intro, then sing your best. If I put my hand up, you need to stop and we'll start again, but you'll be great,' Sami said confidently. He and Karl were naturals. They knew how to make themselves relax and settle into songs while keeping them fresh.

Throughout the session, Sami's hand never went up, not even once. When the song finished, the red light went off. 'That was great. Jimmy, are you happy with that?' Sami asked.

'It's good on my end. Banging, man.'

One by one, Karl, Jay, Nathan and Eddie each sang their best. They were all great, but DeAngelo and Karl's voices were still neck-and-neck for the lead parts, so Sami had them sing lead on all of the songs. His thought was that once the mock versions had been done, he'd leave it to Dizziboy to see which version would be the best model for the project. He was not worried for now, as it all seemed to evolve naturally.

♫ ♫ ♫

It was midday and a convenient time to take a break. Eddie was the last to sing, and he bounced back into the sound room, high on the recording vibes. Everyone chattered away after the periods of silence while recording.

Abi congratulated the boys on their outstanding vocals.

While they talked about their lack of nerves and fears, there was a knock on the door. For a second, everyone stopped what they were doing and turned to see who it was.

Beth waddled in, red-faced from hurrying to get there by midday. Wearing a big smile, she said, 'Hi,' to everyone.

Taken by surprise, Sami walked over to greet her. 'Hi. Are you meant to be here today?' Sami asked, feeling puzzled and embarrassed.

'Yes. Remember last week when I couldn't come to the studio, and we rescheduled for next Tuesday, midday, which is today? I told you this morning that I'd see you later, and you said yes.' Beth couldn't see the full picture. She had no idea why he appeared so shocked.

He rubbed his mouth as if to find the words. Sami had his back to everyone as he spoke to Beth, but when he turned around, he saw Abi and the boys all looking in his direction. From that moment, there was a silence that seemed to linger for ages.

Beth turned to him and said, 'Aren't you going to introduce me?' She paused. 'Hi, I'm Beth, Sami's wife.'

Sami moved around the room, reluctantly introducing his heavily pregnant wife to the boys, who were so excited to know that she was the one who would play the piano on the songs they had worked so tirelessly on.

Beth was equally as excited to meet them because they were the voices she had heard so much about.

'And you must be Abi.' Beth put her hand out and waited for Abi to do the same.

Abi glanced quickly over at Sami, then pulled herself together, cracked a smile, and said, 'Yes, I am,' shaking Beth's hand.

'It's so nice to meet you. You've done an amazing job organising the auditions and practice sessions. You're an angel. In fact, you're the *my bella angelica* that got this project rolling.' Beth continued talking, as she did when meeting new people for the first time. Apart from how stunningly beautiful, slim, and attractive Abi was—unlike her bulging bodily shape, all out of proportion—she was none the wiser about the affair Sami and Abi were having.

Sami quickly sobered up to the reality that his hidden affair with Abi had been exposed, now that at least one party had found out. He was more anxious of Beth becoming enlightened. And the possibility that Abi might be enraged, causing a difficult scene. But Abi was more dignified than Sami gave her credit for. However, one bombshell was more than enough for the day. So, Sami stepped into the conversation and asked Abi for a chat outside. It was an awkward moment for them, but it had to be faced. If there were to be a showdown, Sami didn't want it to be there right in front of everyone.

Abi's heart pounded in her chest from being put on the spot, having seen that Sami's love for her was not real and that he was a married man. Betrayal pumped through her veins, making her feel sick to her stomach.

He smiled at everyone and placed a hand on Abi's shoulder as if to usher her out, but she stepped to one side and said to Beth, 'Really nice to meet you,' before walking towards the exit, swiftly followed by an anxious Sami.

No words were spoken between them as they walked down the hallway towards the garden area. Abi could find no words to express the betrayal she felt at that moment.

She walked towards one of the benches, and Sami sat down, expecting her to sit beside him, but she remained standing. 'Please, sit down,' Sami said.

'No! I will not sit down beside you.' Abi was not having any of it. While standing, she looked over at his left hand and asked, 'Where's your ring?'

'What ring?' Sami asked.

'Don't you play games with me now. You're a married man giving the signal that you're single. I asked you if you had a girlfriend, and you said no.' Abi hissed the words at him.

'And I said no, that I didn't have a girlfriend. I was going to say that I was married, but you didn't give me the chance to finish,' he said, turning it back on Abi.

'So, it's my fault now? For not…what? Allowing you to speak the truth? How ridiculous is that?' Abi spelt it out for him. 'If I knew you were married, I'd never have gotten involved with you like that. We would've just been friends, and I don't sleep with my friends, either. And I don't sleep around.'

'I'm so sorry about this,'

'What? Sorry that you got caught out? Judging by Beth's reaction to me, she's none the wiser, right? A nice, convenient affair behind her back. I can see that you wouldn't be leaving her for me.

'She's pregnant, too. I never saw this coming. After all I've been through in my life, I find myself in an affair, and not by choice.' She continued to talk, taking deep breaths in an attempt to calm her indignation.

Sami let her spout off, knowing that he was in the wrong and not wanting to exacerbate the showdown. 'Abi, I'm sorry. I don't want us to finish like this. Let's meet on Saturday evening when we can talk. I don't want to lose our friendship. What about Oasis Wine bar at 7 p.m.?' Sami thought his attempt to defuse the bomb was working, at least for the time being. Oasis was a place they had frequented many times. It wasn't too crowded and had booths conducive to cosy chats.

'Okay. I'll see you then,' she said, accepting his invitation, hoping she'd find much-needed closure. The next few days away from the studio would give her time to process what had happened. If this was the end, she wanted to let him know how he made her feel and ask what had driven him to cheat on his wife with her.

Abi left Sami in the garden without so much as a goodbye.

Sami stood up from the bench, feeling quite relieved that part one of the showdown was over. He composed himself by doing a quick stretch, tensed, and released his shoulders, putting what had happened to the back of his mind. He adjusted his facial expression so as not to display any tension and walked back into the studio. He had work to do and a week to get through.

Friday seemed to come around quickly, like a blink of an eye. The days before had been more productive than anyone had imagined. Dizziboy came to the studio to add his magic to the mix. It had been planned that way so as not to waste his precious time. All of the tracks were completed and fed back to Dizziboy over the weeks, so by the time he'd come to the studio, he already had a fair idea about what he was going to do.

He asked the boys to go into the sound booth, where there were five microphone stands and headphones, one for each of them. Their faces radiated the joy they felt, not only for the songs they knew and loved so much but for that feeling of accomplishment. There they sat, waiting in the booth while Dizziboy, Sami and the other technicians were on the other side of the glass, carving out their future careers.

Overwhelmed by the moment, Eddie said, 'I'm not gonna lie—I feel quite emotional.'

'Hey guys—no talking in the sound booth. You know the rules!' a stern Sami voiced his disdain. He didn't want any displays of emotional outbursts erupting and spoiling his clean sweep of the weeks of work now that the project had reached its finale. Plus, the faceless people were already upstairs, seated and watching from the upper room through a two-way mirror. Sami had invited them to witness the occasion for their final seal of approval on the project. They would see the fruit of Sami's labour and the reality of their investment in an advanced state.

The boys' voices were both blueprint and prototype for the next phase of the project. This final day would be their one and only appearance in front of an audience, albeit of secret observers, the Faceless People.

It was time, everything culminating in this last stage. The red 'On Air' sign lit up, and everyone was in position, ready to play their parts. There was a short silence, and then the sound of the string intro burst forth into the atmosphere like a gentle breeze, taken up by DeAngelo, leading on the first note. The boys sang as if their lives depended on it, with such passion and conviction in their tones. The stories in the songs were believable. Some were beautiful ballads, while others were stonking, catchy dance tunes. They sounded on par with those forever songs, like 'Every Time I Close My Eyes' by Babyface, which would be played at weddings for decades to come and slow tunes for end-of-the-night smooching at parties and nightclubs. The sound was a turning point for how songs would be produced in the UK and taken out into the world, not just in the US and Europe, but into the emerging markets of the Far East. With pre-recorded instruments, slick mixes of synthesised sounds, and no band in sight, it would be the new way of the world, riding on the crest of the digitally mixed wave.

♫ ♫ ♫

The last song of the session was in progress. The harmonies were impeccable, and they finished with all five boys holding their notes flawlessly before fading into the music outro towards the end.

Just like a movie but without sound or subtitles, the boys saw Sami and Dizziboy jump to their feet, high-fiving one another and flicking their fingers in excitement. They saw them mouthing the words, 'Yes! Yes!' They saw smiles and what looked like laughter and lots of talking. Although the boys were unable to hear what was being said, they had a strong sense that they had delivered the goods.

They sat in the booth expecting to be called back in, but Sami didn't address them at all. It appeared as if Sami and Dizziboy had forgotten they were even there, given that they had their backs to the glass window as they enjoyed their revelry.

While the boys were waiting, something caught their eyes. They looked up above the recording studio at the darkened glass area that had puzzled them all week, and their eyes were drawn to a quick flash of light, like the fire of a cigarette lighter or match.

'Did you see that?' Nathan asked. 'I've had this feeling today, ever since we've been in the booth, that people are up there behind that glass, watching us. It must be a two-way mirror or something.'

'I got that, too!' Karl concurred.

'So, what if people are watching us? We sang our hearts out today! Think about it: when we perform live, thousands of people will be watching us, so we'd better get used to it,' Eddie said, full of enthusiasm.

Suddenly, Sami and everyone in the studio appeared to stop talking. They turned towards the window and looked directly at the boys, having heard the comments made by Nathan, Karl and more interestingly, Eddie. Sami turned on the sound so they could hear him, and he told the boys to come back into the recording room.

11

———

Conspiracy

IT WAS OVER. The boys walked out of the booth on cloud nine. They were confident, knowing they had given it all they had. Rock stars, even, after they'd performed their last song and walked off the stage to be greeted by the production team and well-wishers with backstage passes to shouts of 'Well done, you smashed it!' or 'That was amazing!' It would be a real confirmation of how well they'd held it together, not to mention the rapturous shouts and cheers from the audience's standing ovations, adding their seal of approval to the night's performance.

The boys entered the studio, expecting a ticker-tape welcome. Instead, they were met by Sami, who gave off a mediocre vibe, far, far different from the animated person they had seen only moments ago on the other side of the recording room's window. 'Hi, guys. That was good,' Sami said, subdued. 'I think we're done here. I'll catch up with you soon. Thanks for your time. It's been good.'

The boys didn't quite understand what to make of the vibe they were getting, and it left them confused because they didn't know whether they should ask what he'd meant by 'It was good.'

Jay, who was often vocal about everything, sensed that something was missing. He didn't feel the expected sentiment for their stellar performance and the effort they had given Sami over the past months. He was just about to say something when there was a gentle knock, and someone poked their head round the door to say, 'Sami, they're ready to see you now.'

'I'll be up in a minute. I'm just finishing up here,' Sami said. After delivering the message, the person left, and swiftly, at that.

Sami moved towards the exit, but Jay intercepted him. 'Should we wait for you to come back?'

'No, you can leave now. It's been great,' Sami said with a smile, but he was anxious to leave as he had somewhere else he needed to be.

'What happens next? Will we have to redo any of the songs? Are we signed to Butterfly Records?' Jay asked.

'Those are big questions. I'll catch up with Abi, and she'll get back to you. I've got to go, but well done, guys,' Sami said again, though not in a patronising way, before he left the room, leaving puzzled looks on the boys' faces.

Dizziboy and the other technicians sensed the awkwardness in the air, and they turned away and went back to fiddling with buttons on the sound deck.

Jay was not convinced by Sami's words, and he wondered why he felt as if they'd been shat on from a great height.

'You heard him. Let's go. We smashed it. We need to celebrate,' Eddie said. He was not going to have the moment ruined by some misunderstanding. For him, there had been no crossed wires. The session had been good. It had been outstanding. The best yet. But there was no one around to confirm that.

♫ ♫ ♫

Directly above the studio was the VIP room. It was where the gods of the music industry sat on special occasions, observing artists from behind a two-way mirror, where no one could see in, only out. Sami's plan to use ordinary kids off of the streets, coach them, see what developed, and then copy their voices had reached the end of the first stage of the project. The songs were now ready for the right faces to launch the new pop group and the next wave of iconic stars in the twenty-first century. He had his sights set on number-one hits and albums that would rival the Beatles. It would be the cherry on the top tier of the cake, the proof that singing was so much more than the voices.

The next phase of the project was already in motion. Sami had already prepped the new pop group, selected for their looks, height, physique, and Britishness. Without a doubt, their faces fit, ticking the boxes for Western markets in the UK, Europe and Australia. Then, on the wings of that success, they would take North and Central America by storm.

A team had been working behind the scenes staging choreography and working with top stylists to create their image. From haircuts and trendy clothing (not excluding their underwear) down to their footwear, they were styled to the max. They would be fashion icons, ready to be taken up by brands for worldwide endorsements and sponsorships. The new pop group would show their fans a lifestyle they could only dream of and that they would love to live.

Could they sing? Not exactly, but with a lot of help, possibly. The idea was sold to the Faceless People that their investment would pay out millions for decades to come, and they liked the ballsyness of his suggestion. It was like nothing that they had ever tried in the UK, but it did happen quite a lot in the US. Great songs were written and sung by African Americans before being passed on to someone whose face defined the sign of the times.

Even with the go-ahead and carte blanche to make something happen, the project would never have gotten off the ground in the way it did without Abi. She was so eager to please, but she didn't know that Sami was a chameleon who could not be trusted. She knew talent was out there, as she saw them at church conventions and gospel concerts, but she never had the chance to be appreciated by a wider audience in her own right. Sami had no intention of actually building up her career, nor was he fully intent on starting up singing careers for the boys, but he was willing to see how far he could go with the project, which, to a great degree, was unknown territory. In the end, his interests were purely selfish.

♫ ♫ ♫

Sami entered the VIP room above the studio overlooking the singing booth. He was greeted, through a haze of cigar smoke, by the company's directors and their smiles. 'This was most enjoyable.'

'I thoroughly enjoyed the songs.'

'They are so very talented.'

'Well done for finding them.'

'Who wrote the songs?'

'I wrote all the songs but with a few collaborators,' Sami said. The collaboration had been with Beth — and she didn't mind that she wasn't mentioned in any of the credits.

'And the other group? How are their voices shaping up to sound like these boys?' Jeffrey Smith asked. He was the head of the new band enterprise, pushing boundaries and covering the UK and European markets. It was a recently formed entity and a bold move by Butterfly Records UK aimed at harnessing greater music revenue and boosting shares.

'It's been better than expected. We have a date for their provisional debut performance for private guests only,' Sami said, keen to show how the project was advancing towards its penultimate stage.

'Speak with my secretary and book me in plus four. Great job, Sami,' Jeffrey said on behalf of the Faceless People.

Sami knew that millions of dollars would ride on the performance, after which Jeff would be satisfied, and having met the approval of the Faceless People, he would sign off on the project, bringing him a huge payday. After the sign-off, the project would be handed over to marketing, where it would be full steam ahead for the product's launch. Massive exposure of the new pop group meant using every media avenue available to make their faces and voices known in magazines such as *16* and *GQ,* on TV chat shows and radio channels such as Radio 1 and Capitol Radio, news stories in national newspapers, paparazzi tip-offs and nightclubs. The group had to keep their lives clean from drugs and not overdo it with alcohol, and there was a strict no-girlfriend policy in place. They needed to be single and unattached so the fans would desire them more, feeling as if the boys were available.

The new pop group signed a five-year contract with Butterfly Records. They were owned by the company and expected to be present for every engagement. Whether early-morning TV shows or late-night talk shows, their schedule of appearances was jam-packed. Once their faces and the music became household names, once they were number one on the charts and their album had been released, the marketing team would schedule a summer tour. There could be no concert featuring songs unknown to the fans, so it was up to marketing to provide the exposure that would justify a concert. One or two new releases would be okay, but there had to be songs the fans loved to sing and hear.

Saturday nights at Oasis Wine Bar didn't get busy until after 9 p.m. Midweek was less crowded. Sami had rescheduled his meet-up with Abi until after the boys had finished their time in the studio. She wasn't happy about it, but agreed to the changed date. Sami arrived at the wine bar slightly ahead of time. He surveyed the layout to choose the best vantage point, where his back would be to the wall, slightly away from the other customers and where he would be able to observe the entrance to see when Abi arrived. Unlike the other times when they'd been entwined in a cosy booth, he did not expect this encounter to last long, nor did he expect her to take what he was about to say well. He had no intention of revealing the complete truth about the project, but he knew he had to give her some kind of an explanation. He decided to only say as much as she needed to know. Dealing with the boys was her responsibility, and it would be up to her to tell them the bad news.

While Sami waited, he took the liberty of ordering a JD and Coke for himself and a virgin mojito for Abi. She was not a drinker, but she did enjoy flavoursome, non-alcoholic cocktails with fancy umbrellas. To occupy the time, Sami ran through his end game, checking that no key point would be missed. Then, he put it out of his mind and sat back to listen to the background music.

An hour passed, and Abi was a no-show. He wanted to get another drink, but he was driving. He decided against ordering another JD and settled for just a Coke. He was about to get concerned that she might have changed her mind about their meeting, but then he saw Abi enter the wine bar, beautiful and stunningly dressed, wearing a tight, short black dress, a short leather jacket, and high heels. There was a group of young men at the bar whose heads turned and jaws dropped when she walked in.

Sami noticed the attention she was getting and the stares, and for a moment, he felt jealous, but then he stood up and waved at Abi, one, so she could see where he was, and two, so the onlookers would know she was with someone, and more to the point, with him.

'You've arrived. You look stunning as ever.'

Abi remained standing for a moment. She looked at Sami but didn't say anything.

'Please, please, sit down,' he said. 'The music is a little loud here,' but he knew that would be the case. 'Let's go over to the alcove, where it's private and less noisy.'

Abi looked over at the alcove. It met her approval, and she walked off in that direction. Fortunately, the space was free, as everyone wanted to be seen at the bar and be a part of the atmospheric mix.

The alcove was well-lit, and the music was dampened, allowing them to hear each other talk. The kitchen door was close by. It swung back and forth as the wait staff delivered their food orders, but it wasn't enough to stop them from having a conversation.

'Well, what have you got to say for yourself?' Abi said, getting straight to the point. She wasn't the one who had explaining to do, so she sat there, waiting for him to squirm his way out of being accused of infidelity.

'I didn't mean for this to happen. It was never my intention to cheat on my wife. She didn't understand my culture, and we weren't getting along so well. Then, by chance, I met you. We connected so well it must have been fate. Our cultures are so similar, and I felt as if we had a great friendship, but I'm sorry it progressed much further than we expected.' Sami did his best to put himself across as a man who couldn't help himself and had been carried away by her beauty. Not that she agreed with a word of his explanation about their cultures, but she'd let it pass.

'On the subject of honesty, I have some other news: the directors at Butterfly Records have decided to pull the plug on the project with the boys, so I'm sorry to say I won't be working with them anymore.' The bombshell had been dropped.

'Sorry…say that again?' Abi tried to suppress her hurt by putting it off to one side.

'I know the boys worked really hard, but it was not approved by the board of directors, so the project is scrapped. There's no record-signing, at least, not with Butterfly Records.' Sami held his nerve to affect a sad face of disappointment.

'You know, you are a real piece of work, Sami. Are you telling me that after four months of hard work, including your efforts, the directors don't like what they've produced?'

'Yes, I'm afraid so.'

'That's complete BS. I don't believe it. You took advantage of me by hiding the tiny fact that you were married. You took off your ring to conceal your true situation. It was only by accident that I found out you were married, and your wife, who, by the way, doesn't strike me as someone who deserves a scumbag like you, isn't aware that you were having an affair with me. Otherwise, she wouldn't have greeted me so nicely.

'That poor woman — she doesn't know a thing, and I really feel for her. And now you're dealing me a double blow by trying to tell me the boys aren't good enough? Really?' Abi fumed, unable to process what was happening.

Sami had been the prime instigator of the whole scene from start to finish, leaving out key details in his private life to reel her in.

'I thought you were genuine, but why wouldn't I think that? Why would anyone deliberately do something like this, raise up my hope for a loving, honest relationship and the hopes of those innocent boys, knowing that you were only going to drop us all from a height? It doesn't make any sense.

'Why didn't you stop things at the auditions, or during the practice sessions with Mervyn, or at the studio sessions? And what about Dizziboy? What did he say?' Abi asked.

'He liked it after all the mixing. His job is to make the music, but he doesn't get the final say or sign-off on the project for Butterfly Records. It's the directors.' Sami tried to speak convincingly, and he was prepared to say whatever it took to get the message across that the show was over between him and the boys. He wanted Abi to accept his explanation, but she was intuitive enough to sense he had left out huge chunks of information, though she wasn't able to put her finger on exactly what that was.

Abi couldn't sit there any longer looking into the face of someone who had lied to her about being married and who was now lying again, only this time about the boys. Call it women's intuition, but he was hiding something. Abi briefly toyed with the idea of pouring her now diluted cocktail over his head, but she picked up her handbag instead, stood, and walked out of the wine bar, utterly disgusted that she had been played in so many ways.

'Abi…Abi…' Sami called to her, but she didn't hear him. He decided to follow her outside. He also wanted to escape the happy wine bar's atmosphere now that he had done what he'd set out to do.

Sami stepped out, looked around, and saw Abi sitting on a chair at one of the outside tables. She needed to catch her breath, just for a moment, as her head was spinning with many questions.

Sami went over to the table and said, 'I'm so sorry I've misled you,' which, to Abi, sounded like, 'Blah, blah, blah.'

'Shut up! You're a liar! I can't talk to you right now.' Abi was at a loss for words. She stood up, feeling it would be less humiliating if she went to her car and drove home. Her house was empty because it was her ex's turn to have the girls for the weekend. She didn't have to play supermum or superwoman, masking yet another hurt. Not that evening, anyway.

This time, Sami didn't follow her. He went in the opposite direction from where her car was parked. She got into her car and slammed the door shut. 'Dear God, I feel so stupid,' Abi said aloud. 'Are you really listening?' She held back the tears, deciding to wait until she was home to let them pour out.

Abi entered her house, feeling the girls' absence, the only two beings who would love her regardless. It was just her alone, with no one to console her or ask her what the matter was. It was routine for her to call Candice to have a chat after meeting Sami or any special event she'd attended, but she didn't feel like talking to anyone, and she unplugged the house phone for the night.

It would have been better for Abi if the phone had been on. Then, Candice would have called, which might have intercepted some of the mad thoughts running around in her head, driving her to do what she was about to do, stopping her dead in her tracks, but it was already too late. Her rage had already gone too far, getting the better of her. With no one to talk her down, she was hell-bent on giving Sami a piece of her mind, and she wanted to make sure his wife, Beth, heard it, too.

♫ ♫ ♫

That night, Abi couldn't sleep. She tossed and turned, replaying the time she'd first met Sami, his smile, the way he looked at her, their conversations, and now, the twist of betrayal, not only of her but of those innocent boys who'd been dragged into something she was unable to explain. She was overwhelmed by how they might feel, even though she didn't know the full picture.

Three o'clock in the morning, and she still hadn't calmed down. It was now a case of waiting for daylight and the appropriate time to confront Sami at his house. With that as the solution to her unrest, she was finally able to settle down and sleep for a few hours.

♫ ♫ ♫

Abi remembered Sami's address because in the early days, when they'd first met, she'd given him a lift home from an event one night. She hadn't dropped him off directly outside of his house, but when he left the car, she watched him go into the corner house. The door had been glossy white, with stained glass panels, a brass doorknocker in the middle, and two small potted ferns, one on either side of the door. Never in a million years would she have seen herself going to a cheating lover's house, not even after her ex-husband's philandering with other women. However, after raking through her thoughts, she would give him this: he would never have led her to his house if he'd known he would be having an affair, nor would he have set deliberately out to deceive her. Something had to have switched. Something had to have gone wrong for his demeanour to have suddenly changed.

Shortly after the audition, he'd made subtle advances towards her. She was obviously flattered by his charms and had fallen for it. After all, she was a single woman, and he'd portrayed himself as a single man.

Abi dressed in jeans, white trainers, and a short, dusty blue sports jacket. She put her hair up in a ponytail and tried to make herself look half-decent with a light touch of makeup and some lip gloss. She drove to his house, parked a little way from his door, and waited for 9.30 a.m., which seemed like a good hour for a Sunday. Then again, she couldn't wait much longer to have it out with him.

It was a bright morning with one of those cloudless skies. It was also a good time to clear the air of the bad feelings swirling around in her stomach. She stepped out of her car, pushed aside her fear of humiliation, and gathered her confidence to confront Sami with the many questions she had that demanded answers. She walked up the path, certain it was the house where he lived, and put her hand on the brass doorknocker when, out of the blue, she heard her name being called by someone from behind her. It stopped her dead in her tracks, and she removed her hand from the knocker.

It was Sami who'd called her, approaching with an armful of Sunday newspapers having returned from the newsagent. On her approach to the house, she hadn't seen him coming as Sami had been on the side street and round the corner.

'Abi—what are you doing here?'

'I've had time to think about the last four months, and you're not going to walk out on the boys and me without an explanation.' Abi was doing her best not to allow the emotions to stop her from articulating what she needed to get off her chest.

'Let's go for a walk where we can talk some more.' Sami put out his hand to try to move Abi away from his front door. Beth was inside making breakfast, and he didn't want her to be alerted to Abi's presence.

'Don't touch me! I'm not going anywhere!' She pushed his hand off her back and spoke as loudly as possible. Loud enough to wake the dead.

Sami wasn't about to answer any of her questions. He wanted Abi away from his house. There was a bit of a push between Sami and Abi, with Abi standing her ground. In the process, the Sunday newspapers fell onto the pathway.

Then, the front door flew open.

Beth, even more heavily pregnant than before, had heard the shouting on the doorstep and come out to see what was going on. 'Abi, hi. What's going on? What are you doing here? Are you okay?' Beth asked, concerned.

'No, I'm not okay! Sami took advantage of me, and we had an affair behind your back. He told me he was single.

'Look! He's wearing his wedding ring now, but whenever he met me, he took it off. That means it was pre-meditated. He lied to me, and he's lying to you, too. While you are pregnant, he's been sleeping with me.'

She continued, addressing Sami, 'I feel sick to my stomach. How dare you treat me like a rag you can throw away after you've finished with it?

'And the boys' voices? They are brilliant, don't try to tell me otherwise. What was going on there?

'You've abused them, too, in your own way. Now I've got to tell them that they won't be signed to Butterfly Records.' Abi was on a roll.

'I thought you knew the boys were never going to be signed,' Beth said.

Sami looked over at Beth sharply. He didn't know what to address first: the affair or the boys.

'Thought I knew what? Are you trying to tell me that this was all a complete setup? I've never lowered myself to do this before, but this,'

Abi lifted her hand and slapped Sami in the face, startling him, 'is for coercing me into an affair with you.'

A second slap landed on his face. 'And that is for taking advantage of the boys. You're up to something, and the truth's gonna come out.' Abi carried on, ranting about the indignation she felt.

'I'm calling the police,' Beth said, but Sami said not to.

'Don't worry. I'm done here, but I know that whatever this is, you're not going to get away with it.' Abi turned and walked back down the path towards her car. Safely within the confines of her car, she wept aloud over her hopes and dreams of being a star remaining unfulfilled, as well as for her overwhelming loneliness.

Meanwhile, Sami had to explain to Beth what he had or hadn't done to make Abi turn up on their doorstep and accuse him of having an affair.

12

Time to Shine

THE JOURNEY HOME to a place of safety was a blur, partly due to the tears welling up in her eyes and partly due to driving as if on auto-pilot. There was no cheerful music playing for her to sing along to as was her custom, but then she reached into her cassette collection, found Mahalia Jackson, and inserted it into the player. 'Trouble of the World' was the first track. Mahalia knew the struggles and pain of life. If she didn't, how could she sing like that? Abi loved to listen to deep, southern gospel music because it was honest. It held a truth that could only be sung, and you had to have been there to sing it. It was one of those moments that outstripped the fear of losing her voice or never having it heard anywhere ever again, not in public and not at church. Like a carpet, her hope and confidence had been pulled right from under her feet, and Sami was the one who had done it.

'I am done,' Abi said out loud, exasperated by her emotions, as if telling the universe it was so.

♫ ♫ ♫

Abi arrived home safely and without incident. She opened the front door, tossed her keys into a turquoise glass dish on the side table, and made her way towards the kitchen to put on the kettle for a cup of chamomile tea to calm her nerves. The girls wouldn't be back until later that evening, which meant there was a whole day ahead of her to wallow in the sadness of her humiliation. She hadn't eaten or drunk anything since leaving early to have it out with Sami, but the thought of food didn't interest her at all. She stood away from the stove, her eyes closed, waiting for the kettle to boil. Then, almost at the same time, the kettle whistled loudly, and the doorbell rang, jolting her eyes open.

She turned off the stove and made her way to the door. She wasn't expecting anyone and had no idea who it might be, as it was still before midday on a Sunday. She had a mind to pretend that she wasn't in, but her car was on the drive.

She opened the door.

'Abi — what's wrong with your phone? I tried ringing last night and then again this morning, but it just kept ringing. Not even your answer phone came on. Is there something wrong with your line? If so, you'll need to report it and get it fixed.' Candice was in full flow with energy, but then she noticed Abi's demeanour and that her eyes were puffy likely from having cried for a time.

'Sorry about the phone. I'll check. I must have accidentally unplugged it.' Abi knew she had deliberately disconnected it beside her bed so she wouldn't have to take any calls.

She ran upstairs, plugged it back into the socket and returned to the kitchen to continue making tea with Candice, who had a lot of questions to ask. The answer phone kicked in, stated the date and said, 'There are no new messages.'

'What happened last night with you and Sami at the wine bar?' Abi hadn't told her about the studio episode that occurred, when she found out that not only was Sami married but that his wife was pregnant. It had taken all of her energy to conceal from Candice the depth of what she had discovered. And now the bombshell about the boys being dropped from the project.

'I can't even bring myself to talk about it, or talk to anyone, for that matter. I'm so ashamed of myself. I'm completely out of words to describe how humiliated I feel.'

'Abi, we're friends, right? You don't have to be a certain way with me. Made up, not made up, got it all together or not, we can be who we are, however we're feeling. Don't think I haven't noticed. You've been pretending that everything was okay for weeks. Something was up, but I thought you needed space and that you'd tell me whenever you were ready. '

'Candice, I'm sorry I didn't tell you anything because I knew how you get anxious, and I didn't want to worry you while I was struggling with my own anxieties.' She suffered a surge of emotions that pushed out more tears, but she prepared herself to tell her story, putting together the pieces she'd found of the puzzle…

'*Ring-ring, ring-ring.*' The phone stopped Abi from going into her explanation. She walked over to the phone on the wall in the kitchen and picked it up.

'Hello?'

'Hi, it's me, Justin. Remember me? The piano player at the Bromley Shopping Mall event a while back.'

'Yes, I remember you. How are you? It's been a while.' Abi was about to brush him off by saying she was busy and would call him later, but Justin had called to give her important news that couldn't wait until Monday. He needed an answer that day.

'Those three demo tapes you gave me and your profile? Well, they got into the hands of some very influential people with links to a music company. They absolutely loved your voice and want to meet you to discuss options.'

Abi was stunned into silence. She looked at the phone, then back at Candice.

'Hello? Hello? Abi, are you there?

'Yes, I'm here.'

'They'd like to meet you tomorrow at their offices in Knightsbridge at 11 a.m.—can you make it?'

'Are you for real?'

'I'm deadly serious. I'll also be there because they want me, too—are you up for it?'

'What can I say? I don't know what to be excited about, if at all.'

'Then, tomorrow will be the first day of finding out. I've already met these guys. They're genuine and serious about making something happen. I'm talking Whitney Houston, Donna Summers, Diana Ross big. Real singers.'

'But I'm not them. I'm just me.'

'Exactly. They want just you.

'Can you make it for 10.15 a.m., Knightsbridge Station?' He didn't give her a chance to answer. 'We can have coffee and a chat before we meet the company. I'll meet you at the Brompton Road exit. That's the one that leads to Harrods.

'See you tomorrow, and don't worry: you'll be great.' Justin hung up the phone.

Abi stood there with the phone still in her hand, pressed to her ear, and the dial tone playing.

'Abi? Are you okay? What's going on? You were about to tell me about Sami.'

'I don't know what to tell you first. Something has just happened, and now I'm confused.'

'Tell me: what is it?' Candice didn't know whether to be lost in the tragedy or uplifted by something almost supernatural.

'I'll tell you about Sami but later, not now.' She jogged Candice's memory about the time she'd sung at the shopping mall and met Justin.

'I don't know whether this is genuine, but he seems to believe it is. This company has listened to my demos, and they want to meet me tomorrow morning.'

'That sounds like great news to me,' Candice said apprehensively. 'This is what you've always wanted, right?'

'I don't want to get my hopes up about anything anymore. Look at me—I'm a complete mess. I feel sick, and I have a headache from crying so much. I can't do this.' Abi began to spiral into a meltdown.

'Hey—yes, you can. You can't give up on your hopes and dreams over Sami. Forget about him. You've got some important people to meet.'

'But I haven't told you that the boys were dropped from the project, Sami's a married man and his wife's pregnant—'

'Stop! Stop, Abi.' Candice put her hand up, indicating that Abi should say no more. 'Not now. We can talk about it another time when you're up to it. Sami's lies are not gonna bring you down. Don't allow him to ruin this for you.

'Have you eaten?'

'No!'

'I'll make us some brunch and then we can talk about getting your head straight for tomorrow. Whatever it brings, you'll be ready.'

Candice opened the fridge door wide and rummaged through it. 'What have you got? Eggs…bacon…beans…bread…' Abi sat down at her kitchen table as if at a restaurant, waiting for her order to arrive. She sighed. 'Either this is a miracle from God, or I don't know what. Or, if it's some sort of hoax, it would be a cruel joke on me, played when I'm at my lowest. Then again, if this is my destiny, I'd better face it. I'm all out of shots.'

''Course you'll be ready. You've been preparing all your life. Even if it looks like a carrot being dangled in front of your face or that you're about to plunge into a rabbit hole, I'd go for it. Your luck must be turning.'

Abi folded her arms. 'I don't believe in luck. Destiny and fate, yes.

'Anyway, I'm not gonna second guess what will or won't happen tomorrow, but I'm gonna be me, Abi Jackson.'

Her thoughts and attention switched to what she might wear and doing her vocal practice. Each time Sami's image entered her head, she told herself, 'Not now.'

'As for the boys, I'm happy to call them to break the news that things didn't work out and the project has been axed.'

'No, as bad as it is, I'll be the one to tell them. I'm the one who started the whole thing. I'm the one that got everyone involved, so I'll be brave and do it myself. Thanks anyway, Candice. I got you involved, too. You must be pretty pissed off.'

'I know it's not your fault. You were only trying to do something good, something you believed in. This guy, Justin, seems to believe in you. This meeting has come at the right time.'

A thought popped into Abi's head like a lightbulb going on. 'I know what I need. I need some music.' Abi had a stack of cassettes in a rack in the living room. She looked through it and selected Commissioned, an American gospel group that never failed to lift her spirit and make her want to dance. She turned the volume up and danced her way back into the kitchen.

'That's it, girl. Yes, dance.'

Abi loved the song, and she sang it as if she were a part of the group.' Still finishing off the brunch preparation, Candice caught the vibe and moved along to the beat.

Music was Abi's answer to everything, be it feeling sad or happy, be it fast or slow, or at weddings, funerals, celebrations or commiserations. It was her elixir, and there could never be too much of it.

♫ ♫ ♫

The next day, everything moved like clockwork. Children were up without incident. They ate breakfast, dressed and were dropped off at school. The drive to the train station was uncannily seamless. There were no major road works to interfere with the early morning traffic. There were no issues on the tube, which was always touch and go for a Monday morning. Abi arrived on time to meet Justin at the Brompton Road exit of the Piccadilly line. Justin was already waiting. He was thrilled to see her again since the performance at the Bromley Shopping Mall, which was a long time ago. She had called him once since, to follow up with the contact, but there had been nothing since then. Abi had forgotten about him as if he were nothing more than a blur in the distant past.

'Hi, Justin. I've just one question for you: how did you know I'd come today?'

'I didn't, but I went ahead and arranged the meeting anyway. You're already in, but you don't know it yet. You will.'

'And if I didn't make it today, what would you have told them?'

'I'd tell them something, and I'd be left with egg on my face in front of the people I wanted to impress. That's how much I trust in the universe. It's your time now and mine — can't you see it?'

'My trust was always in God, but I lost that for a moment. Let's see whether God is with us or not today.

'Oh, just so that you know, if this doesn't pan out, I won't hold anything against you. Just…thanks for thinking of me.' She truly meant every word she said, not allowing her soul to see beyond the current moment. The plan was to take things one step at a time and have both eyes open. 'Words that come cheap have no honour. Let's go meet these people and hear what they've got to say.'

Outside of the huge corporations that dominated the world's music industry, there was a new landscape emerging: the Middle East. They loved Western music but weren't expected to want a seat around the table of the well-established, tightly controlled industry. The Faceless People owned the markets, and they would never allow the Middle East to be given a place at the table. Their inherited wealth, earned by converting oil into dollars, was not welcome, but the Middle East coveted Western education. It was a must for sending their children to UK universities, and though they attended classes, they also partied hard to Western music. Ideas eventually surfaced about investing in the growing industry, and they used their wealth to try to get into the business without success. Seeing that there would be no place for them, the wealthy sheikhs in the United Arab Emirates decided to make their own table, knowing that, one day, the Faceless People would come to them and want a part of their action. To that end, a group of businessmen determined to be involved in the music industry set up a record label in the heart of London, Knightsbridge.

The prestigious address was owned by Gulf Records. Justin rang the buzzer and stated their names and who they'd come to see into the intercom, and the door clicked open.

A smartly dressed receptionist greeted them with a welcoming smile. 'Good morning. You're Abi Jackson and Justin Palmer.'

'The last time I checked, yes,' Justin said, hoping to lighten the mood.

'Welcome. I'll let the directors know you've arrived. Would you like coffee, tea or a cold drink?'

'I'm okay for now. Perhaps later, thank you.' Abi wasn't there for a tea party, but she appreciated the offer. Justin nodded to show he concurred.

They didn't have long to wait before Amir came into the reception area to greet them. 'We're so happy to see you in person. Come this way.' Amir took them into a plush boardroom with a large French polished table and finely upholstered chairs with décor to match. 'Take a seat. Mostafa, my partner in this venture, will be joining us shortly.' As soon as Mostafa's name was mentioned, the door opened.

'Hi. Forgive me. Sorry, I'm late. I was delayed on a call. Nice to finally meet you, Abi. Great to see you again, Justin,' Mostafa said. He began to pitch their plans to Abi. They offered Justin a music director position for the jazz genre, R&B crossovers into pop, and other collaborations. They'd had previous meetings and believed he was the best fit for the programme. Although initially the meeting appeared to be informal, they'd chosen the boardroom for their first encounter to show Abi the bigger picture of where the label might fit into the European market.

Mostafa picked up a glossy brochure profiling the company from a few copies stacked on a side table and gave one to Abi. There was no question they were legit. She would come to that conclusion even if she were to research the company herself.

'Let us cut to the chase—I believe that's what you would say. We love your music and your style of singing, and we want to sign you. We have big ideas for this venture. Our record label has been running in the UK for around five years. We are taking our artists into Europe and other worldwide markets. We have the backing from our investors, teams to support our projects and a legal department, so if you have an agent or lawyer, we're happy to work with them to strike up a contract that's mutually acceptable. When we've finished here, we'd like to give you a tour of our studios.'

'Abi, you must have many questions,' Amir interjected. 'What would you like to know?'

For the second time in less than two days, Abi was stunned into silence. This was the best and only offer to sign she'd ever had. She needed a moment to catch her breath as it was so unexpected, but her gut told her this was the option for her. This was not a job offer as an employee but as a respected artist. The package she was being offered seemed sound.

'Send me the contract, and I'll have my lawyer look over it. They can do the back and forth until we're happy, then we can have another meeting about what we've agreed to.' Abi didn't have a lawyer, but she took the initiative, knowing she'd have to find one to make the deal legal.

'So, where are your studios, Mostafa? I hope they're as impressive as your pitch.'

'We are in the business of making stars. Money is no object. We want to sign you on a three-year contract, renewable if you wish. You'll have creative license to bring your ideas forward, and we'll be your seal of approval. We have offices and studios in London, but we're an integral part of a bigger project in Dubai, one of the states in the United Arab Emirates. One of the initiatives in progress is building one of the biggest, fun, luxury attractions in the world to be opened by 2020. The tallest hotel in the world is already under construction, complete with entertainment arenas and Formula One racing. It will be the Las Vegas of the Middle East. When we build it, the people will come is one of our mottos. In terms of music, we already have a record label. As we speak, we have been in talks with Sony and other top record companies. They'll be floating on the US stock market because they want to raise more cash to expand. We'll buy as much stock as we can, or at least a percentage of it. What we really want is a Middle Eastern arm of Sony.

'The Arabs are very patient people and we can wait, but that's our politics. We want you to write songs or source the songs, sing them and build this wonderful platform for music. You'll also have access to the best musicians and people who appreciate talented, iconic singers. We want to transform the mediocre into the spectacular.' Abi was learning that once Mostafa got started, there was no stopping him. She saw the passion and commitment he had for the programme. The door of opportunity had truly been opened for her. It was not blind faith, but she was prepared to enter into the unknown without questioning that divine intervention had actually come at a time when she needed something to pick her up from the pits.

13

Faceless People

THE UK MUSIC Awards was a coveted event that everyone in the industry wanted to attend. It was there that Sami was introduced to Theodore Crabtree, Theo for short. They became good friends and socialised in each other's circles. Sami attended events like this mainly to find new contacts to advance his career. It was not what you knew about the music business but who you knew that got you the opportunities. Alcohol always flowed at these places, and wine was great for loosening the tongue. Sami took whatever was promised in these conversations, even if said in a drunken stupor, and followed up.

Theo had many connections in the industry. He pushed Sami to aim high and go for a talent scout position he'd heard about at Butterfly Records. Artist and repertoire man was his official title; in short, an A&R man. Sami was willing to work hard just to find that next up-and-coming star.

Theo talked to Sami about his own goal, to build an empire one day. Academics weren't his strong suit, which was evident by the numerous failed exams throughout his schooling career. He spoke of the influence his favourite aunt, Beatrice, had had on him. She had once asked him, 'Theo, my darling—what are you most passionate about?' Her advice had been to find his passion and plant the seed by starting something in that area. Theo thought about her words and *bam*! It came to him.

It felt so right—his passion was music.

Yes, he liked the classics: jazz, rock and a bit of pop, but nothing too mainstream. He loved music coming from the underworld of talented artists who were, in some way, disadvantaged, either financially and/or socially: the underdogs. Their music was authentic and alive, a moonshine of tunes that often never saw the light of day in the mainstream world of music, owned by the Faceless People. They were the puppet masters who pulled the strings on a grand scale, and they were behind every big money-making industry on the planet.

Take radio, for example. Anyone thinking of going it alone was sure to stumble at the first hurdle. The transmission costs alone would be impossible to maintain. Ordinary people didn't have that kind of money, so many of their ideas never got off the ground. The BBC owned the airwaves on radio and in TV. To play anything in the UK, you needed an approved license, costing thousands of pounds, plus the ongoing costs. The popular TV programme *Top of the Pops*, owned by the BBC, was a part of this consortium, and only broadcasted approved artists who were allowed on the music circuit. The industry was tightly controlled.

Theo was the stepping stone that led Sami to meet the Faceless People. Timing and location were everything. Theo had his ears to the ground when he heard that Butterfly Records had brought in a new UK director to boost sales. They'd put out word they were enlisting talent scouts to find a new wave of music, with a view to signing artists to their record label. They were open to new ideas and would support anyone they felt worth backing.

The Faceless People had a solid bond, and they met every five years to make big decisions on the direction of mainstream music in the world. They were part of an elite inner circle—strictly invitation only—organised by the firm of the Faceless People. This time around, they all agreed the industry was stale and in need of new blood and fresh ideas, and they were ready to take a chance by taking take music in a new direction.

The word about the change in the industry trickled down. Sami followed up on Theo's lead and applied for an A&R position at Butterfly Records. After a group interview with other potential hopefuls, he was offered a three-year contract. It wasn't just Sami who was picked from the selection—they had taken on seven in total. They planned to start in London and do the same in areas like Manchester, Liverpool, and other big city hubs for a particular genre of music. If they got the expected results, they would employ more people using the same model.

It was a lucky break that Sami had come in at the start of this new initiative. He promised the management team that, come hell or high water, they wouldn't regret selecting him. Sami worked long hours, scoping out the club circuit and gatherings of artists, including the Isle of Wight Festival, Glastonbury and Wired, and come festival season, he'd travel anywhere that unique artists or bands might be looking for management.

A number of times, his efforts paid off, and he presented a few indie bands he could plug into the mainstream.

Two and a half years later, his three-year contract was coming to an end. Sami wanted to show the Faceless People he could think outside the box. He didn't know what he would present, but he knew that when he saw it, he would recognise it.

It was by trawling through the many invitations he received, one event leading to another, and through the rounds of socialising that ensued, that he met Abi. She was so easy to talk to. Sami never missed an opportunity to meet up-and-coming artists, so after a conversation, he agreed to listen to Abi's demo cassette tape, which she gave him on the spot.

Sami wasted no time in letting artists know his opinion of their talent, and Abi was no exception. Her genre and style were okay, but she was not the fresh, zesty vibe he was looking for to impress the Faceless People with.

He knew that his connection with Abi wouldn't go anywhere, but after that meeting, he'd kept in contact. He couldn't put his finger on it, but there was something about Abi he liked and not just her beauty. He enjoyed being around her, and he was intrigued by her innocence and naivety. There was also a positive energy about her that inspired him.

On the flip side, Abi liked the idea of having a friend who was an actual A&R man for a record label. She was fascinated by the fact that he was a genuine contact in the industry.

Then, one day over lunch, Sami mentioned that his contract at Butterfly Records would come to an end unless he came up with something that might cause the management to reconsider renewing it.

'I'll be gutted if my contract doesn't get renewed. I've worked really hard to bring talent with the potential to make it big in the music business,' Sami said as he considered how the Faceless People might see him.

'If you're looking for the next wave of talent, you don't have to look too far. Think about it: real talent is homegrown within the belly of community halls, recreation centres, churches and even playgrounds. They're the ones who have a hunger for fame.' As if a light bulb had switched on, Abi had an idea. 'I know what! Why don't you hold an audition for a boy band? You could select five singers with the best voices and appearances and take that raw talent and turn it into something unique, get a vocal coach, give them some songs to sing that fits the profile you're after, let them practice and practice, and see what comes out of it. You've got six months left, yeah? What have you got to lose?'

It seemed like a slam-dunk of an idea that might just be the saving grace for his contract extension and career at Butterfly Records

'I really like it, but if it were you, how would you do it?' Sami didn't know where he would begin to construct something like that, but he was intrigued to hear what she would say. He was looking for something that would draw hidden talent from the woodwork out into the open, something that wouldn't otherwise cross the paths of A&R scouts.

He knew this could go one of two ways: either it would raise him up the ranks at the record label, or it would go down spectacularly in flames. The more Abi talked about it to flesh out the idea, the more it became clear and viable. He was happy to see what Abi would bring to the table.

That was how the whole thing leading to the auditions started, with Sami using this angle of opportunity to advance his career and extend his contract at Butterfly Records, all credited to Abi. She'd worked hard for his cause and had actually pulled it off.

Amazingly enough, the auditions produced a promising selection of singers, and it would have all worked out well for Sami, who was on the cusp of going down in history as the creator of a fashionable boy band handpicked for success, not to mention the royalties from the songs he'd written that would be immortalised around the world. But the final approval was not with him. That rested squarely with the Faceless People.

Having done the first phase of the project, getting the boys together, he eagerly arranged to meet the Faceless People to present his plan. He asked Jeff, his line manager, if he could assemble them. It was going to be a big moment when he could show them just what he had been doing with his time and get their total buy-in to launch the boys as stars, waiting to be adored by millions.

In the head offices of most organisations, there is often a floor at the top of the building. When you are on that floor, it is referred to as being 'up there with the gods'. It was a floor you never visited unless you were invited. Butterfly Records was no exception. The top level was where nobody but the board members and executives went. As well as stairs leading up to the room, there was a lift from the ground floor straight into the boardroom, designated for use by only the elderly Faceless People, who met there once in a while and who didn't particularly want to take the stairs with the common staff. Besides, their knees wouldn't hold up, so the lift was the safer option.

'Are you ready? Have you got everything?' Beth asked Sami as he stood admiring himself in the mirror, checking out his outfit, which was a petrol blue suit, pale blue shirt with a faint check, a paisley print tie, black brogue-type shoes, and black socks. The ensemble looked sharp and spoke of success, confidence and trustworthiness. Sami's aim was to make a good first impression when he met the Faceless People at his appointment. He had never seen them before, but Jeff, his manager, often asked for updates on Sami's work so he could attend various meetings to talk about his UK region and progress on the A&R scouts' programme.

'Have you seen my briefcase?' Sami asked. A minor panic clouded his brain, and he couldn't remember where he'd left it.

'You left it over there by the front door so you wouldn't forget to take it with you,' Beth said reassuringly. Sami was accustomed to throwing his rucksack over his shoulder on his way out through the door. Everything was flung into it. This time, he had a briefcase in which things would remain flat.

'You'd better leave now to give yourself plenty of time to settle down before your presentation.'

With those words of encouragement and a kiss for good luck, Sami was off and out the door, like a warrior determined to conquer his territory and come back with the spoils: a promotion, an extended contract, more money, or even a permanent position at Butterfly Records. Anything that said victory.

♫ ♫ ♫

'Good morning, Sami. You are looking hot today! Look at you! Where are you going? What's happening? Tell me, tell me, tell me,' Amie, the receptionist at Butterfly Records, greeted him. She had never seen him dress that slick before.

'I've got a meeting with the board today. Could you call Jeff and let him know I'm here? Thanks.'

'Hmm…I saw Jeff and some big guns getting into the lift this morning. So, they're here for you, then? Well, good luck.' Amie called Jeff, who was already waiting in the boardroom with the Faceless People. She relayed his message to Sami: 'Jeff said to take the lift to the top floor, and he'll meet you there. Go gettum, tiger!'

Sami couldn't help but smile at Amie's sassy comments. Cracking jokes were her thing, which was just what he needed to break any hint of nerves he might be feeling, but he was, nevertheless, confident that he would win over the Faceless People with his plan.

'Good morning, Sami,' Jeff greeted him as he came out of the lift. He offered him a handshake and a warm smile.

'Good morning. Are we good to go?' Sami asked.

'Yes. We have five board representatives present. They don't get out much, so make it worth their while. Be yourself and relax.

'I'll do the intros, then hand the floor over to you, okay?' It was true the board members were not often in London, but fortunately, they were there now for various other business interests, trying to kill multiple birds with one stone.

Sami and Jeff walked over towards the Faceless People, who were sitting at the back end of the polished, rectangular oak table. Bottled water, small tumbler glasses, and paper coasters had been carefully positioned near where each person sat. The Faceless People were in their seventies, bronzed by a lifestyle of yachts and visits to private islands in the Caribbean. They were called upon to make big decisions in their spheres of expertise, and they made themselves available only when needed.

Jeff was the go-between on the project, and the Faceless People were intrigued to hear about its progress. It was more than just casting an expert eye over things; their opinions were the ones that counted.

'Welcome, everyone. Thank you for taking time out of your busy schedules. I'd like to introduce you to Sami Achu, one of our A&R scouts working on the new talent initiative. I'm excited about this, and I hope you will be, too.'

The Faceless People smiled at Sami with their bronzed faces and silver-grey hair. Sunlight streamed through the huge windows, making their faces shine even more.

'Thank you for your time. Before I go into details, I'd like to start by playing you something I believe represents a new wave of music that will create massive revenue in the industry.' Sami wanted to hold off giving his full pitch until he'd given them a taste of the product. This wasn't something with which he might get the Faceless People to approve with a few enticing words. The music would have to speak for itself.

'Here's track one.' Sami pressed play on the cassette player connected to the built-in Bose surround sound speakers in the boardroom (it was nothing but the best when it came to their needs).

He had them at the first few bars of the musical intro. Then, when DeAngelo's lead voice pierced through the music with that unique voice, he won them over. Track after track, the voices moved from strength to strength. Based on the nodding of the heads, the Faceless People were captivated. Sami was now ready to sell the dream behind this new wave.

'Music evolves every decade or two, from the "Sound of Silence" era with Simon and Garfunkel and Carly Simon to Pink Floyd, Alice Cooper, Queen, The Jackson Five, and The Osmonds—you can place those artists in their own times to shine. But we are fast approaching the year 2000—what will be the sound to propel the music industry into its long-awaited evolution? Anything a new young audience can latch onto, imitate, and rave over. We are way beyond the post-war era and have moved through the cries for peace era. Back then, songs emerged about making love, not war, and all you need is love. Now that there has been so much peace, everyone wants to have fun. From "Girls Just Want To Have Fun" to boys who want to look and act cool.

'With your endorsement and investment, these are the voices that will show up to shape the next decade. The fruits of my strategy will transcend the UK market. The European market has always been on our doorstep, but our aim is to start this trend strongly and light it up like a torch set on fire as far as Asia, Japan, Hong Kong, China and even the Middle East. Dubai is on track to be the next Las Vegas, and the Arabs want this new wave of music, too. The global market is our oyster, the revenue is colossal and this sound is our vehicle.' Sami paused for a breath, and there was a minute's silence. He knew he had the Faceless People in the palms of his hands.

Sami moved around, no longer talking from the front of the boardroom, handing out files to the Faceless People. In them were the promo pictures and bios of the five boys who had auditioned to be in the group and to whom they'd been listening for the past fifteen minutes. His presentation spoke of more money for the Faceless People, innovations leading the way for the next few decades, and voices that others would imitate forever. The presentation spoke of longevity into the future.

'Now, how does everyone feel about the voices you've just heard?' It was a 'how do you like that?' rhetorical question, knowing full well what the answer would be as he had already observed their responses, which appeared to be favourable.

Not that Sami was aware of it, but the Faceless People had already seen pictures of the boys and been given a vague heads-up by Jeff, the UK director, but they hadn't yet heard their voices.

One of the Faceless People responded almost as if they were all in agreement telepathically. 'Don't get me wrong—these voices are incredible, and I agree they are the voices of the future, even without the finishing touches by the studio—but I'm sorry, the singers will not work going forward into our future. As hot as this is, it does not represent what we see as our "brand". It's not the direction we want to go, so unless you can find other boys to push this new wave forward, it's a no from me.'

An echo of that single word, a resounding 'no', went around the room, ricocheting off the walls.

Sami interjected as he saw the big opportunity he'd worked so hard for slowly slipping through his fingers down into a pan of nothingness. 'What if I can find you five new boys who can sing like these boys can? Would you accept the project?

'Well, if you're able to do that, find other boys that fit the brand who would spearhead our cause, then, yes, I'll back it.'

Like a chorus, Sami heard yesses for the idea all around.

'That's great. I'll find you the boys, then I'll arrange a private event for you to give the final sign-off—does that work for everyone?' Sami had redeemed himself, getting back into play. He didn't know where the suggestion to find other boys who could sing just like the current ones had come from. Perhaps it was a straw of hope he'd grasped when he saw it. His contract with Butterfly Records hung in the balance.

He loved his job and the industry he worked in. He knew it would be a long shot, but he could feel it in his soul that success was right there in front of him. He just had to be patient and do whatever was needed to make it happen, just as he'd described to the Faceless People. There was nothing more that could have been added to the presentation.

Sami smiled a positive can-do smile as he took one last look at the Faceless People, but when he shifted his gaze and stared into space for a few seconds, he saw a picture of Abi and the five boys in his mind's eye—and even Mervyn—and all they had done to bring the product this far.

He took a breath in, breathed out, smiled at them, and pushed the others out of his mind. He'd get around that small issue somehow. The boys were not under contract, besides. They hadn't signed anything.

'It was a privilege meeting you all,' were Sami's parting words.

14

The New UK Group

THE IMPACT OF what the Faceless People shared at the presentation hit Sami like a fast-moving freight train with him firmly pinned to the front, on the outside and holding on for dear life. He left the boardroom, smiling at everyone as though everything was just peachy and going to plan. Their suggestion to change the group to boys who were more to their liking was no trouble at all. They expected it to be as easy as waving a magic wand. Then, the right boys would appear in an instant as if they'd pulled a rabbit out of a hat, only this time, they would be parrots instead of rabbits. Sami was a quick thinker, but this monumental change would require thinking at lightning speed.

♫ ♫ ♫

It was midday. Sami had plans to meet another musician—a violinist—to lay down some tracks to mix into a few of the songs. The thought of giving up flashed across his brain, but that was impossible. From past experience, he knew better than to engage in such thoughts. He'd learnt that hard lessons lead to success, which often comes from hard experiences and how we respond to them in the moment.

Sami shook off these thoughts as if they were pieces of fluff on his jacket. He needed to find some space, somewhere he could sit down to think things through. Finding new boys with the same voices as the originals weighed heavily on his mind. It was a thought he could not brush off. The studio was already booked for the next few weeks—should he cancel the studio? Change it to another week or another month? How long would it take to find new boys to step into the original boys' shoes? These were valid questions he could not ignore. Sami pondered on what he might do as he made his way to the atrium leading out to the gardens in the middle of the Butterfly Records complex, hoping to find solace along the way.

♫ ♫ ♫

Bright lights, big cities, flashing cameras, the media, and adoring fans—these had all been predestined for the new group. They were what the world—and not just the UK—were waiting for, and they would take it by storm, if for no other reason than their marketing and media force. Meticulously packaged, piece by piece, construction by construction, come hell or high water, the new boys would be found, assembled, prepped, and made ready.

And so, the dream building began. On a piece of paper, Sami penned the phrase, 'The world is my oyster, and delved into his treasure trove of possibilities, drawing up scripted scenes for future performances, stage by stage, all culminating in the birth of a phenomenon.

It was Friday at midday when the Faceless People gave Sami a partial yes for the new group with the proviso that, with the right boys, they might give the project their full backing. Up until then, the Faceless People had been completely sold on the practice recordings he'd pieced together from the best of the weekly tapes Mervyn had sent him. As a result, the studio was locked into a schedule as protected time. If it didn't work out, there was enough time to pull the plug on the whole thing, call it off, and not spend any more from the budget. It would all be chalked up as something he'd tried that didn't bear fruit, but even with the best intentions, it would be impossible for him to coach the boys through the studio sessions while simultaneously developing the new group. He felt sure that new boys would be found, and one would segue into the other in a kind of osmosis.

♫ ♫ ♫

Sami's plans with Beth over the weekend were meant to be a way to chill before the intense studio sessions started and the project moved into its next phase. He knew what he was doing. To some degree, Beth was his wingman, though he didn't always tell her the full story about everything he did. He did, however, have moments of bravado, in which he wanted to show her how bright, clever, and intelligent he was.

Beth was clear-headed whenever he engaged in conversations about what he was working on, and he respected her abilities as a classically-trained pianist who could read music, unlike himself.

'Beth, the board of directors loved the voices, but they couldn't see how they would make money for the company. They said that if I found another group of boys who could sing like the original ones, they might consider backing the project.' Sami spoke with tones of half-sadness mixed with the occasional bit of optimism.

'Right. That's a dilemma. Are you going to pull the plug and tell the boys? Everyone has spent months on this. Cutting it short won't be easy,' Beth said, sharing his pain and naively expecting that Sami would tell the boys and do the right thing.

'The studio is already booked, so I'll go ahead with the sessions. I'll let the boys know that they weren't accepted by the record company, but I'll use them again for jingles in advertising. I have contacts always on the lookout for singers to back their ads.' Sami had pulled that answer from thin air. It was not what he intended to use their voices for; the Faceless People's suggestion was still in play.

Sami planned to finish the studio sessions before moving on to the next stage of forming the new group. Telling the boys the news too early would only be shooting himself in the foot, halting everything when he was only partway into his mission. Instead of focusing on what he couldn't change, he intended to spend the weekend dreaming, constructing the fantasy into reality, and flat-out working.

In his house was a room he used as an office. It was his sacred space, calming and not overly cluttered with furniture. There was a rough oak wooden desk, a computer, a printer, and a kneeling chair tipped to the best ergonomic angle for working long hours at the desk without causing mobility issues in the future. But that wasn't the focal point of the room. That was an array of scattered cushions with vivid African prints and black lines partitioning tribal images. It was a haven that represented his home in Cameroon. There were pictures of ancestors long passed away, and a large, stunning landscape painting that reminded him of Yaoundé, the capital of Cameroon, where he had lived, though he was born in a Bamenda town. In the room, he sat on the fluffy rug on the wooden floor, pen and notebook in hand, and gathered his thoughts, ready to create.

It served as his retreat — Beth rarely entered it — after suffering through this challenging experience. Sami thought about the task that lay ahead, and the title of a song came to him: 'Fantasy to Reality'. He scribbled down a few words as they sprung to mind, never losing touch with the magic of the moment.

♫ ♫ ♫

The weekend was over. Sami had written a new brief: five English boys from anywhere in the UK who were native English speakers, with a mix of dark-hair and perhaps two blonds, if they fit the profile. They must be able to sing in tune and dance in time to the music, have gone to acting school, and be able to perform in front of large audiences. They must be good at mimicking accents and learning lines, have fresh faces, model looks and athletic or sporty builds. They should be the same age and height as the originals. Most importantly, they had to be willing to put whatever they had on hold for three months to relocate to a luxury house in Coulsdon, Croydon, where they would be trained for their roles in the new UK group.

That Friday afternoon, Becky from the marketing and entertainment team had sent out a memo to all established agencies that a record company was looking to form a group. It was not just any mundane group, but one that would change the landscape of music and would be loved forever. Once the group was unveiled, it would be their time to shine.

Early Monday morning, just before the original boys arrived to start recording their live vocals, Sami was sitting with Becky. It was as if the request had only just rolled off his tongue when the agencies began ringing the switchboard to speak with the team.

'Talk about the word spreading like wildfire. There must have been a fly on the wall when we discussed our plan last Friday.

'I can't look at anything until the next few weeks are over. Ask the agencies to send only what I've asked for, or they'll be wasting our time, and I won't use them again. You tell them that. We're on a time-critical path here.' Sami trusted that, within those weeks, they would have a selection of boys who met the new brief whom they could mould into whatever he needed.

'Right. Do you want the boys to come from the same agency, or don't you mind?' Becky asked, thinking ahead that if the boys were from the same agency, they might already know each other, and that would be half the battle as they would be entering into something new with friends, or at any rate, people they knew instead of strangers.

'Not necessarily. We're going on looks, height, performance, acting ability, and all the other criteria,' Sami said. A picture not unlike a mirage and ideas were slowly emerging in his head, even before seeing the candidates. He wasn't asking Becky to do the selecting for him, only that her team eliminated anyone who didn't fit the brief. He trusted the process would produce something, and he was confident the right boys would shine through. 'Oil, no matter how much it is mixed with water, will, without exception, float to the top,' Sami said. This was followed by the unspoken thought that oil makes money, as would the new boys.

♫ ♫ ♫

The result from the intense weeks in the studio with the original boys was abundantly fruitful. As always, Dizziboy came up trumps with the mixing. Even though Abi briefly crossed paths with Beth, it was never Sami's intention that they should meet. That notion busted apart that fine Sunday morning with the confrontation on his doorstep and their dirty linen being washed in public (as witnessed by at least a few of their neighbours). It also sealed the fact that he and Abi would never be friends again. As a result, Abi was now well out of the picture, and the new boys were right on cue.

♫ ♫ ♫

Becky had plenty of profiles for Sami to look through to give the final yay or nay. The next step required that the new boys be called in for a round of auditions. This time, Sami was flanked by Becky and Tommy, who were purely there to comment on the looks and the style (Tommy's forte was in detailed entertainment personae). The boys would need a lot of charisma and a formidable presence if they were to be in the public spotlight, and Tommy was the man who could make it happen. He'd styled the Beatles, Pink Floyd, Jimmy Hendrix and the like, all iconic images. Sami just needed to know whether they could hold a note and didn't have two left feet, as, at some point, there would be dance routines.

♫ ♫ ♫

Abi had been left to deal with the original boys, whose expectations were crushed during the phone calls. They were devastated and emotional and burst into tears, and there was nothing Abi could do to console their broken hearts. It was a time of sadness for everyone. From Shirlee and her husband, Robert, to Candice, none of them saw it coming. How could they?

Mervyn was the most surprised. He'd worked those boys to within an inch of their vocal breaking points. By the time they were ready for the studio, they could have sung the songs in their sleep. The phrasing and tones were fresh, unlike the usual soulful African-American sounds, where you could tell, blindfolded, whether they were Motown, Atlantic, or Tamla singers. If you closed your eyes and listened to those boys singing, you wouldn't have known they were first-generation boys born in the UK to immigrant parents from the Caribbean. Their voices were unique, unlike any others, and Mervyn had honed their skilful singing.

He was also sad for the boys because he'd been their vocal coach, and for a long time after, Mervyn would question himself as to how he could have gotten their voices so wrong, feeling responsible for what appeared to be a failure. He reached out to the boys individually to express how sad he was, as well as encouraged them not to give up. He let them know that everything they'd done had been right, and he knew that something good would come from it. When he said it, he sensed a knowing in his gut that it was true.

♫ ♫ ♫

Sami recovered from the showdown outside of his house with Abi and Beth. He managed to convince Beth that he had rejected Abi's advances towards him, but after a few drinks at her place, he'd had a weak moment and slept with her. Beth was left unsure as to whether she could trust him again. It was going to take some time to heal from the embarrassment of the public humiliation, having her neighbours watch and listen to the argument as it played out on the street, not to mention the hurt it had caused, but Beth loved him. She was with child and vulnerable, and she couldn't kick him out now, not at a time when she needed his protection the most.

♫ ♫ ♫

It is written that it took six days to create the world plus one in which even God needed to rest and admire His handiwork. What he'd done could never be compared to something as magnificent as Creation, but within three months of going full tilt, a new group had been formed in that tiny speck known as London on the planet Earth, and it was designed to rock the world. All that was left was to find an iconic name that would withstand the test of time, up there with the likes of Elton John, The Jackson 5, Duran Duran, Simple Minds, Madness, The Bee Gees, The Beatles…

'The' or not 'The'? Sami couldn't decide. Such groups were invited to Hollywood to immortalise their names in stone. The name had to have that kind of ring to it. It had to be memorable and translatable into something that meant fun and excitement worldwide that was also desirable, emotional, upbeat, fresh and young, all mixed into a single phrase. Sami didn't know what to call the group, but that would come later, and when it did, it would be the cherry on their sundae.

The hard slog of no stone unturned and costs running into thousands was what it took to perfect the new group. This, compared to the few hundred pounds for the original boys, where most of the money had gone towards their vocal coach, Mervyn, who had patterned the voices and style. It seemed like a long time ago. The new group was primed and ready for the Faceless People to see whether Sami had delivered on his promise to find new boys who would fit the brand. Their endorsement meant everything for the project.

♫ ♫ ♫

Gusto Restaurant was chosen as the place to unveil the new group. It was one of those places with a discreet entrance on Charlotte Street in Central London. On the outside, the decor didn't shout, 'I'm here, come dine with me,' and one would likely pass by it without noticing it, but on that special Wednesday evening, which was usually a quiet day at the restaurant, there was a private event, strictly invitation only. Twenty guests had been invited to the presentation, which included the original five Faceless People plus another five, all of whom were capable of influencing decisions.

The project would still be under wraps until it was declared official, but Beth was allowed to attend, which was special for two reasons: one, she would be by Sami's side to support his potential success or commiseration, and two, it was her first time out six weeks after the birth of their son, Zak.

Beth's mother had travelled down from Lancashire to stay for a while and get to know her new grandson, which was a treat for her and a blessing for Beth.

Gusto's reception area was more like a cloakroom, but it doubled as a place where people were greeted, checked off of the list, and led to the restaurant down a tiered stairway with black marbled walls. Lights shone down on black and white portraits of famous Hollywood actors and directors: that iconic, saucy picture of Marilyn Monroe, captured with her dress blowing upwards; Doris Day, Humphrey Bogart, and Marlon Brando looking as commanding as ever; and finally, a stoic, Alfred Hitchcock. As guests descended the last tier of stairs, they were met with a bar on the back wall and a display of a colourful array of bottles of alcohol—rum, whiskey, cognac, vodka, cocktail mixers—stacked high up the wall. There was a ladder on the side in case someone asked for a special brand that might be sitting on the top shelf. Bar stools were scattered around the dark, marbled bar, encouraging people to relax, talk and drink. Generally, Friday nights heaved with people who knew about their happy hour, which ran from 5–9 p.m., featuring two cocktails for the price of one, but this was Wednesday, which didn't have the same feel.

Gusto had also been chosen because it was the only restaurant that doubled as a cinema, its projector facing the back wall. When the restaurant floor had been cleared, the area could be used as an entertainment venue, which made it ideal for unveiling the new group.

On that evening, the bar and restaurant section were set up with tables and chairs enough for the twenty guests, positioned in a way that would allow people to mingle. Canapes would be served. Then, when the event began, people could either sit at the bar facing the entertainment area or at one of the tables. Adding to the ambience was music, which added an air of sophistication. Wafting through the restaurant were the sounds of Billy Holiday, Nina Simone and Ella and Louis Armstrong. The music would play its mellow tones until it was time for the presentation. The aroma of expensive cologne only served to add to the exuberant luxury.

Tommy from entertainment, the evening's compere, had a great voice. In a toned-down fashion, less glitzy than usual, he walked over to the entertainment area to get the evening started.

'Welcome, everyone. Thank you all for coming to this exclusive, top-secret event. We know many of you have travelled far, and your presence is much appreciated.' Tommy was referring to the Faceless People who lived abroad that had come in especially for the presentation. 'We believe we've found a hidden treasure here, and we want you to be the first to see it. Their fate is in your hands, and we respect your decision as the thumbs-up or down on this. After all, it's your investment, so your approval means everything for the project going live. We don't have a name just yet, but that will come later.

'For now, we have a presentation and two performances, so enjoy your evening.' Tommy signalled to his team by lowering his right hand, the code for 'cut the lights', and the presentation video began rolling on the back wall.

An old-fashioned white background like a cine camera started rolling, then the flickering of numbers: five…four…three…two…one.

Pictures of five fresh-faced children flashed on the screen, one by one. The photos were of them singing into hairbrushes and clowning around. Some of them had funky hairstyles, and some wore shades.

There was even a young Elvis at a children's fancy-dress birthday party. The pictures told the story of the individual boys' dreams to become superstars one day.

It was Tommy's job to influence the audience by appealing to the hearts of the decision-makers.

Next came a fast-forward, as if someone had pressed a button into the present day, stopping on the individual profile pictures of each boy, almost like police mug shots, showing first the front and then the side profile views, and ending in a line-up of the five boys on a white background, as if in a police station line-up.

The new boys were depicted meeting up outside of the Coulsdon Train Station, hopping into a taxi, travelling through town and arriving at a gravelled-drive, double-fronted house, where they entered and were given a quick tour of the house. After the intro, there were scenes of their sheer hard work, vocal-coaching sessions, the boys practising, scenes of their singing and rehearsal performances of their choreography and drills that carried on for weeks. There was footage of pizza nights, card games and singing beside the piano. One of the boys played the piano and used it for practice. They were generally shown enjoying their temporary habitat at the house.

Finally, though their faces were not shown, a taxi picked them up from the house in Coulsdon and drove them into London. That was where the presentation ended. The lights gradually came up, and the boys walked from the back of the restaurant into the entertainment area.

Live in the flesh, looking well-groomed and fashion-coordinated, they held their microphones and awaited the cue to sing.

'I'd like to introduce our hidden treasure: the new UK group.' Tommy nodded as a signal to play the first track.

The boys seemed relaxed and comfortable on stage, showing a level of confidence. Even though they had only met three months prior, they sang as if they had grown up together. Their voices were an exact replica of the original boys. Their movements were simple as they swayed to the beat. There was nothing wild like the old school, Black-American, doo-wop groups, but they owned the stage and seized their time to shine.

The second song was less energetic. Five stools were surreptitiously brought out into the area for them to rest on while singing. It was a beautiful moment.

Sami, who sat in the audience but off to the side, couldn't resist glancing at the Faceless People. He was burning to know their thoughts. The final song was 'My Bella Angelica'.

The song ended, and it was followed by a silence that seemed like an eternity for Sami, Tommy, and the rest of the team. In reality, it was only a few seconds the audience needed to register that the performance had ended. Then, simultaneously, everyone rose to their feet to give them a standing ovation, clapping and cheering as if it were a performance at a concert. It was rapturous, and it continued as if there would be no end.

The boys took their bows graciously and sat half-perched on their stools, looking directly into the eyes of the audience, smiling.

Tommy came onto the stage. 'That was a wonderful performance, but I'll let you all be the judge of that.' Tommy didn't want to put the Faceless People on the spot when it came to giving their answers on whether or not to proceed with the project. If it was bad news, the team would rather hear it in private, so he had prepared a place in the office, away from everyone, to ask the original five Faceless People about their verdict.

Before he could invite them to the area, one of the Faceless People said, 'That was amazing. It's a yes from me.'

Then everyone said, 'They get my vote,' or 'That was incredible,' and the applause started up again.

Tommy joined in, shouting over the clapping, 'There are so many people to thank here. First and foremost, you gentlemen, the investors, thank you for taking a chance on this project. We know you'll not regret it, and you will receive dividends for giving your approval.' He turned to the boys and said, 'The hard work begins now, so you'd better get some rest in because you're gonna need it.'

Everyone laughed at Tommy's comments. 'And I'd like to give a special thank you to Sami for presenting the idea that something like this could work in reality.'

The applause began again, directed towards Sami, who graciously accepted it with a smile.

Beth was beaming by his side, proud of her husband's achievement. His past indiscretions were furthest from her mind.

'And, of course, I'd like to thank Becky and our marketing and entertainment teams for working tirelessly to join the dots.'

Sami turned towards Becky and applauded her, smiling and nodding because she had been his wingman when contacting the agencies to find the boys. From the least to the greatest, everyone's efforts had paid off.

The evening ended with Champagne being served to celebrate the monumental moment when the new group had met the approval of the Faceless People, bound to make millions of dollars and pounds for Butterfly Records. There was a buzz in the air as people chatted while the Weather Report's *Birdland* album played the track 'Heavy Weather' in the background, adding to the energy and leaving the guests on a high. The music soon changed to the smooth sounds of Kenny G and Chet Baker.

'Sami, we did it!' Tommy said. He exhaled as though for the first time since the event had ended.

15

The Revelation

THE SHOCK OF not being signed with Butterfly Records hit the boys hard. The sessions at the studio and the connections they had with the songs ran deep into their souls. They'd put every ounce of effort into making the songs sound incredibly spectacular, and the results were natural and flawless, or so they'd thought.

Abi reassured the boys that this was what happened all the time in the music industry and that thousands of talented singers didn't make it for whatever reason. Still, the project had been her first and last experience as a manager-slash-mentor, and she was at a loss for words. On top of that, she was hurting for so many reasons. Yes, the boys not getting signed was a big one, but there was also Sami's betrayal, and she still struggled to get her head around it.

The whole experience had her on her knees crying out to God, 'Why? Why have you abandoned me?' After the tears subsided, she sensed something she hadn't in years and heard gentle words in her head which said, 'It was not I who abandoned you, but you who rejected me.'

Like a spear, she felt the conviction of that statement being directed right to her spirit. It was a truth revealed that she could not deny. And along with the revelation, her spirit came alive, igniting something like goosebumps and butterflies in her stomach. Where could she go after that other than to ask for forgiveness?

'I'm so sorry I ran away from you,' was Abi's response. She used to have these kinds of thoughts all the time. She called them her conversations with God. In this conversation, the truth had called her out, but it wasn't the only thing revealed. It's strange the way truth doesn't stop until everything is all out in the open, and she had no doubt there would be more to come.

♫ ♫ ♫

'Good morning, everyone. I'm Lorraine Kelly from GMTV. Welcome to our live breakfast show. We've got Mr Motivator ready to get you moving with some gentle exercises. Sindy has some quick, wholesome recipes for those hungry kids when they get back from school, and the news round-up is at the top of the hour, but first, I want to introduce you to a brand new boy group that will be taking the UK by storm.' This was followed by at least two minutes' footage of X-Gen singing 'My Bella Angelica'.

Watched by millions, GMTV was a favourite programme in Jay's household. In particular, his mother, Hyacinth, got ready for work, listening to the light-hearted morning show before preparing cases for work or court. Jay happened to be passing through the living room on his way to the kitchen area and stopped dead in his tracks, when he heard singing that sounded like DeAngelo's voice. Immediately, he sat down, stunned into silence. It was as if he had seen a ghost and had done a double-take, because the boys in X-Gen sounded just like his boys, but they were not.

Jay felt sick to his stomach and confused. He did, however, have the good sense to switch on the VCR and record what was left of the performance. He didn't capture it all, but there was enough to tell that it was the same song he and the other boys had rehearsed and sung at the studio.

♫ ♫ ♫

'It's our exclusive pleasure to reveal, X-Gen. Welcome! Welcome!' The cameraman expanded his lens from Lorraine, the programme host, to include X-Gen.

'Thank you for having us.' Their words had been perfectly scripted by the entertainment team at Butterfly Records. As actors, their lines flowed seamlessly from their lips. Throughout the interview, they would be asked the questions for which they had prepared.

'So, who's who? I've got Jack, Wills, Matt, Robbie, and Drew —'

'That's me,' they each answered to their names when called.

'It's a beautiful song, and your voices? I look forward to hearing more. My daughter is too young, but I know my nieces will be mad about you.'

Jack was the spokesman for the group, and he answered all of the questions thrown at them.

'How long have you been together?'

'Just under a year. We were spotted by agents working for Butterfly Records, and they put us together.'

'Who's the lead vocal?'

They all said, 'Wills.'

'You have an amazing voice—where did you learn to sing like that?'

'Growing up, I listened to a lot of music styles with my parents—the Beatles, Elton John, Jimi Hendrix, David Bowie, jazz—and I developed my own style,' Wills said, chuffed at her comments.

'You've perfected quite a unique singing voice.'

While watching the interview, Jay shouted at the TV, 'You liar! That's not your voice! You cheat!'

Jay's mum heard him shouting. 'Jay, who are you talking to?'

'No one, Mum. It's nothing.'

Jay struggled to contain his anger and frustration, putting both of his hands on his head as he continued watching the programme.

'So, Drew, earlier, when we were talking, I detected that you don't have a British accent—where are you from?'

'Actually, I was born in the UK, but when I was five, my parents moved to Detroit in the US for business. We've been back in the

UK for the past three years, and I love London. It's way different than Detroit.'

'Well, you haven't lost your American accent. What part do you play in the group?'

'Mainly harmonies, but sometimes I lead. I'm versatile, but we all blend well together.' Drew smiled at the others, who confirmed what he'd said with a nod of their heads.

'I'm so excited about your group—when will we get to see you all?'

'Well, we'll be performing live on *Top of the Pops* at 8.30 p.m. this evening.'

'I'll certainly be watching, and all of our young viewers shouldn't miss this exclusive performance. Thank you all for coming. No doubt we'll see you here again.'

'For sure,' Drew said.

The cameraman panned away from the boys and rested directly on Lorraine. 'Yes, X-Gen is the group to watch.

'Next up, we've got Sindy with her recipes. Do you struggle to find something nutritious to give your famished kids when they get back from school? After the break, Sindy has some tasty tips, so don't go away. We'll be back. Stay tuned.' The outro music played before the adverts came on, and Lorraine leaned in towards the boys to continue her conversation, congratulating them on their first live interview: 'Guys, you did well!'

Jay leapt to his feet to set up the VCR to record the *Top of the Pops* show in the evening. He wanted to keep it in case the other boys didn't get to see it. He had to call someone.

Eddie was the closest to him in proximity. 'Eddie, something weird just happened. It's unbelievable. Can you come over? I've got to show you this. And whatever your plans are for this evening, man, you've got to be here at 8.30 p.m.'

Eddie wondered what the fire was as he sprinted over to Jay's house. He arrived at the door in record time. It seemed to Jay as if he'd only just put the phone down, and Eddie was already there.

'Hey, hey — what's up, man?' Eddie asked.

'I'm not going to tell you because I want you to tell me if I'm going mad or what.' Jay led Eddie into the living room. 'I want you to watch this. Don't say anything until the end.' Jay had the VHS tape in the machine and primed to the right place. He pressed play.

Eddie's facial expressions moved from a blank stare of confusion to raising his eyebrows to a terrified look of fear, and then his stomach began to churn.

He could no longer hold back his feelings when Will, the lead singer of X-Gen, was praised for having an amazing voice and asked where he'd learnt to sing like that, Eddie exploded with, 'You're a bloody liar!' too uncomfortable and quite offended by what he saw to hold his tongue.

'Man, just watch it until the end.' Jay wanted to see if he really had come to the same conclusion as him. He felt an alliance with Eddie, who'd bore witness to the copycat group. The biggest revelation would come that evening, at 8.30 p.m. on *Top of the Pops*.

'Is this a joke gone wrong, using us like that? Is what I'm seeing and thinking real?' Eddie asked Jay.

'I don't usually watch GMTV, but my mum has it on in the background in the mornings. I just happened to be going to the kitchen and heard that song we sang, "My Bella Angelica". How could I forget it? I swear we sang it a thousand times. I couldn't record it all, but I got about one minute of it.' Jay sighed and shook his head as if to say he couldn't believe it either.

'I'm just as shocked as you, but what are we going to do about it?' Eddie asked.

'I'm going to record the full version of the song with those imposters singing at 8.30. Look, we've got to tell the others before we do anything,' Jay said.

'What about Abi, Mervyn, and Sami? We've been set up, man, and we need some answers from them, don't we?' Eddie was moved to the point where tears sprung from his eyes.

'This is no time for boohooing. We've got to think straight,' Jay said, allowing his level-headedness to take control.

'I'll call the guys. I'll think of something to say, but I don't want to cloud their judgement by giving them our opinions.' Jay was already thinking like a lawyer. After the group had disbanded, he'd given up on the idea of becoming a professional singer, seeing it as a dream that was not meant to be. With his grades, he'd already been offered a place at Birmingham University.

'No one is to confront Abi, Mervyn, or Sami until everyone has seen the imposters for themselves.' Jay glanced at the clock on the wall. 'Look—it's 9.30 now. We've got the whole day to get on with whatever we were going to do, but be back here for 8.30, right?'

♫ ♫ ♫

Jay called everyone individually to tell them he had something important to discuss, and he couldn't do it until after they had watched *Top of the Pops* at 8.30 that night. They all promised to watch it, but they didn't know why.

Karl hadn't spoken to the others in over two weeks. They usually kept in regular contact, catching up on each other's plans for further education and exchanging general guy-banter. The previous year, they'd attended each other's birthday party celebrations. They were still very much part of each other's lives.

♫ ♫ ♫

Candice, Karl's aunty, stopped by his house with her two sons, Reece and Jake. That particular Thursday evening, she had arranged to see her brother—not for anything special, just to catch up—plus, it was a half-term school holiday. Although the group was no longer together, she still felt guilty, as she'd been the one to introduce Karl to Abi and encourage him to go to the audition. Karl had moved on since then and was at a sixth-form college, studying his A-levels. He wanted to go to university.

'Hi, Karl, how's it going?' Candice loved Karl. He had overcome so much in his young life, yet he remained positively optimistic.

'I'm good, Aunty.'

'Are you still in contact with the boys?' Candice's question was meant to start a polite chat, but she liked to hear they were okay, too.

'Funnily enough, this morning, I got a call from Jay. He sounded odd. He asked me to promise him that I would watch *Top of the Pops* tonight. I'll watch it, but I don't know what it's about,' Karl said.

'We're not leaving until later as it's not a school night, so I'll watch it with you, okay?' Candice didn't mind watching it. 'When I was younger, *Top of the Pops* used to be one of my favourite shows.'

'Aunty, you make yourself sound like a dinosaur,' Karl said. '*Top of the Pops* is not that ancient.'

'Cheeky! You'd better watch yourself, or I might just get up and dance to the music. They used to have dancers on the show called Pan's People. They were rubbish at their dance routines, but I imagined that one day, I would also be a dancer on *Top of the Pops*.'

'Aunty, I don't usually watch that programme — it's old-fashioned, anyway. I prefer to watch MTV music videos.'

♫ ♫ ♫

Evening came quickly, and it was packed with the tastiest Caribbean food that only Karl's mum could make. There were conversations about everything, and they all sounded heated, but that was just the loving energy of the house. Finally, it was time for *Top of the Pops*.

Quite an audience had gathered in the living room, each of them intrigued to know what was so special about the show. Perhaps Michael Jackson was about to release another of his new, chart-topping hits along with an outstanding dance performance from him and his brothers. They didn't know, but they were nonetheless excited to find out.

The host for the show was Simon Mayo, a Radio 1 show DJ. He promised to keep everyone up-to-date on the latest chart-topping hits, but they had an exclusive new group performing their debut song.

Halfway through the show, there had yet to be anything spectacular from any of the artists. Karl got up to leave the room to go to the kitchen for something—anything—to escape the monotony, but then he heard the song 'My Bella Angelica' playing. Karl turned back to listen, and he could not believe his ears—the singers sounded just like him and the other boys.

'Aunty, is this a joke? Remember that song that I rehearsed with the others? It was called "My Bella Angelica", and that's it! That's the song.

'Who are those guys? Do you know them? They sound like us—yes, us. Their voices—how could this be?'

When the performance had finished, Karl left the room and headed for the phone to call Jay.

Karl got the busy signal, waited a minute, and dialled again and again.

Candice was just as confused as Karl. 'I heard you sing that song—how could it be an exclusive when your group were the only ones to know it? You worked so hard to perfect not just that song but a whole album. I don't know what's going on, but I'll call Abi.'

'No! I want to speak with Jay first. Don't say anything to anybody.' Karl would never dream of being rude or flippant to an elder, but he lost it for a moment.

Eventually, he got through to Jay.

All five boys concurred that it was the song they had rehearsed day and night, and recorded at Butterfly Records Studio.

'Before we go confronting Abi and any of the others, we've got to meet up somewhere to talk this through. I don't want them to know before we've had the chance to discuss it.' Jay paused to think of someplace they could meet.

'Jay, my aunty, Candy, saw the performance, and she's going to talk with Abi about it to get some answers,' Karl said.

'I told you I don't want them to know until after we've met.' Jay started to feel as if he was losing control of the situation.

'I didn't tell her anything! I didn't know what to tell her, anyway. She happened to be at my house, watching *Top of the Pops* with us. You were so secretive about what I was supposed to be doing,' Karl hit back.

'Look, I'm sorry. It's not your fault.' Jay couldn't have known that Candice, would be with Karl on that particular Thursday, much less, sitting with him watching the programme.

Unbeknownst to Jay and all the other boys, Abi and Mervyn were watching the show, too, not because they had an inkling that anything was going on but because they generally watched the show for midweek entertainment to keep up with what was happening in the UK music scene.

Mervyn called Abi to find out what was going on. She had also seen the performance and was in shock herself until she got the call from Mervyn. He had questions that needed answering, as he felt used, confused, and discarded by Sami. He insisted that Abi assemble the boys and tell them what she knew about the whole business directly to their faces. Saturday was only two days away, but it would be enough time for Abi to accumulate some details about what Sami and Butterfly Records were up to.

Mervyn, who was just as much in the dark as the boys, wanted an open conversation, and he expected nothing to be held back. Also, he'd insisted that Abi get there at least an hour before the boys arrived to give him the answers he needed. Jay didn't have to wait too long to find his next move. It seemed like the decision had been escalated to a higher power when Abi called him directly to pass on the message for the boys to meet at Mervyn's house. She had no idea whether he had seen the performance on *Top of the Pops* at that point in time.

'Hey, I'm sorry to have to call you so late to tell you this,' Abi said, 'but something has gone terribly wrong, and it involves you and the other boys. I don't know all the details, but I'll find out as much as I can.' Abi didn't give Jay a chance to say anything. 'Please, can you contact the boys and ask them to meet at Mervyn's house on Saturday at 11 a.m.? This is very *important*.'

'I'm intrigued to know what's going on here, just as I'm sure the others are, too, but you need to be the one to call them and not me. I'll see you on Saturday.' Jay put the phone down abruptly. He didn't want to hear anything other than honest answers when he and the others got together. He wasn't going to give her the opportunity to fob him off. He was in no mood for that.

Jay wanted to arrange his own meeting in which everyone would have the liberty to speak openly. They couldn't get together in each other's houses because their families hadn't yet known the full extent of what they were involved in. Nathan was with foster carers, and besides, they were not interested in him to that degree. They were paid to keep a roof over his head and provide him with some structure and regular meals, and not for his emotional or social well-being.

Eddie, however, had come full circle with his mother and stepfather. When everything was going well with singing practice sessions and at the studio, his behaviour had changed for the better. He'd actually allowed a relationship to develop between him and George, but when it all went wrong and they weren't signed to Butterfly Records, his mood swung back to the old Eddie, who was rude to everyone except his sisters. George did, however, have a genuine connection with Eddie now. He understood that he was hurting about something important for which he must have cared deeply, and he invited Eddie to go out with him for a drive to clear the air. They didn't go far—just an open space in Brockwell Park—but George asked him what happened.

Teary-eyed, away from any onlookers, he told him the whole truth about the audition, that he'd found the opportunity on his own, and that he was going to make it big and live his own life, but the whole thing had crumbled when they were told they would not be signed, and they were dropped with no real explanation. Eddie described the details of the effort and time he'd put into making his singing perfect. Every day, the whole family had heard him practise in his room.

George stepped in to encourage him, and not just with words to pacify his ego. He told him to stand tall as there was no shame in trying to make something of himself.

Now, with the fresh development, Eddie toyed with the idea of telling George about the whole thing just to get his take on it, but he went along with the consensus to meet at McD's at Waterloo station. They all knew there was an upstairs area with some booths that were generally empty, and Jay felt they might get some privacy there, but they had to meet immediately, and it had to be before Saturday.

16

The Case

It was short notice, but it had to be done. Friday before midday at Waterloo Station was like Heathrow. Nevertheless, amongst everyone trying to get somewhere fast, the boys met at McD's on time. Jay wondered whether it was the best choice of venue for their discussion, but it was too late to change his mind now, so they had to make the most of it.

Jay and Eddie had travelled together. Throughout the journey, they talked nonstop about what they had seen. In some ways, it wound them up even more, as they had each other to bounce their thoughts off, guessing and second-guessing what Abi and Mervyn were going to say when they met them on Saturday. As far as they knew, they were also in on the whole scam.

They arrived at McD's slightly earlier than the others and began scouting the area upstairs to secure some privacy. There seemed an ideal spot over in the corner, near the door, that said STAFF ONLY.

At least customers wouldn't be continually walking by. The staff weren't around that frequently either, so there would be minimal interruptions.

'I'm going downstairs to get a milkshake, and I'll look out for the others. You stay here. I can get you something,' Jay said, but then he saw Nathan, Karl, and DeAngelo come up the stairs.

'Hey!' Jay's hand went up in the air to call them over. 'I'm just going to get something to drink. Get something for yourselves, then come back, and let's talk.'

Everyone seemed to talk at once. They were getting louder and louder. 'Hey, let's tone it down,' Jay said slowly, raising his right hand. He took a notepad and pen from his rucksack. 'We've met here for a reason, not just to discuss how bad we're feeling. We can't let whoever they are get away with this. We've got to be clear about what we think happened. Yes, I personally feel as if I've been violated and used for something I sure as hell didn't give my consent to.'

'Write down the name of that group,' Nathan said. 'What was it again?'

'X-something…yes—X-Gen. They stole our voices,' Karl shouted.

'Were they miming to our voices?' DeAngelo asked. 'How did they get it sounding so clear and in sync?'

Jay had decided to lead the discussion to make sure no point was missed. 'We've got lots of questions. We'd better get them down on paper, shall we?' he said. 'Let Abi and Mervyn answer them for us,' Jay said.

'As far as I'm concerned, Abi was working for Sami, and Sami was the one calling the shots. Remember when we were at the studio, and we sang that last song? I think it was DeAngelo…when you ended the song on that wicked final note? Then we saw Sami and that other guy, Dizzi-something —I can't remember his name—high-fiving each other. We left the sound booth and walked back into the recording area, and just got a blank "That was okay" from Sami. At the time, it seemed whack, and I've had a bad vibe about it since then,' Jay said.

Nathan joined in by voicing his suspicions about something not being right, too.

'Do you think Mervyn was in on this?' Nathan asked. He'd trusted Mervyn because he came across as if he cared. There was a time when Nathan was not getting the breathing technique right, and Mervyn gave him extra tasks to make his singing better, but Sami was a big disappointment. 'And Sami—he never once called us to say anything about not being signed. He ignored us.'

'You know what? I don't care who said what. Everyone's guilty until we hear otherwise. We were used and treated badly. My question is, can they get away with it, and what can we do about it?' Jay said, plain and straight.

'We gotta bring them down, man. Butterfly whatever. Dizzi-cockroach. Sami acted so innocent, so high and mighty, and he used us like pawns. They worked us hard, man.' Eddie was working himself up, wanting to demand recompense and an apology. 'I should go down to that studio and mash up the place.'

'That would be stupid, don't you think?' Jay said, quashing Eddie's idea. 'We only need to know the facts.'

'To be fair, Mervyn did call us to tell us how sorry he was that we didn't get signed. We've got to give him that. He didn't sound like someone who knew about Sami's ulterior motives. You hear about it in America all the time: Black singers getting ripped off in so many different ways. The record companies don't want to pay the people who got the real talent,' DeAngelo said. His mother, Shirlee, had sung in the States for many years with a lot of success, but she told him about this type of thing going on. He never thought he would be in a similar position.

♫ ♫ ♫

Like a blast from nowhere, X-Gen was everywhere. Even as the boys left Waterloo Station, some of the billboards showed pictures of them clowning around as a group, with the song title, 'My Bella Angelica', written underneath it. There was no escape—X-Gen was out of the bag! 'Buy the single now in Woolworths, HMV, and all worthwhile music stores!'

Even Blockbuster had their music video for hire. Everyone worked together to make sure the launch would catapult them to the very top of everything in the UK. The marketing spinners had them on TV promoting their single; they were on the playlists at Capital Radio, BBC Radio One, Kiss FM—anywhere young listeners would hear it, and the disc was spun every hour. They were the talk of the country.

Record sales soared into the thousands. X-Gen was going to have the fastest number-one single since The Beatles. It was like a genie had been let out of a bottle. X-Gen's name was on everyone's lips, and 'My Bella Angelica' was on everyone's minds, just like 'Back to Life' had been for Soul II Soul after they appeared on *Top of the Pops* but with more marketing clout.

♫ ♫ ♫

That Saturday, it rained throughout the night with no sign of letting up. That was not uncommon for April, but it was beyond the usual showers and more like a flood of biblical proportion. Mervyn answered the door for Abi. Without a hello, he led her into the living room and said, 'Who dreamt this up? If I hadn't seen this with my own eyes, I wouldn't have believed it.'

'Well, hello to you, too!' Abi said.

'Sorry. I couldn't sleep last night thinking about the hard work I put into those boys, only to be told they weren't wanted.

'Did you hear those guys—X-Gen? They stole my boys' voices. Ah, man—the UK's just as bad as the States. In fact, it's worse. They smile when they talk to you, and then, behind your back, they do something like this. In the States, they'd at least tell you to your face they'd found someone else to sing your song or whatever. At least it's the truth. Abi, what happened?'

'I'm just as much as upset about this as everyone. Even more so because I got you all involved.'

'Blaming yourself isn't going to solve this. I know you met Sami someplace at an event, but I'm struggling here. Man, help me out—how did the auditions get staged? What was the real reason for finding these boys?' Mervyn wanted to give her some benefit of the doubt, but he couldn't see past his thoughts about being ripped off.

Abi recounted everything she remembered as fact but made no mention of the messy business of her affair with Sami.

'From what you've told me, I still haven't heard that he promised anything, much less a signing—how did we get here, Abi?' Mervyn was trying to work out how his misunderstanding clouded his own judgement of the situation. 'I thought the boys were being prepared for singing careers with Butterfly Records, and I worked my butt off to make it happen. I've coached other artists far less talented than these boys, and they still got signed. I've blamed myself for months for not getting their vocals right, but I can see now that I didn't get it wrong.'

'I don't know what to say,' Abi confessed. 'I've been calling Sami since Thursday night, but he hasn't returned any of my calls.'

'He's not going to return any of your calls because he knows exactly what he's done! He shafted those boys, and you know what really ticks me off? The fact that he used me to do it.

'Ahh! This really infuriates me.' Mervyn was interrupted by the doorbell ringing.

'Look, the boys are here, and I'm none the wiser, Abi.' Mervyn went to get the boys, leaving Abi alone with her thoughts.

Abi sent up a prayer asking for courage and wisdom: 'Dear God, I need help. I don't know what to say or do,' but there was no magic wand that would get her out of this situation. She was going to have to face it head-on and walk through the fire.

♫ ♫ ♫

'Hi, guys. Thanks for coming.'

There were man-hugs all around so Mervyn could show that he was genuine, albeit under troubling circumstances.

Abi said hi to the boys as they entered the room, but their responses were faint.

'Take a seat. Can I get you anything — tea, coffee, a cold drink?'

'I'm cool, thanks.' Jay led the way for the others who had similar responses.

'Okay. Let's just get right to the point. From the bottom of my heart, I want to say that I've never seen or heard of X-Gen before until I saw them on Thursday on *Top of the Pops*, but they sure as hell sounded like you, and they were singing one of the songs you guys rehearsed for that final recording session at Butterfly Records.' Mervyn needed to get that off his chest. 'Were they miming? Lip-synching to your voices?' He shrugged his shoulders. 'I don't know.'

He turned and asked, 'Abi, can you shed some light on what's going on?' Mervyn had no qualms about throwing her under the bus. In their talk before the boys arrived, he never said he would pull her arse out of the fire. It was him or her, and it certainly wasn't going to be him.

All eyes were on Abi. The room appeared as if it had been divided in two, with Abi on one side and Mervyn and the boys on the other. It was how the seating was positioned, but they'd chosen to sit that way.

Abi made an attempt to defend herself from any accusations of being in on the conspiracy. 'I swear I've never seen or heard of them either.'

The boys concluded that both Mervyn and Abi were drowning in quicksand and failing miserably to get out.

'When you've both finished—because we,' Jay pointed to the others and himself, 'haven't said anything yet…some injustice has happened here.' Jay pulled the list of questions, the one they had prepared the previous day, from his rucksack. 'So, one: Abi, did Sami ever intend to sign us to Butterfly Records?'

'Yes.'

'Did he say that, or did you assume it?'

'Well, yes, that's what his plan was. That's what he told me. Sami is a talent scout employed by Butterfly Records to find new artists, and we found you guys.'

'Two: did he tell you we weren't good enough and that he was going to find another group?'

'No, he did not to answer both of those questions.' Abi was holding up under pressure.

'Three—Mervyn, this one's for you: how do those boys sound like us? Were you their vocal coach?'

'I don't know how those boys sounded so much like you, and I've never seen them before, much less coached them. Whenever I had a practice session with you, Sami asked me to record you and send it to him. I did that every time you had a session with me, and you guys knew about it. I didn't know he was collecting the tapes so he could give them to other boys to practice with. He's a low-down dirty rotten snake, but I don't know if there's anything we can do about it,' Mervyn said.

'Up until now, I haven't said a word to my parents about this, but I'm going to have to tell them everything, and I know my mum will have something to say about it. Sami didn't kill anyone, but can we try to sue him and Butterfly Records and get a judge to decide based on the evidence we have and our statements. Do you have copies of those tapes you sent to Sami?' Jay asked.

'Yes. Every last one. Labelled up with the song titles and dates.' Mervyn was ready to retrieve them.

'Good. If you're okay with it, I'll take them now.' Jay thought it was better if he took them so they wouldn't go mysteriously missing. The tapes were proof they'd sung the songs before X-Gen, and they had to be guarded as evidence.

'If there's anything I can do to help, I'll do it,' Abi offered.

'Don't you worry. When the time comes, we'll need your help, I'm certain of that. We're gonna nail Sami's arse.' Jay was ready for a fight, and it would be a legal one against Sami and Butterfly Records. He was the only boy in the group who could take it forward because his mother and father had legal connections and felt it up to him to do this for the others.

There wasn't much more that could be discussed about how and why it happened, but Mervyn added that as painful as it would be to watch again, they should stay a while longer so they could watch the footage together and try to see if they were actually miming or not. 'Even if they weren't miming, who taught them to sing like you guys?' That was the big question they were left with.

♫ ♫ ♫

Jay's parents, Stanley and Hyacinth Braithwaite—Stan and Cynth, for short—were well-established in the legal profession for over twenty years. They hit the roof when he told them about his secret singing escapade and that the group had been exploited for their voices. First, they were upset because he'd planned to have a singing career behind their backs without any discussion. Second, he hadn't trusted them enough to support him on his journey, which they would have done, even if their preference was that he follow the family's footsteps into the law. Uncannily enough, things worked in their favour, and they had got their wish. Jay's disappointment was, in some way, a blessing in disguise, as it nudged him towards focusing on getting a law degree.

It was an eventful weekend in Jay's household. His mum and dad had spent Sunday calling trusted colleagues at their firm, scoping out the merits of the case, and arguing whether Sami and Butterfly Records had committed an infringement of rights and whether any safeguarding or consent issues had been taken into consideration due to their ages. Some of the boys were under eighteen, and some were under sixteen. The facts were the facts: had Sami and Butterfly Records done anything illegal?

♫ ♫ ♫

Cynth wanted to put the case forward as pro-bono work at their weekly Monday morning staff meeting, where they presented all of their cases. This was done to keep everyone abreast of the jobs the firm was working on.

Monday was always a hive of activity and an exciting kick-off to the week. A breakfast of croissants, pastries, percolated coffee, and teas for self-service was always available on the back table in the boardroom. The boardroom itself was big enough to hold the thirty-strong full-time staff that worked for James, Mason, & Braithwaite, where Stan and Cynth jointly formed the Braithwaite arm of the partnership. They were an international, commercial business law firm. Sadly, Matthew James had passed away five years before, at the age of ninety, but the firm was still renowned for winning litigation cases, and it had a good reputation. The firm was reluctant to remove James' name, as James, Mason, & Braithwaite were a brand, though legally, it was Mason & Braithwaite who were still registered as running the business.

The format for the meeting was always the same, with the minutes being taken by the clerical admin team. At the meeting, they signed off on closed cases. Ongoing cases and tricky, complex ones were put forward for discussion. These were usually cases being litigated by new solicitors in need of the partners' advice as to which particular direction they should take the case. There was, however, an open-door policy, which meant that if anyone needed to discuss anything, they could approach one of the partners. No special appointment was necessary, but they could make one if they so wished. This included pro bono opportunities, as the firm always wanted to give something back to those in need of legal support who couldn't afford it.

The boys' case was presented in such a way that only the partners would know that Cynth's son was involved. It had been written up as an untitled pro bono case involving five Black boys who had been coerced into working long hours without pay—essentially slave labour—so a large corporation could benefit by exploiting their talents. Someone in the room cracked a joke and said it sounded like what happens in Pakistan.

Without disclosing that her son was one of the five, Cynth said, 'No, it's much closer to home than abroad. We're a long way from the days of young kids being chimney sweeps in the 1800s, but we are talking about modern-day exploitation of talent, young boys being asked to sing as professionals, and broken promises, with their only reward being pizza and a trip to Chessington World of Adventure. While, 'the corporation' makes millions off the backs of these kids who get nothing for their talent and who are forced to remain invisible.'

'I know this case is probably for a good cause, but won't it take up a lot of time in litigation fees?' Michael Johnston, one of the solicitors, asked.

'Yes, it may well take up a lot of time—that's the nature of pro bono—but we can still create a bill for it.'

It was standard practice that, when this type of case was won, they'd claim back their time plus damages. If they lost, it would be written off as a lost case, and they would be liable for paying the other party's costs. But all loss case fees, came out of their losses account fund. That's was how this type of work was done, but highly rewarding when they won.

'Who wants to take up this case?' There were three solicitors who were new to the firm that put up their hands. They were young and hungry when it came to making an impression on the partners and a name for themselves. The other partners looked at those who'd offered, then back over at Cynth.

Charles Mason, one of the partners, said, 'I'd put Michael and Penny on it. Combined, these two are like setting hounds on a trail to find a rabbit.'

'I agree with that. Sorry, Tom, not this one. Next time, it'll have your name written on it.' Cynth didn't want to leave Tom thinking that he had no place in the firm, as recently, he'd been putting himself forward whenever an opportunity arose. For this case, even if it was pro bono, she wanted the right people on the job.

'Can I support Michael and Penny? I promise I won't get in the way, but I can assist whenever they need it.' Tom wasn't about to give up so easily. He had the feeling that the case was going somewhere, pro bono or not.

'If that's okay with you guys?' Cynth looked over at Michael and Penny.

'Yes, that's fine with us. We wouldn't say no to an extra pair of legs.'

'Great. That's set, then. Any other business?' Cynth asked. She was always the chair in these Monday morning meetings unless she was away.

With 'Nothing from me' responses around the room, Cynth concluded that the meeting had ended. 'Good. Let's make it happen.'

Everyone filed out of the boardroom, talking as they left, having received their pep talk from the mouth of the firm, leaving them feeling like a family and ready for business.

'Michael, Penny — see me in my office. Let's say 10 a.m.?' Cynth called out to them as they were leaving.

17

The Court

MICHAEL AND PENNY made their way to Cynth's office at 10 a.m. sharp to receive the briefing on the pro bono case. They had done this type of work before and understood that pro bono work represented practical experience for their resumes, and it would be for a good cause, besides.

'What are your thoughts on the case?' Cynth wasn't initially ready to let on that her son was involved. Although she had already scoped out some ideas with the other partners, she wanted to hear what the young solicitors would do first.

'Well, there's a law against youth working more than four hours a day, and there is an expected pay that applies to young adults. That could be a breach, but it's nothing worth pursuing. Coercing someone into slave labour; not knowing whether they'd get paid or what they were truly agreeing to; holding them captive as if they weren't free to leave until they'd been used; after hours and late into the night could be emotional abuse, but I get the sense it's something more, isn't it?' Michael said.

'You're right: there's more. These boys responded to an advert in the newspaper, asking for boys aged fifteen to seventeen years old to audition to become a part of an up-and-coming boy group. There was a selection process, and five boys were chosen. I'll let you know now, but my son, Jay, was one of those boys responding to the advert. He joined the group on the premise that he and the other boys were being scouted to sign with Butterfly Records. Over the course of three months, there were practice sessions, trips back and forth to Coulsdon, and finally, solid weeks of recording from 10 a.m. to sometimes 1 a.m. the next morning. The boys worked hard to get themselves ready for what they believed was a singing career. On the last day of recording in the studio, it seemed to them as if they had finally finished the album, accomplishing their mission, but the following day, they were told that Butterfly Records had decided against signing them up.

'That would have been the end of it—sad as it might have been, the boys accepted that they hadn't made it—but then, six months later, on *Top of the Pops*, they heard one of the songs they had sung in the studio being sung by that popular group called X-Gen. Jay recorded X-Gen's interview on GMTV with Lorraine Kelly and then again on *Top of the Pops*. The boys recognised their voices, including the harmony styles they worked on.'

'I'm sorry to hear your son got caught up in this,' Penny said. 'What are the backgrounds of the other boys?'

'They're ordinary local kids with boyish dreams of one day becoming stars, but they might as well be bus drivers or postmen in the community. Even if they were ripped off, they would never have had the funds to be able to take anything like this to court.

'Fortunately, Jay happened to be involved, and he is passionate about getting some compensation for them. He knows he'll be all right in life, but the others? It might well make a difference for their trajectory.' Cynth wanted Michael and Penny to see where giving something back to the needy came in, and she aimed her compassion at the young boys, as the case would never have been brought to her attention otherwise.

'So, you'll need to find a cause for the case and present it to the rest of the partners and me. Get answers to the questions. You'll be thinking along the lines of if it is illegal to steal someone's voice without them knowing for business gains, and take note: these are voices that were not in the public domain. There are many Michael Jackson and Elvis Presley impersonators out there, happily earning a living in Las Vegas, so don't go down that route. These boys did not give permission for their voices to be used in this way, nor were they aware their voices were only being harvested for another boy group to use.'

Having brought them up to speed, they were sent off.

Michael and Penny were fresh from being university interns at the firm along with other candidates. They were the lucky ones who were offered positions as they were the most promising of those from the intake. They loved their jobs and the opportunities the firm had for growth when it came to commercial business and litigation cases.

News about Cynth's son, Jay, and the case spread like wildfire, but none of the staff dared to convey feelings of support to Cynth or Stan. It wasn't a subject they were willing to broach with either of them because they had not been told about the case directly.

Tom was, however, the only one to say something to Cynth when he passed by her office and saw her on her own. Although her door was open, he knocked on it and asked permission to come in. 'I'm truly sorry for what happened to your son and the other boys. I know I've not been assigned as lead on this case, but if there is anything you want me to personally check out, please let me know,' Tom offered.

'Ah! There is something I'd like you to do for me.' She moved her left hand from her chin, where it had been resting, to her lap. 'Where do you live in again?'

'I live in Notting Hill, West London,' Tom said.

'Just what I thought. I've got an idea. Michael and Penny have a lot on their hands at the moment, so I'd like you to find out when Sami Achu and Jeff Anderson are at Butterfly Records. They're the two who will need to be served with papers in relation to the case. As soon as you get it, feed it back to me. Oh, and keep this to yourself for now.' Cynth had known that Butterfly Records was based in Notting Hill as Jay had told her about his trips back and forth to their studio. With Tom living in the area, he could find out any extra bits of detail she needed, even though it was technically Michael and Penny's case.

'I know where it is. I walk past the studio every day on my way to work.

'No problem. I'll be discreet,' Tom said. Even if it was one little piece of the puzzle, he was determined to make it count.

Yahoo was the great phenomenon of its time. Businesses used it, and it was starting to become a go-to source, for anyone with access to a computer and a dial-up connection. Using the new Yahoo search engine to gain access to the World Wide Web, it would be easy enough for Tom to find info on Butterfly Records. He came across material on Jeff Anderson, who was currently the UK director, including pictures, but there was nothing on Sami at Butterfly Records or anywhere else. It was, nevertheless, imperative to get a picture of Sami so the right person could be served with the papers when the time came for court.

Michael and Penny were like a dynamic duo. They agreed the case should be based on the boys' voices and how the record company had capitalised on it without their permission or knowledge. They were looking for compensation for time and expenses while hiding the true nature of their plan, their hurt feelings, the trauma and stress to their young minds, and the fact that they were used as slave labour. Plus, they were seeking royalties on every record produced on which their voices were used and distributed, including worldwide distribution. The case would be lodged at the High Court, as it dealt with complex claims in the nature of intellectual property rights. Their claim would be that X-Gen couldn't actually sing live, and they were lip-synching. Although they had no evidence at that point in time, they were willing to stick their necks out to win the case. Let X-Gen prove otherwise.

Statements were taken from everyone involved as evidence. Appointments were made with the boys to come in on the same day.

It was a trek for the boys, travelling into the city of London, where the offices were located. EC2, was the heart of banking and multi-national corporations. Nevertheless, they were committed to seeing this thing through to the end, whatever the outcome. It had almost been a year since they'd first met, and they had grown even closer than before.

Eddie was the only one to regularly visit Jay's house, as he lived close by. His initial opinion of Jay's house was that it was rather swag, and he had commented to Jay that he must be rich, living in a house like that, with a fitted kitchen and loads of fancy gadgets. He was mesmerised by the soda maker that made cool, fizzy drinks on tap—not that it affected their friendship; it had only been a passing comment. Everyone knew his parents were lawyers, but that day was a huge eye-opener as he realized they were partners in a top firm in the City of London. Eddie now saw where the wealth had come from, though Jay wanted to be seen as an ordinary kid.

'Wow! Do your mum and dad own the company?' Nathan asked, his eyes widening. He had never been inside a company like it before.

'Yes, man. It's their company, right? Didn't you see their names written on the door?' Eddie said this in a tone that implied, 'Isn't it obvious?'

One by one, they went into a room to give their statements to either Michael or Penny.

Abi and Mervyn couldn't make it on the same day as the boys, but Penny felt it was probably wise to keep their days separate. It all worked out, as Abi and Mervyn still felt responsible for what had happened to the boys, and seeing them at that point in time would have been awkward, to say the least. Since Abi's traumatic split from Sami, her life had changed for the better. She had signed with Gulf Records and had the creative license to write, sing and produce the songs for her album under their label. In some ways, it might have looked as if she had dropped off the radar, and very few people knew she was becoming successful in Europe. What happened to the boys and the mess with Sami was a past she hadn't expected to revisit, but she was willing to cooperate in whatever way she could and to be one of the key witnesses at the court hearing.

Once all of the statements had been collected, Michael and Penny slotted them into their case preparation folder and ran it by the partners to check that it met with their approval.

Cynth requested that the summonses for the hearing be served on the same day the affidavits were filed in the High Court. Michael asked Tom to lodge the papers, book the earliest possible date and report back to him.

'How are you going to serve the papers?' Cynth asked Michael and Penny.

'We've been thinking about using a bailiff company from within the Notting Hill area,' Penny said.

'Have you spoken with Tom? Butterfly Records is in Notting Hill, where he lives. Ask him to deliver them. Get the papers ready by this afternoon.'

'We didn't know that,' Penny said. 'We've already made some inquiries about the bailiff.'

'It's a pro bono case. First, let's exhaust our in-house resources. If Tom's not able to do it, then, by all means, use your local source, right? Get Tom on it. Tell him to report back to me by phone when it's done. There's no time to waste.'

Michael and Penny took the hint to get on with the job.

♫ ♫ ♫

Penny went to see Tom. 'Do you mind going down to the court tomorrow morning to lodge the affidavit and get a hearing date?' she asked.

From his research, Tom knew that both Sami and Jeff were at Butterfly Records all day on Wednesdays as it was a catch-up day in the office with staff and meetings. 'Wednesday is a better day for me,' Tom said, knowing what he knew.

'The case is ready to go now. We need you to do it tomorrow so we don't hold anything up,' Penny insisted.

'I'm sorry, but Wednesday is better for me.' Tom knowing that both Sami and Jeff would be in the office, stood his ground on his statement.

Penny wasn't happy with his response as it seemed like he was being stubborn. She left him to find Michael, who was discussing the details with Cynth and Stan in her office.

Penny stuck her head through the doorjamb. 'Can I come in? I'm assuming you're discussing the case, right?

'Just need a bit of advice. Now that we're ready to file the papers, I've asked Tom to do it tomorrow, but he is refusing. Can you have a word with him? Perhaps if he hears it from you, he might do it.'

'If Tom said Wednesday is the day, then I'd go along with him,' Cynth said, to their surprise. Both Michael and Penny's jaws dropped. What did Tom know that they didn't?

'Okay. No problem. Wednesday, it is.' Penny sheepishly, backed out of the room and went to find Tom.

♫ ♫ ♫

On Wednesday morning, Tom left early to file the papers at the High Court. He wanted to be the first one there as soon as the court doors opened.

It was a grand old building, with its Gothic stone masonry representing the institution of civil justice, dating back to the early 1800s. Tom had been there many times before, so he was familiar with how to navigate the labyrinth of first getting through the security checks and then going up the stairs on the left to the great hall. Across from the hall was a heavy swinging door. He had to go along that hall and up two flights of stairs to find the cashier's office on the right.

There were two early birds before him, though the office wouldn't be open until 8.30 a.m.

As a requirement, he presented three copies of the papers to the cashier, paid the fees, and had the documents stamped, but his job wasn't over yet. He had to run down the flight of stairs to the ground floor, exit into the courtyard and go across the courtyard to the door to the Thomas Moore Building.

He located the lift and took it to the office holding all of the court listings for all of the cases. Tom waited his turn before presenting two of his documents and requesting the earliest dates. He was done by 9.30 a.m., which put him in good time to make it back to Notting Hill by black taxi to serve the papers to Sami and Jeff.

Jeff was easy to recognise—Tom had found his picture on the World Wide Web Yahoo search engine. He studied Jeff's features intently to make sure he got it right.

Sami, on the other hand, would be more difficult to identify as he was not on the Web. Fortunately, Tom reached out to Abi, who had a photo that was taken of him with the other judges at the audition. He contacted her before she came into the office, and she brought it with her when she came to give her statement. Tom also studied his profile.

Tom's taxi cruised up Cressington Gardens, home of Butterfly Records, and asked the driver to stop a short distance away from the office's entrance as he didn't want to be noticed. He stood back at a vantage point that would allow him to see anyone coming in any direction.

He didn't need to wait too long before recognising Sami.

'Hi, are you Sami Achu?' Tom asked.

'Yes…do I know you?' Sami asked, thinking that he might be someone in the industry.

'My name is Tom Parker from Mason, James, & Braithwaite Solicitors. I am serving you these papers to appear in court on Monday, 17 June 1996. See you in court.' Tom turned away, leaving Sami holding the envelope.

Sami was puzzled. He tried to ask, 'What is this about?' but Tom carried on, walking slowly away. Now, he only had to wait somewhere for Jeff.

Tom turned to watch Sami enter the building, looking somewhat bewildered.

It wasn't long before, Jeff Anderson arrived, and Tom called his name. When Jeff turned around, Tom said, 'Jeff Anderson, I am serving you these papers for you to attend court on Monday, 17 June 1996. See you in court.'

Jeff asked the same question as Sami: 'I'm sorry—what's this about?' Also like with Sami, Tom just walked away, only this time, he headed for the red telephone booth at the end of the crescent. He went in and called Cynth to tell her the papers had been filed, stamped and paid for, a hearing had been booked for Monday, 17 June, and the papers had been personally served, first to Sami and then to Jeff. Cynth thanked him for his efficiency and said she'd see him when he got back to the office.

His job was done.

Sami didn't have his own office at Butterfly Records. His area was a type of hot desk, where the first in got to choose where they wanted to sit. He chose a spot in the corner near an open window as he needed some air. He sat down, looked around to see if anyone was coming in his direction, and opened the envelope that had been given to him.

'Hi, Sami. Are you coming to the meeting at 11.30 a.m.?' Becky asked him. 'X-Gen are hitting it out of the park on the UK charts, and we've even had requests for them to appear in Lithuania. Would you believe it?'

The Lithuanian request had been Tom asking a secretary at the firm to pose as a music promoter's PA who wanted to be the first to invite X-Gen to perform in their country.

Sami was startled by Becky's vivaciousness. She was excited by the progress her marketing team was making, and their efforts were paying off. Record sales on 'My Bella Angelica' had sky-rocketed, holding the number one UK spot for over six weeks. Since the interview with Lorraine Kelly on GMTV and *Top of the Pops*, requests for their appearance were coming in.

The weekly Wednesday meeting had a slot for each team to either talk or present their figures and plans for X-Gen's future. These were exciting times for the group. They were on the move and seemed unbeatable against some of the US imports that had previously dominated the UK charts. X-Gen were true Brits, and they did well for the UK brand.

Sami smiled to show his approval of the work her team was doing. 'Yeah, it's great. Of course, I'll be there. Save a seat for me.' He didn't mention anything about the lawsuit or that he had just been served.

'See you in a bit,' Becky said, and she bounced away to talk with some of her colleagues at their desks.

Sami didn't want to be disturbed while opening the envelope, so he went to the bathroom, locked himself inside a toilet cubicle, and read the summons. 'Oh, my God,' Sami shouted.

'Hello? Hello? Are you okay?' Someone had come into the bathroom and heard him.

'No. Yes. Yes, I'm fine. No problem.' Sami was embarrassed. He didn't know who was asking, nor did he come out of the cubicle. He waited in the cubicle until the person had left.

Thinking quickly on his feet, he decided to see the legal team, who dealt with things like this all the time, but he had to move quickly before the Wednesday catch-up meeting started at 11.30 a.m.

He walked back to his desk to get his things. Jeff was waiting for him there. The blood seemed to drain from Sami's face, and he felt lightheaded.

'Sami, have you got a minute?' Jeff asked. It was not an optional request.

'Sure,' Sami said. They walked away from the hive of activity in the open-plan office to a quiet, empty room in silence.

'What the hell is this, Sami?' Jeff asked.

'I have no idea. I never saw this coming.'

'What do you mean, you never saw this coming? They're claiming X-Gen is lip-synching, which can't be true, and then there are all of these other damages,' Jeff said.

'Can we talk this through with the legal department?' Sami suggested.

'I've just seen them, but they want to see you to get some facts.

'This is all on you, Sami. You're the one who met these people.

'I'm not getting mixed up in this.

'And by the way, you'll have to go to court to testify and answer their questions. I'm not in the country on Monday, 17 June,' Jeff said, 'so you'll have to go with the legal department's representatives'.

'Look, these things happen. The legal department is good at smoothing things out. This can't harm X-Gen's brand, so work with them to get it sorted as soon as possible.'

They left the room. Jeff turned in the direction of his office while Sami turned towards the legal department.

'Are you coming?' Sami asked.

'No, I'll go to the 11.30 a.m. catch-up meeting and make some apologies on your behalf. You can ask Becky for the highlights later, but this accusation needs to go away and fast. X-Gen is exploding across the country, and we don't need the bad press. Not a word to anyone about this,' Jeff said.

18

The Victory

IT WAS TRULY a bittersweet time for Sami. Sweet, because he'd finally had a breakthrough with the songs he had written as they were being sung by a boy group who were fast becoming popular. He was already accumulating points on the royalties, far more than he could ever have dreamt of. Now, it would be muddied with the bitterness of Butterfly Records being sued for plagiarism and the other claims he found himself in the middle of. Jeff had quickly turned his back on Sami, leaving him to liaise with the legal team all by himself.

He felt lonely. His mind ran to Abi, with whom he hadn't spoken since the bust-up outside of his house. She tried to call him in April, but he didn't want to get involved with whatever it was she wanted to talk about. Perhaps that had been what her urgent calls — which he'd ignored — were about, but it was too late now. Then again, he could try talking with her. As soon as he finished with the legal team, that's what he planned to do.

Inch by inch, the legal team at Butterfly Records examined the documents. They'd also received a copy of the affidavit, one delivered by courier, another by DX No 37892—the legal system's private postal service and a fax to let them know the documentation was on its way, plus the date of the hearing. All bases were covered. No judge could say the papers had not been served correctly, nor could the defendants say they had no knowledge of the claim or had received nothing from the plaintiff.

Sami spoke about how the original five boys had been solicited, but he categorically denied the claim that he'd made the promise they would be signed to Butterfly Records. When it was obvious they would not be using the original boys to form the band, he'd informed their contact, namely Abi, and asked her to let the boys know. There was never any signed agreement between him and the boys or between him and Abi.

'What about the claim that X-Gen were only lip-synching—is that true?' Ryan Hillcrest, the one assigned to protect the company's reputation, who was skilled in IP matters, asked.

'That's not true, I swear. I can assure you those boys used their own voices, and I can prove it. I can get the recording of the final approval presentation from the live performance at the Gusto Restaurant. There were around twenty guests and teams that witnessed it,' Sami explained. 'I'll get you the recording. It's with the marketing department.'

That was all true, but was it enough to ensure the claim and charges against Butterfly Records would be dropped? Could the legal department sue for damages? These questions hung in the balance as the team pondered the case.

'How on earth did a bunch of kids get that kind of money to bring a case against Butterfly Records using a top firm like Mason, James, & Braithwaite?' Ryan asked Sami.

'I'm sorry, but it's a mystery to me, too,' Sami said.

'Give us your statement in writing by the end of the day, and we'll run through any possible questions you might get asked in court. We'll send a barrister and members of our team to be with you on the day. Let them do all the talking. If you have anything to chip in, just pass a note to the team to consider. It should all be over with very quickly, I promise,' Ryan said, confident the case would fall apart upon examination.

Sami left the department and headed out of the building to find a telephone booth. He wanted privacy when he called Abi to ask her to stop all of this foolishness, though he knew he was clutching at straws.

Abi happened to be at home when he called. She was surprised to hear his voice after all the time that had passed. 'Oh, it's you—what do you want?' Abi had no time or patience for Sami anymore, nor did she have any respect for the position he'd put her in.

'I was wondering…could we meet to talk about the case the boys are presenting against Butterfly Records and me?' Sami hoped she might see reason and let him have a chance to make things up in some way.

'So, your arse is on the line, and you want me to get you off the hook?' Abi asked. 'Don't ring my number ever again, or I'll report you for harassment.' She hung up the phone.

Sami's plan to soften her up had backfired. How could he tell Beth about the situation? Abi was already a woman scorned, but his career would be left in tatters if Butterfly Records lost the case through his negligence.

Upon hanging up with Sami, Abi immediately called Michael at Mason, James & Braithwaite. 'Hi, just keeping you up-to-date,' she said. 'Sami had the cheek to call and to ask me to meet up with him to discuss the case. I told him in no uncertain terms never to call my number again.'

'You did the right thing. I'll make a note of it. If we need to use this to prove harassment, then we will. Don't be rattled by him. He must be scared to have called you about it.' Michael assured her.

Next, Abi made a quick call to Candice. As her best friend, she had always been her sounding block, and she could speak openly to her.

The months passed, waiting for the case to be brought to court, but that didn't distract Abi from working. In fact, the whole Sami experience had prompted her to write even more songs, as it was a way to expose the rawness of being caught up in someone else's lies. Her signing with Gulf Records was one of the best things that had happened to her in a long time. She hadn't shared her success with anyone other than Candice, but it wasn't the time to sing the praises of her personal successes, as the boys were already emotionally charged.

♫ ♫ ♫

Monday, 17 June 1996 arrived. The date was etched into everyone's calendars. The boys had nothing to lose and everything to gain. If they lost the case, they'd walk away without being liable for paying costs to the other side, which could be huge. Nonetheless, it was a pro bono case taken up by Mason, James & Braithwaite, who was willing to bear the brunt of the expenses. Still, if they won against a giant of an organisation like Butterfly Records, it would be a miracle.

They were set to attend Court No. 8. 'The case of DeAngelo Persaud, Karl Brown, Jason Braithwaite, Nathaniel Allen, Edward Francis, and Abigail Jackson jointly Versus Butterfly Records' was listed on the board. They were second on the list for that courtroom. The first hearing was already in progress.

Judge Curtiss, the judge hearing the case, was always punctual, and she didn't mince her words.

The boys all turned up wearing mismatched suits, but they were very smart, nonetheless.

Abi arrived early, not wanting to miss anything. She looked respectable, wearing a burnt orange button-fronted dress, smart, fitted black jacket, tights, and black kitten-heeled shoes. There was a time when it mattered what Sami thought about her, and she would think about what she should wear to impress him and hold his interest, but now she didn't care what he thought. She looked the part, not for him but for her own self-respect.

Michael, Penny, and one other barrister were there for the hearing, and Abi and the boys felt supported by the firm. Tom had been invited in case there were any questions as to how he'd served the papers directly to Sami and Jeff.

'I want to say that I'm so sorry it came to this, but whatever happens, I'm here for you all,' Abi said to the boys.

'Don't worry—we stopped blaming you ages ago,' Jay said, speaking on behalf of the others.

As they waited their turn to go into the courtroom, a group of people, about ten strong, arrived together. Two were wearing black gowns and wigs. The others were suited and booted. The entourage was Sami's legal team. Some were from Butterfly Records' legal department, while the others were from Whittaker & May Solicitors, a firm they often used for cases when needed.

Michael and Penny looked at each other. 'This must be them—are you intimidated?' Michael asked Penny.

Penny looked at Sami's team, shook her head, and replied, 'Hell, no!'

'Neither am I,' Michael said.

Sami glanced over at Abi as he walked with the group. For a moment, their eyes locked, but the intensity of her stare caused him to drop his gaze. He also saw the boys, but he couldn't face them either.

Their timing was perfect. The people previously in Court No. 8 came out. They were next.

Michael and Penny went to the group standing around Sami, having recognised one of the barristers. 'Hi, Simon. Fancy seeing you here,' Michael said.

'It's a small world, but I've got to make a living somehow,' Simon fired back. Before they could get into the conversation, they were called into the courtroom.

They all took their seats. Penny directed the boys to where they needed to be. If needed, they would be called to give evidence. There was a transcriber taking notes and a clerk ready to collect papers from either the defendant or the plaintiff.

'Will you all rise? Judge Curtiss is presiding over the case between DeAngelo Persaud, Karl Brown, Jason Braithwaite, Nathaniel Allen, Edward Francis, and Abigail Jackson jointly Versus Butterfly Records,' the clerk said. This was a formality to ensure the right people were present in the right court.

They all stood. Judge Curtiss entered the room briskly and sat in her chair, ready to hear the case.

The defendants were the first to speak. 'My Lord,' the wigged barrister stood to address the judge, 'this seems to be a complete misunderstanding. The whole case hinges on the sole evidence that these gentlemen's voices were used on the songs sung by the boy group X-Gen, who have become famous. We have evidence to the contrary and can prove that the boys in X-Gen did, in fact, sing the songs themselves. We have a recording.

'Judge, if I may, we would like to take the liberty of presenting it to you.'

'Okay, let's see it.' Judge Curtiss asked the clerk to switch on the television and use the VCR attached to play the recording.

It was only a three-and-a-half-minute recording, but it showed X-Gen singing live at Gusto Restaurant in front of a private audience. There were also a number of witnesses who could testify to the performance.

'Thank you for that.' Judge Curtiss took off her glasses and looked directly at the boys and their group. 'I can see that you have come here expecting something, but unless you have evidence to the contrary, I stand to dismiss your claim that Butterfly Records has used your voices in any shape or form. This case is dismissed.' The gavel went down with a loud bang.

The boys turned to each other. 'What's happening?' they asked Michael and Penny.

'All rise,' the clerk said.

Judge Curtiss left the courtroom as briskly as she'd entered. It took almost fifteen minutes for the hearing from start to finish. The trial was over.

'Did we lose?' Eddie asked. 'They never gave us a chance to say anything.'

'What about our day in court and all the evidence we've got? Did the judge look at any of it?' Nathan asked.

'I'm telling you, they used our voices. The album was released last week. Those songs are being played everywhere, and not just 'My Bella Angelica'. We rehearsed twelve songs. Those recordings are what we did in the studio,' Karl protested. The others agreed.

'I'm sorry, guys. We can appeal, but unless we get some new evidence, we have nothing to appeal with,' Penny said.

Sami and his team of ten left the courtroom, smiling and chatting with each other, congratulating themselves on their win against Mason, James & Braithwaite. Sami couldn't help taking one last look over his shoulder at Abi.

Abi kept her chin up and held back her tears. She felt so humiliated, but when Sami left the room, she could no longer hold her tongue. 'I'm so frustrated by this all. So, so, sorry, guys.' She wiped away the tears running down her cheeks.

'Let's leave before we get thrown out. There's another case coming in here soon,' Tom said to lighten the tension.

'Never say never. Things have a funny way of turning around.' Tom could be philosophical at times, and he was never phased by what might appear to be a loss.

Wednesday, 19 June 1996 — two days after the case…

There were a number of people who knew the original singers of the songs on the X-Gen album were suing Butterfly Records. This included everyone in the studio at the time of the recording, as well as Dizziboy and the sound engineers. Even Amie, the receptionist, had to look back through the sign-in book to show how many times the boys had visited the studio.

The legal department did a thorough job of ferreting out the facts. The news that the boys had lost their case in the High Court was not publicised, nor did it reach the national newspapers, but two days after the case had been tried, a package arrived at Mason, James &

Braithwaite's offices, addressed to 'The Legal Team against Butterfly Records'. Inside the package were twenty-four tapes, twelve of them dub master tapes. Each of them was labelled.

They were the individual song recordings that made up X-Gen's recently released album. There was a handwritten message attached to it signed by Jimmy Fraser, one of the sound technicians on the project at the studio throughout the recordings. It read:

My name is James Fraser (Jimmy). I was one of the sound technicians at Butterfly Records assigned to the project when the original boys (DeAngelo, Jay, Karl, Eddie and Nathan) came into the studio to lay down their vocals for the songs now being used by X-Gen. I'm sorry I didn't come forward earlier, but it wasn't until I saw the legal team come back into Butterfly Records like heroes that I realised something had happened. I was interviewed by the legal dept to explain how I came into contact with the original boys. I wasn't asked to hide anything. They were only interested in the new group and whether I recorded them live in the studio.

In fact, I did, and they did sound a bit like the original boys. Someone may have trained them to sing like the boys; you can train a parrot to sing like Elvis, but that doesn't make it an original. That's all I'm saying on that.

There were some issues with the new boys getting the harmonies to work. No matter how hard we tried, they couldn't do it, so on Sami's instructions, we took a shortcut and used what we had, which was the original recording with the harmonies. So, on every track of that newly released album, the harmonies are those done by the original boys. The master tapes used for pressing the records, singles, and CDs are enclosed.

The recordings were also used as backing for TV performances, interviews, and radio. I hope this helps.

From my heart, those boys deserve better. Sorry about that.

I would prefer to remain anonymous, but if I am summoned to court, I will tell the truth and nothing but the truth, so help me, God.

♪ ♪ ♪

It was a major breakthrough and a scoop that didn't seem possible. It was a miracle, handed to them from the heavens. It was the game-changer they needed to force an appeal because the boys now had everything to gain and nothing to lose. Their previous loss was no longer on the table.

'Get me Colin Whittaker at Whittaker & May Solicitors. Thanks,' Cynth instructed her PA. Colin was one of the main partners she personally knew at the firm, which was one of the top hundred in their field.

'Colin? Great—you could take my call. I hope your family is doing well. How's Merilee?' He'd nearly lost his wife to cancer, but it wasn't terminal.

'Yes, Merilee is doing great after her op. By the way, thanks for the flowers, and your note was such an encouragement. Thank God she's still with us,' Colin said. 'Colin, I want to cut to the chase and give you the heads up: your firm recently won the case representing Butterfly Records against the five boys who took them to court for infringement rights.'

'Yes, I heard about it, but that was only two days ago. What was it…Monday?'

'Correct, but today, Wednesday, we have new, solid evidence in favour of the boys, so we'd like to give you two options: come to our offices this afternoon at 3 p.m. or tomorrow morning at 10 a.m. to see what we have and settle the costs out of court, or we go for the appeal and make the whole thing public.'

'Cynth, you always drive a hard bargain. I'll get the client's legal team and ours to be with you by 3 p.m. today. Don't do anything hasty now. They are one of our best clients,' Colin said.

'You know how I don't like to play,' Cynth said, knowing that all the balls were in her court.

'I'll get my PA to arrange it.'

Two million copies of the first X-Gen album had already been pressed. Distribution was worldwide. It was too late for the brakes to be applied to stop the flow of the singles and the album from getting out there. Though they were still in their infancy, X-Gen were megastars and in demand. Butterfly Records could not afford a scandal coming out about their vocal credibility at that time, as it would cripple their brand. The Faceless People who had given the go-ahead for the project would also lose their investment, which hinged on their success. There was much at stake, and Butterfly Records had a lot to lose when it came to the group.

True to his word, Colin Whittaker arranged for the legal representatives managing the client along with their legal team to attend the meeting at Mason, James & Braithwaite. The big boardroom had been booked from 2 p.m. which comfortably seated twenty around the grand, polished oak table.

It was rare for both Cynth with Stan to work on the same case as they were far too busy, but they both planned to be at the meeting. Michael, Penny, and Tom had already been briefed on how the meeting would go before they'd filed into the room. Michael would be the one to present their demands using a newly-trained solicitor to help handle the huge request, a ploy that might be viewed as a weakness by the other party, but if the representatives showed signs that they would not agree to their terms, Cynth would come in with her strong arm.

They all sat on one side of the table, with Cynth and Stan sitting in the middle, Tom on one side and Michael and Penny on the other. 'There's strength in numbers. We need at least another five people. These are our offices and our domain. Bring in Sarah-Jane, Jonathan (their PAs) and three others who can stay until 6 p.m., if necessary,' Cynth said.

Penny went to assemble the others. She returned in no time. Perrier water, sparkling and still, was on the table alongside glass tumblers.

The phone rang in the boardroom. Tom got up to answer it, and he was told that the representatives had arrived. 'Send them into the boardroom,' he instructed.

There were two key senior members of the legal department who were prepared to protect Butterfly Records' assets and two advisers from Whittaker & May Solicitors. They were there to talk business and shut down any claims.

'Thank you for coming. This case was dismissed because you presented evidence proving the X-Gen boys could sing, so we are not disputing that, but we have a written statement plus copies of twelve dubbed master tapes of our boys recording all twelve songs from the X-Gen album. The songs were re-sung by your X-Gen boys, but the harmonies on those tracks are, in fact, recordings of our boys. Whether you like it or not, our boys deserve their dues, so here's our claim.'

Michael read: '"Two points of royalties on the twelve named X-Gen songs released as singles and assembled as either an album, EP, or any type of compilation.

'"Royalties whenever the song is played in any public place, concert, event, TV, radio, pub, and jukebox unless X-Gen is singing live with a band of musicians. However, if the original backing track containing the boys' pre-recorded harmonies is used, they will be entitled to royalties on any gigs. The instructions for the distribution will be logged with Performing Rights Society (PRS).

'"Fifty pounds each per hour for every hour involved in practice and training, plus twenty-eight days at ten hours per day at a time and a half for their studio work for the unsocial hours, i.e., after 7 p.m.

'"Compensation for emotional damages in the amount of seventy-thousand pounds per person.

'"Compensation for Abi Jackson for the time and effort she spent arranging the audition, managing the boys, and administration in the amount of one hundred thousand pounds.

'"Written apologies on behalf of Butterfly Records for the lack of clarity of their intention to use the boys to form a group, and all legal costs and expenses covered by the firm."

'These are our terms — do you agree?'

'Can you give us twenty minutes to discuss the offer between ourselves?' Ryan asked.

'No problem.' Cynth got up to leave the room, which was the cue for everyone to follow.

The legal representatives knew there was nothing to do but agree with the request or the client would stand to lose far more than they would by paying the boys. In time, X-Gen would be one of many other groups, but the deception would never happen again, and Butterfly Records would see to it that Sami Achu would not be able to work in or for another record company. They would see to it that word got around.

Everyone came back into the boardroom to hear the decision.

'We agree to everything you have requested and will get the papers drawn up by Friday at the latest for you to go over, but we would like a disclaimer included that receiving this out-of-court settlement does not wholly admit complete liability. There must never be mention of this in any media. These are our terms,' Ryan said, being the spokesman for the team.

'Are we done?' Cynth asked.

'I do have one final question: just to satisfy my own curiosity — how did you get involved in a case like this?' Ryan asked

'Our son is Jason Braithwaite—didn't you notice the name in the affidavit? He was one of the original five, which was fortunate for the boys but unlucky for you guys because you would have otherwise gotten away with it.

'Thank you for your time.

'Please show the gentlemen out.

'Good day,' Cynth said curtly.

The team rose to their feet and said good day in return. They left with red faces, looking (and feeling) as if they had been royally slapped.

When the legal team had finally left the building, and the coast was clear, Cynth congratulated her staff for their time and effort. 'Well done, guys! Great teamwork. If you are still working at the firm when I retire, I know the business will be safe in your hands. You all did a marvellous job.

'Now, we need to tell the boys. And Abi. She must feel terrible, but this victory changes everything. Bad news travels fast, but good news should spread even faster. I'll tell Jay. Who's going to tell the others?'

19

The Epilogue

SEVEN YEARS WENT by in the blink of an eye. X-Gen had become a raving success worldwide, but in the lifecycle of a new group, their shine would lack its lustre at some future date when they would be superseded by other stronger, emerging artists in the same genre who were just as young and just as fresh-faced as X-Gen had been back when.

The concept that a tightly scripted formula could make big money had been proven. Catching the fire of the successful formula, copycat groups would perfect their craft in East Asia (Taiwan), South Korea and Japan, introducing their language in a pop style with the same look and feel as Western artists. The tide was certainly turning for countries predominantly used by the West for cheap labour and workhouses for manufacturing. As their wealth slowly increased, there was more exposure to Western themes, movies, and music, and the home-grown talent that eventually matched it.

New digital sound technology emerged, allowing producers to add echoes, synthesisers, reverbs, and overlayed filters on the singers' voices. Anyone able to hold an appearance on stage was worth the investment. Could they sing? That was the multi-million-dollar question.

The UK had lacked real talent for many years. The original boys—DeAngelo, Karl, Jay, Nathan, and Eddie—had talent, but whether you had a voice no longer mattered. It was all about looks and saleability, and the music industry didn't want to wait to find that diamond in the rough.

Butterfly Records was on a roll, churning out group after group, but without Sami, whose name was mud, never to be mentioned in the music industry again. Losing the court case had almost rendered the Butterfly Records name disreputable, but the Faceless People put out the subtle word that it was Sami who had almost ruined the brand.

Sami disappeared into the woodwork, and the name Sami Achu was never heard publicly again, at least not in the music arena, but like a cat with many lives, Sami bounced back, reverting to his birth name of Simon. On official papers, he was Simon Achidi Achu. After thinking deeper about it, he decided to change his name to Simon McKenzie—McKenzie was Beth's maiden name, which she'd kept as a double-barrelled name: Beth McKenzie-Achu. He felt the new name would bring better opportunities for him, and it did.

He started his own business, falling back on his earlier days of talent side-hustling. He created jingles for radio and TV commercials. Being at the top of the food chain meant he called the shots. Of course, he still received royalties from the songs he'd written that had been sung by X-Gen. They were still making their rounds across the world and would do so for a long time.

Beth, forever his dutiful wife, was made a director in the business. Her talent in classical music and piano helped put the finishing touches on some of the most iconic advertising commercials in the UK. Working with the likes of Saatchi & Saatchi, Ogilvy & Mather, and other seasoned creative agencies, their portfolio contained many top A-list clients, such as M&S, IBM and the memorable British Airways ad, where the passengers board a plane to 'The Flower Duet' by Lakme.

Their son, Zac, was now seven years old and had learned to play music, but they decided not to push him in that direction. They wanted him to be a doctor instead or anything but a musician.

Beth fell pregnant again when Zac was six years old and had a girl they called Zara, but a leopard never changes its spots, and Sami had a brief fling with someone from one of the advertising agencies. The relationship didn't go anywhere, and Beth was none the wiser.

The fruit from the hard labour of those difficult times had turned into success for the five boys, not necessarily in music but in so many other directions. They all made it to university. The money they received from the case and ongoing royalties sured-up their futures, in which they could be anything they wanted to be.

Karl became a primary school teacher, as he loved children and sports.

After seven years of studying at Nottingham University, Nathan became an architect and got a job as a trainee in a London practice.

He also bought his own house, a two-up, two-down in Kingston. He renovated it so it would be just how he wanted it, fulfilling one of his hidden dreams. He and Sarah (from his days in the care system) remained friends. Now in his early twenties, Nathan was quite a catch. No matter how many times he introduced a prospective girlfriend to Sarah, the girls found it hard to believe she was just a friend. Sarah had grown to be a beautiful, caring person despite her troubled childhood. As innocent as their friendship was, they would, one day, wake up to realise they were meant to be together.

Jay went on to Birmingham University. He studied law and got a first degree, which made his parents and grandparents proud. Everyone expected him to work as a solicitor at Mason, James & Braithwaite, but he wanted to experience the hard graft of working in another top firm and took on an internship at Whittaker & May, the same firm that had negotiated the Butterfly Records deal with his mother, Cynth. Jay wanted to explore different work perspectives before joining his mum and dad, but one year into his plan, his father took sick with cancer, rapidly declined, and passed away six months later. It was then that he got the urge to join the firm to support his mother.

Although it was a sad situation, Jay was proud of all his father had achieved, and he had been fortunate enough to tell him as much while he was still living. Jay didn't think he could fill his father's boots, but he was prepared to take those first steps to find out.

He wanted no special privileges in the firm as a result of being Stanley Braithwaite's son, and he requested to work his way up to becoming a partner one day.

Eddie, considered by the boys as the live wire, went to Kingston University. He and Nathan had a patchy friendship. Eddie's blowing hot and cold rubbed Nathan the wrong way. If there was anyone who would fly off the handle in the group, it was one of those two who were always happy to be on the opposing side of any argument. Despite their differences, they hung in there where the relationship was concerned.

Eddie turned his petty gambling on scratch cards and lottos to understanding stocks and shares. He studied business and also got a first degree. While he was still at uni, he worked part-time for a company selling commodities to professional people like vets and doctors, who had money to invest. The income was commission-based, with no base salary. Working down a list of names and making sales pitches to prospective clients was like a baptism of fire when it came to selling. On the other hand, Eddie learned the RPP method: resilience, perseverance and patience. The team supervisor had told everyone that, after so many nos, there was bound to be a yes. When he joined, he made his first thousand-pound commission in the first week, and he was happy. Others couldn't hack it, so there was always a high turnover of staff, but Eddie was of a different mindset, as the thousand pounds spurring him on gave him the taste for more money. His team leader took an interest in anyone who could make money for the company, and he encouraged him, saying that Eddie was naturally gifted.

Then, JP Morgan had an exhibition stand at the annual recruitment fair on open day at the university, inviting students to apply for apprenticeships. On a whim, Eddie applied and was accepted, giving him a job working in derivatives investments in the UK. He went on to learn everything about trading investments and moved up to becoming a stock market trader. He was very smart, but he always took risks. As long as everything worked in his favour, things would be all right. However, in times to come, the joy of working fast and loose would eventually catch up with him, but if ever he needed legal advice, Jay was his man.

Out of the five, only DeAngelo continued with his music career to become an independent entertainment solo artist. He had huge hits in the Caribbean and even in the Middle East and European countries. He was inundated with invitations to perform at events and was busy and happy with how things had turned out. Another one of his successes was helping his mother open a Caribbean restaurant called Rum and Black, based in South West London, that served the finest Caribbean cuisine in Clapham. Besides the food, there was space for entertainment. Shirlee and Robert often sang to customers, which made everyone love the ambience, and they frequently returned.

It wasn't only a place for Caribbeans, as all nationalities were welcomed. There was also a Friday evening DJ night with a popular happy hour for the early evening revellers before they went out on the town. The restaurant opened for lunchtime from 12 to 3 p.m., then in the evenings from 6 to 11 p.m. during the week. They had a late-night license for Friday and Saturday, where customers could stay until 2 a.m. before being thrown out, by which time, they were well-oiled from the rum.

It was Wednesday, just after lunch at the restaurant, on a day when DeAngelo was not touring or out of the country. He offered to be on standby to help out at the restaurant, as well as invite the boys for a catch-up. It was end-of-term for him, and everyone's diaries worked, but they couldn't be certain that Nathan would turn up because, on their last trip abroad, Eddie and Nathan had a big falling out again.

Karl was the first to arrive. He entered through a decorative array of palm trees, greenery and bamboo. Light 'soca' music played in the background, which was quite fitting for a perfect escape from the mundane.

'Come in, man,' DeAngelo said. They exchanged big man hugs, smiles, and laughter. 'What can I get you to drink—rum and black?' DeAngelo laughed. 'A cocktail?' He proceeded to list off other possibilities.

'You know me by now: I'm not a drinker.' That was true. Karl had to watch his alcohol intake because of the medication he was on. 'I'll have a cocktail, but non-alcoholic, okay? Surprise me?'

DeAngelo called out to one of the bartenders to mix a surprise non-alcoholic cocktail for his good friend.

Shirlee knew the boys would be coming that evening. She heard DeAngelo talking with someone and popped her head through the kitchen's swing doors. When she saw it was Karl, she said, 'Hi,' but she apologised for not having the time to join them. Her once-white apron was covered in stains from cooking with spices, and her hands were full of flour from preparing bakes and fritters. There were also requests for takeaways she was dealing with; plus, Wednesday was open mic night, and she often sang as a warm-up act to encourage others to come forward. Everyone was welcome to sing as long as it wasn't in a drunken stupor. It usually turned out well.

Jay arrived next, followed by Eddie. After hugging DeAngelo and Karl, they headed for the kitchen to say hi to Shirlee. They'd just finished work and wanted to see what was cooking.

'I know you guys must be hungry. Go ahead and choose something from the menu, and I'll get it ready for you,' Shirlee said. It wasn't quite opening time yet, but she treated the boys as she would her son.

They wasted no time placing their orders: jerk chicken, rice and peas, mac 'n' cheese and coleslaw.

Eddie went over to the door of the restaurant and called out to Karl, 'What do you want to eat? Mum's preparing some food for us.' Eddie called all the boys' mothers 'Mum' when he met them. He truly felt as if they were a part of an extended family.

'I'll have ackee, salt fish, and white rice if she's got it,' Karl said. It was one of his favourite dishes.

Everyone ordered something, but Nathan was still MIA.

All of the boys had become professionals as the cash that had been injected into their young lives allowed them to further their education and set them up financially for better things.

True to his word, DeAngelo had taken the guys to Disneyland, Florida, so they could get a real taste of how a theme park should be done. That time, Nathan was fully aware of his limitations. He didn't try anything extravagantly wild, like the top-listed roller-coaster rides. There had been plenty for him to do in the endless world of entertainment features they had at the park without them. He was just happy to be a part of it all.

After that first holiday abroad, they vowed to go somewhere together every year. They went to Egypt to see the pyramids, which was reminiscent of Rameses's Revenge at Chessington World of Adventure. They thought it was pretty cool going there. They also went to Paris to see the Eiffel Tower, and South Africa on safari was unforgettable, giving them the once-in-a-lifetime ability to see real animals in their natural habitats. Year upon year, they added to their list of adventures.

The most recent trip was to Las Vegas. Eddie had lost his mind and went on a mad, drunken spree, spending money on the slot machines. He was totally mesmerised by the whole experience. Nathan had tried to tell him to get a grip, and that's what caused the argument. They hadn't spoken in the months since.

They were talking about their adventures when Nathan suddenly turned up. Everyone's face lit up when they saw him, including Eddie's. There were hugs all around again.

Eddie went up to Nathan and said, 'I'm sorry, man. I got wasted.'

Nathan stopped for a second and looked at him with a straight face. Everyone thought, here we go again. Then he said, ''Course I forgive you.' He burst out laughing, and they hugged it out.

'Anyway, I've got something I need to tell you guys,' Nathan said, getting their attention. 'I'm getting engaged, and when I get married next year, I want you guys to be my best men.' They all congratulated him.

'So, who's the lucky — or should I say unlucky — girl?' Eddie couldn't resist.

Nathan smiled and said, 'I'm going to marry Sarah.'

'What? Sarah? You sly fox, you,' Eddie said. 'I've always thought there was something between you two.'

'No, seriously, I never saw it until recently. She's been a constant in my life for many years, supporting me through difficult times. She's beautiful inside and out. It's time for me to have my own life and family, and she's perfect for me.' Nathan was pleased to have the approval of his closest friends.

'Let's get a round of drinks in to congratulate the bachelor,' Jason said.

'Oh, my God! I can't wait to plan the stag night for you. Guys, where should we take him?' Eddie said.

Nathan wondered if it was a good idea to allow Eddie or any of the guys to be in charge of organising the stag.

Abi was not in contact with the boys, but Shirlee often told her everything about DeAngelo's successes. If she heard anything about the other boys, she'd mention it in passing. Secretly, Abi reminded herself to consider how something as messy as her experience with the band had turned out to be a blessing in disguise. The boys were still young enough to get over it and enjoy their lives. She had no idea they were having a whale of a time or that they never spoke badly about her or Mervyn.

'Hi guys—how are you all doing?' Abi said, surprising everyone when she walked into the restaurant. Shirlee had invited her along to the gathering. 'I bet you didn't expect to see me here, did you?'

There was a lot of screaming and shouting from the boys, who were so happy to see her. They tried to get in for a hug, fighting each other off to be the first. That evening would be a great celebration of how the 'Hand of God' could twist fate to bring strangers together to partake in a remarkable blessing.

Abi and Candice were still friends, but it was not as intense as before. Abi had turned her life around and found her voice, not just in singing hit songs, but on all levels, and she attended a church whenever she was in town, while Candice still had not experienced a spiritual awakening. Their paths had changed, and they found they had less and less in common.

Since signing with Gulf Records, Abi excelled as an artist. There were no hit songs in the UK, but her songs were played in so many other nations. With the wealth she accumulated, she offered to buy her ex-husband out of the property she was living in. He was happy to take the money, so legal agreements were drawn up and signed, and his name was removed. She was now the outright owner.

There was so much for Abi to be grateful for. The real Abi emerged, the old, unhappy person gone. She had changed, became stronger, used her feminine beauty and charm with grace and took nothing for granted. No longer a troubled soul, she made amends with God and found her spiritual path again, which led her to a partnership that formed the London Gospel Choir (LGC). This didn't interfere with the agreement she had with Gulf Records, but it did mean she had a busy calendar. The LGC were so much in demand that they toured Europe, Australia, and even parts of the states in the American Bible Belt in communities craving gospel music. LGC took a bit of organising, but Abi had a clear vision as to how to make UK gospel music crossover into the mainstream just like the other genres. Because of the LGC, there was now a place for gospel in the UK.

On special invitation, they were invited to sing before Prince Charles at the Royal Albert Hall. They never knew what invitation would come next, but they were ready for any and all requests.

Abi did well with her compensation, although money was never her problem. Rather, it was having taken her life growing up in the Church for granted and how greatly different it was from the outside world. Prayer, meditation and fasting became her ritual in a way of life that would take serious believers through any stormy situation. Abi accepted that there would always be storms, but she now knew that she was more than able — if not above — getting tossed about in it, as long as she kept her eyes on the One source, who was greater than herself.

Here, it ends. Without fail, there is always an answer when the Divine interlinks with the lives of mere mortals. Some might have called her experience with Sami and the boys a lucky break, but Abi knew otherwise.

About the Author

Saleah Micci was born in Shepherd's Bush, West London, to Jamaican parents who came to the UK during the Windrush period. Her love for all things creative began around age 6 after her father passed away. At this tender age, she was a runner-up in a national newspaper children's artists' competition. Coming from a Caribbean household, music was also a big part of her life, where music was played all day long.

Having worked in the commercial world of oil and gas, she became interested in information technology, sparking a desire to know how things fit together. Saleah enjoys injecting creativity into figuring out how to make complex things simple.

During the Credit Crunch, she created the Money Workshops programme, now called *'If Money Had Wings...'*, helping others to gain a better relationship with money.

For fun and escapism, Saleah likes to delve into a book and appreciates the fictional world of the stories. She believes writing can help others get in touch with their feelings, which led her to write 'Make Friends with Yourself', a non-fiction account of how to do just that.

Saleah lives in North London with her husband and has a blended family of four children.

www.saleahmicci.co.uk

Conscious Dreams
PUBLISHING

Transforming diverse writers
into successful published authors

www.consciousdreamspublishing.com

authors@consciousdreamspublishing.com

Let's connect